Divided Sky

Divided Sky

Elizabeth Moses

DIVIDED SKY

iUniverse books may be ordered through booksellers or by contacting:

iUniverse
1663 Liberty Drive
Bloomington, IN 47403
www.iuniverse.com
1-800-Authors (1-800-288-4677)

ISBN: 978-1-4917-4713-1 (sc)
ISBN: 978-1-4917-4714-8 (e)

Library of Congress Control Number: 2014917544

Printed in the United States of America.

iUniverse rev. date: 11/05/2014

For The Wook and The Boo,
as is everything I do

The Poem that took the Place of a Mountain

There is was, word for word,
The poem that took the place of a mountain.

He breathed its oxygen,
Even when the book lay turned in the dust of his table.

It reminded him how he had needed
A place to go to in his own direction,

How he had recomposed the pines,
Shifted the rocks and picked his way among clouds.

For the outlook that would be right,
Where he would be complete in an unexplained
completion:

The exact rock where his inexactness
Would discover, at last, the view toward which they had
edged,

Where he could lie and, gazing down at the sea,
Recognize his unique and solitary home.

—Wallace Stevens

BOOK ONE

Where you find your pain, you will find your soul.

When the world spun too fast the pain set in. It set deep into his lungs until he gasped for one last breath. The white, mesh bed canopy twisted around his body, seemingly lifting him upward into the eye of a tornado. His feet dangled crucifixion style. His weightless body was swaddled so tightly that he couldn't move. His bones cracked. The pain was excruciating. Antonio's untethered soul floated skyward. He listened to his cracking bones until a cathartic release of weightlessness swept over him. The pain ceased. His lightness carried him higher and higher.

He could smell the ocean. He deeply breathed in the salty whiteness. Blue bands softly wrapped around his head, turning his thoughts to the vast, open expanse surrounding him. It was the largest, calmest sea he had ever seen. After decades of Italian exile to Portugal seas, and a lifetime exploring the world's waters on the most magnificently built sailboats, Antonio Capricio was set free. His version of complete freedom was a calm ocean with opportunities on every possible chosen course. That is what he saw; blue, white accented waters surrounding his soul with piercingly clear starlit constellations in perfect astronomical formation to guide his way. It was what he had waited a lifetime to see while combing the European and African waters. The stars and waters harmonized into Antonio's path of unquestionable guidance. He knew he was home. He had finally found his way.

The world stopped spinning.

He looked down at his body lying bloated on the canopy bed. His billowy white shirt reminded him of his sailboats' sails. The same sails which took him to the Cape Verde Islands off the west coast of Africa and carried him around the horn, up to the Indian Ocean, where he found the Seychelle Islands. The voyages were long and hard. Sailors were lost. Lives were torn apart. Children were abandoned, but Antonio didn't stop exploring…until he could no longer leave Isabel.

Antonio Capricio saw his own serenely closed eyes and pale cheeks. He noticed his own dark hair covering the white, down-filled pillows. The bed was carefully tended to with eyelet, white-cotton bedding accentuating four, tall, mahogany bed posts. The posts almost reached the ceiling. The tips were crowned with ornate seashell carvings.

He saw that his head was still. His body was frozen. For a brief moment Antonio's soul spun wildly further upward, intertwining in the blue ribbons. Red overlay auric rings meshed into the blue ribbons, binding Antonio's now free soul in a purple haze. The blue and red auras blended into a reverberating purple aura as his soul confusingly looked at its most recent incarnation lying in the bed.

The purple cyclone spun wildly out of control in confusion. He floated up, wondering where he was, wondering, most importantly; where was Isabel? He could not feel her. As he anxiously looked for her, a void crept inside him. His vision darted wildly to the bed. He saw himself still lying there alone, on his side of the bed. His soul was confused. Emptiness encompassed him.

Her side was untouched, unwrinkled. Her bed stand was empty, save for an unlit lantern.

His bed stand glowed. The lantern flickered life into the darkness. Next to the lamp sat a tan, leather-bound journal. The cover was blank. The spine had no writing. A fringed gold tassel protruded. Antonio's identity was lost in the abyss of that journal. His curiosity caused his soul to float effortlessly down to the bed. His soul sat next to his life-less body. Isabel was nowhere to be found. In this moment he understood that he was dead. He understood that he had only returned from a year long voyage days before. From this understanding, a calmness came over him, releasing the red fire ring, which allowed his blue aura to encircle him.

Isabel walked into the room. Her presence gave him insight. Suddenly he knew who he had been. Antonio knew he was dead. He knew he had been a great Italian and Portuguese sailor. He knew he had lived on the ocean. He knew he had loved her, and he knew he had unexpectedly left her.

Isabel softly climbed into the bed, trying not to wake her lover. She anxiously waited for him to notice her and reach over and pull her body next to his. When she felt his coldness she shuddered. Antonio's body still lay in the exact spot it had been for the last three days, valiantly fighting off the pneumonia he contracted on his last voyage. Isabel had known his death was possible. She bowed her head in grave grace. Isabel twinkled with light green beads of energy dancing around her head as she began to sob. When Antonio's soul saw her sobbing, panic gripped him. His spirit turned grey with fear. She was so young and so beautiful. She would now never know how deeply he loved her. He had loved her for a thousand years and would for a thousand more. A life cut short was a life unlived. His spirit spun more and more frantically, like a cyclone going nowhere, grasping for memories. Lightning bolts repeatedly zapped him until he fell into an electrocuted heap at her sobbing feet. He rested in the middle of nowhere. His nowhere was dark grey fog.

Lights bounced around him, nudging him to get up. The lights were familiar. Each one had a different knowing energy. A loving, white Bullmastiff spirit, Tiberius, pawed at Antonio's spirit, licking his face. The dog's warmth lifted the grey fog. His huge paws waved through the air, leaving iridescent, radiant streaks with each swat. Incandescent droplets floated into the emptiness surrounding Antonio. Tiberius, danced and wiggled wildly in circles around the spirit heap until Tiberius began encircling Antonio's soul. Tiberius dropped down into a sleeping position, making a proper resting place for his and Antonio's spirits. Tiberius's soul hugged Antonio's. The dog buried his short muzzle into Antonio's malleable neck. Radiance filled both their souls. The closest thing to contented breath that any mortal could understand emanated from their physically connected energies. They folded into each other, as they had done life-time after life-time to stay warm on cold nights. Orange enthusiasm encircled them. This time it was Tiberius who had waited in the stratosphere above. He had waited thirty years for Antonio to die, a mere glimpse of time in the spirit world. It had been their fifth earthly life together. They both knew it was not their last.

The power of the past gave them strength; a

perfect, unbreakable, vibrant dark blue strength which comes from the trust and familiarity of life-time after life-time together. It allowed them to settle into nothingness together. White radiance emanated from their physically connected energies.

This strength allowed Antonio to adjust to his surroundings. A sense of knowing came over him. He remembered constructing this life and remembered Tiberius preparing to wait for him. He remembered this white radiance, but something must have gone wrong. He hadn't completed the last chapter. Isabel was alone. Antonio was gone to Isabel, by any worldly, physical definition. With Tiberius's head on Antonio's lap, the dead man flew softly past kneeling Isabel. He knelt next to her and began to flip the pages of the leather bound journal lying next to his dead body.

He was still, but still moving. All Antonio's spirit had to do was effortlessly exhale and the pages turned, as if blown by a gentle, timely breeze. The book blew open and closed three times as Antonio's spirit practiced his new powers. He focused all his consciousness on the book.

Isabel, thinking it must be the wind, rose to close the window. She went to her daughter's, Princess Isabel's, basinet and picked up the serene baby. She hugged her child as close to her as possible, allowing her daughter to absorb the emptiness she knew she would forever feel without her lover. She wrapped

Princess Isabel tighter in her blankets to cover the child from the continual draft. Wind blew wickedly through the open window. The window panes knocked on the majestic house's stone frame.

The journal on Antonio's side of the bed fluttered open. Life moved with the pages. It wafted off the pages into Antonio's heightened senses.

Being that he had just died hours before, his senses were slightly mortal. He could smell sea salt coming off the pages. He could feel love coming off the bed sheets. He could also sense death and blackness within Isabel's soul. He could make the pages move with his sheer will to understand what had happened to him.

Even after Isabel closed the window, she gasped in amazement as the pages continued to seemingly, methodically turn themselves. Isabel solemnly read the pages, not knowing that Antonio was reading with her. Antonio reviewed his most recent past life.

May 20, 1470 Lisbon, Portugal, el vaca del mar port cerca de la sur de Portugal

I will embark on a voyage to the New World Today. It has taken many months and many men to assemble my ship, La Tomales. There is a place I need to go. I do not believe my voyage can be frivolous for I know I am meant to discover something that will shape mankind's destiny.

The Queen Isabel has been generous with her gifts. We have plenty for the voyage. The supplies are abundant;

flour, whisky, goats, cornmeal, sugarbeet, eleven million pounds of salt pork, ten million pounds of ships biscuits, forty thousand gallons of olive oil, fourteen thousand barrels of wine, five thousand extra pairs of shoes, and equipment to repair ships; axes, spades and shovel.

I have many men: six surgeons, six physicians, one hundred eighty priests as spiritual advisors, nineteen justices, fifty administrators, one hundred forty young gallants who brought seven hundred twenty eight servants with them. We are missing astrologists, so I will do all the navigations. I have brought three telescopes for my personal us; as well as compasses, binoculars, and maps.

I have everything I need except the Queen herself, and my faithful canine companion. Leaving dear Isabel is not an easy task. My brother, Bartholemew, will ease her loneliness. I never felt loneliness before loving her. I hope with every cell in my body that she never feels this pain, even if it means her not loving me. Her husband, King Ferdinand of Aragon has given her a daughter;. born in Duenas in the early spring of 1470. There is now another Isabel to beautify this world.

The waves are tumultuous. My heart beats in rhythm to their breaking. The rocks are sharp. The salt air awakens me. It will be a rough voyage across the Atlantic toward the large continent. When I arrive I shall dedicate the new land to my Isabel, my Queen.

Isabel eyes were filled with tears as she read the pages and held her baby, Princess Isabel, to her heart.

She recited over and over again the only soothing ablution she knew: *Angels of Love*

> *Our Guardians dear*
> *To Whom your Love*
> *Commits us here*
> *Ever this day*
> *Please be by Antonio's side*
> *To Light to Love*
> *To Guard and Guide.*

Listening to Isabel recite the ablution, Antonio's spirit shook. He remembered the night before his death being truly in love. He remembered feeling warm and safe. He remembered Isabel lying next to him, dozing off to sleep in that grand canopy bed under the fluffy white down comforter. Their souls astral traveled into a spiraling blue ribbon.

"Meet you at the fire," he had said, as their souls drifted into the clouds.

"The hearth," she corrected with a laugh.

"Yes. The hearth *is* the center of the universe." They both laughed. The blue ribbon spun onto a pile of pillows in front of the fire. Their souls danced amongst the clouds and felt a freedom known only to those who are truly in love.

Their bodies slept by the fire until their souls returned to their bodies just before dawn. Flesh entangled flesh. They inhaled each others' scents as if it were necessary for survival. The bed's aura was turquoise with lavender iridescence. They remembered what seemed like a dream of dancing in the clouds. They knew it was real.

Antonio now remembered that he had everything he ever wanted in life…and now she was alone. His spirit panicked. He had promised never to leave her. Just because he had everything he wanted shouldn't mean his time was up. What about Isabel? She had to have been written into his chart. He needed to find the Hall of Records and find out why his life ended so abruptly; why some lives continue to linger on and on without meaning, and why his was cut short. He needed to know if some karmic force tore him from his earthly existence for a reason…or if there was an ethereal mistake. "There has to be some mistake," he whispered. "My life was for her and now I have failed. I learned nothing from this life."

It was at this point of sudden death that Antonio was able to evaluate his most recent incarnation. It was at this point that he could start to remember why he went to that earthly planet, why, even in death, he could feel such pain. Tiberius assured him that the pain would pass, but Antonio knew that until Isabel was at peace he would always feel pain.

"Take me to the Hall of Record," he exclaimed to Tiberius. "Take me where I can end this pain. I have learned nothing from the earthly existence if she is still in pain. Please, tell me what I went down there to learn."

Tiberius fixed his knowing glance to the north.

"You remember don't you?" Antonia asked his dog without uttering a word. Signaling Antonio to follow, Tiberius galloped toward a large, white Romanesque style building. It had massive pillars and white marbles stairs that seemed to go on forever. It resembled a cross between a gargantuan library and a Supreme Court building. Antonia quickly followed. Their five thousand year old souls were headed to the Hall of Records.

"You must remember for yourself," Tiberius said. "But soon your brother Bartholemew will be here to help you understand. Do you remember writing your charts together?"

"I remember writing a chart with Isabel, as we have done many times. Why did we not have a life together? I need to understand now," Antonio said impatiently.

"You are still bound by your earthly desires. They will pass, along with your impertinence," Tiberius said. "See, you can't separate the past from the future anymore than you can separate your right arm from your left arm. The Hall of Records will show you this."

"This pain will not pass. Make me understand," Antonio said.

"The darkest moment holds the deepest truth. Maybe a look at your journal will shed some light," Tiberius said

The brown, leather bound journal still lay on the night stand. Antonio had to read it. "Maybe the answers lie in my journal?" He said to Tiberius.

"Maybe," Tiberius said. "Your journal will help you understand your most recent earthly life, but The Hall of Records will show your chart and all your past lives."

Antonio deeply concentrated on the leather journal with its gold tassel protruding. Again, with focused breath he turned the pages.

Journal ledger, July, 1470

We have passed Cape Verde islands, although the men question why. They do not seem to understand that I am looking for something unknown. We are rounding the horn of Africa. It is a deadly place and I fear for alls' survival. Our supplies are still strong, as is my loneliness without Isabel. I comfort myself knowing that her princess Isabel is alive.

Journal ledger, Sept. 1470

A set of islands of seemingly French inhabitants has given us renewed life. We are at 16 degrees latitude, only a boat's ride from the Eastern Coast of Africa. It seems we circled the continent and found hidden islands. They have

white sand beaches and bountiful food. The men dove off the ship and swam to their coconut trees. I will not try to over-take these lands. They are too beautiful to conquer. But like the siren's song, I do not have any expectation of leaving soon.

Journal ledger, 5, October, 1470

There are nationless inhabitants on these islands. They are extraordinarily graceful for being uncivilized. Their bodies flow with the ebb and wane of the moon. They live by the stars and superstitions. They are peaceful and tribal. It is unlike any civilization I have encountered. They do not mate for life. In fact, many bare children randomly, without familial ties or genealogical records. They seem to all know where they come from and have a superstitious sense of where they are going. There is one woman in particular. She is more hospitably civilized than the others. I believe she is of English heritage. Victoria. She will not tell me her last name, as is the case with everyone here. Maybe they no longer need surnames. My hunch is that a divulgence of surnames will turn up too many bastard children who could be taken by the guise of official English dictates to London, and under British law be forced to remain in the English isles, away from their mothers. But most seem French and dare not use their surnames; Deveaux, Deveralee or Deroaches.

Victoria's head is always wrapped in brightly colored scarves. I am sitting quietly still in a bamboo chair watching the tortoises waddle into the water. With a cup of port, I am also watching her walk across the beach. Her head is luminous, with deep ocean blues, blood-red oranges, palm frawn greens and vibrant purples stacked perfectly balanced on her head. She is in reticent contrast to the white sandy beach. It is as if she doesn't belong here. I wonder if she ever wants to go back to England. She would never survive the staunchly English moral, not with her enthralling eccentric beauty and superstitions. She walks with a sense of magic surrounding her, as if she knows answers to questions I couldn't even possibly think to ask.

She has stopped as close to the water's edge as possible without the sea foam encroaching upon her bamboo mat. She sits, spine perfectly straight, as she dares to roll a cigarette. Most women on these islands do not know how to roll their own tobacco, or at least I have never seen them. Maybe I have barely noticed women here, with my heart eternally bound to Isabel. It is the men and their business bartering that I pay close attention to. They do not scream and pound their heads in dramatic displays if they do not get their desired price. They are more reserved. The dealings all seem fair and the men part with gracious, slight bows of their heads. Life moves peacefully on this island. Many of my sailors are showing signs of not wanting to return to Portugal. I fear I will lose most of my crew to this paradise.

No one country has claimed this paradise and I dare not try to capture it for fear of ruining it. There is no strife and I will not have it upon my conscience to create it. I will responsibly map their existence and move on.

Journal Ledger, 6, October, 1470

There is a group of women who sit in the same shaded spot each day plaiting hair. The women seem to span three generations. The grandmother makes the beads which hold the plaits in place. The children's fingers move so swiftly that I can't tell the difference between skin and hair until the masterpiece is finished and the grandmother threads a bead onto it. They do this all day, eating mangoes from the tree they sit under. I heard them talking about the woman with 'echarpe'. They refer to her as Victoria. I can see her all the way at the water's edge. She is so far across the sand that she seems like a mirage. Heat fumes and waves of energy swim over the sand between her and me. I wonder why she does not play the hair games with the other women. She still sits, perfectly still at the water's edge. Were it not for the colorful head scarves I would not notice her. It is her colorful delight that entices me. Her vibrancy gives me a sense of happiness I have never felt before. What must it be like to be that unabashed with ones own appearance. I cannot take my eyes off of her. It is her exuberance for life which mesmerizes me. I would give almost anything to capture that exuberance for myself. I must be closer to her.

Journal Ledger 7, October, 1470.

I was wrong about the colorful scarves. They are not what draws me to this woman. Her piercing turquoise eyes are as vibrant as the scarves. Her elongated, giraffe like neck emits awe. The flowing movements of her body, more graceful than a classical ballerina, wake and wane like the moon and tides . She picked up an apple from the dirty market place floor. It was as if she was swooping her arm to wave at someone. Her back remained perfectly straight. Her head adornment did not topple. The apple miraculously appeared in her hand as she ambled her body upright, with the mere swoosh of her arm. She carried the apple through the market place. We don't talk. I outstretched my arm to ask her if I may carry her burlap bag for her. She placed the hemp purse onto my arm. It was unexpectedly heavy. She carried the heavy bag effortlessly. Everything she did seemed effortless. When the wind blew, her body swayed with it. She did not expend any energy fighting the wind, or holding her ground. She became one with the wind and the heavy afternoon rains. When is started raining she didn't run for shelter. She opened her mouth, tilted her head poetically backward, and let the rain hydrate her inside and out. The scarf woven headdress held its' position when she craned her neck backward. The headdress touched her shoulder blades. Although probably English, she looks French and African. She speaks French in a dialect I have never heard and barely understand.

Today, it was obvious that even the other islanders regarded her as affluent. A few people at the market greeted her with bows. The common street venders placed their hands in the prayers position and nodded to her. She responded by placing her hands in the prayer position and expressing softly, "cava?" as both a question and an acknowledgement of greeting each other. She did not bow in return to these people. Instead she smiled. It was the first time I had seen her smile so sincerely and graciously. It was the most authentic smile I had ever seen. It was a perfect smile. One that usually appears after laughing until one's stomach tightens and cheeks turn red, yet it was instantaneous and immediate, with complete composure and sincerity. It warmed the soul of the person whom Victoria gave it to. For a short instant, I felt a pang in my heart. I wanted her to give me that warmth.

When we arrived at a ramshackle panateria she walked behind the oven, without asking the workers, and washed the apple. The man pounding on dough simply nodded at her. She nodded back. She understood people and the grounded, smart ones understood her. She was at home in this borderline savage land. She had made it her home. Where she truly called home I will probably never know. Much like myself. I had the feeling that her home, like mine, was buried deep inside her own heart and no matter how many oceans I sailed and how many sunsets she watched, we were always home.

It was that contentedness which made her irresistible.

We were alone walking through the market and seconds later crowds of people surrounded her. The merchants offered her whatever they had. They did not try to sell it to her. They begged her to take their things. An old lady followed her, placing first a purple scarf on Victoria's shoulder, then a red one on her bag, then a deep blue one in Victoria's hands. Now I understood the colorful headdress. It didn't matter what Victoria wore, she would always be adorned with vibrant colors. It was as if her soul searched out color to nourish itself. On days when she wore all white, she inevitably picked handfuls and handfuls of deep purple lavender plants from the lush meadows adjacent the beach. I must admit that I knew this from following her. If she didn't consciously decorate herself, colors found her. It was as if her life was a void without colors, and the universe hates a void. Today she was not wearing her head scarves. Without the colorful scarves it was as if she, or the universe, was calling for some soulful warmth to rise up from the ground. The warmth would be red and it would come from the deep red clay which I know is what lines the caves hidden in these island jungles. The buried red earth was being summoned to warm her, to warm the universe. I decided that her addition to the world's energy was through color. Some people paint. She didn't paint. At least, not that I have seen. I'm not sure if she is literate. She looks like it. Her part in the grand scheme of things is to add color and beauty. Her mere existence causes this cellular reaction. The drabness of

England must have been what forced her to leave. I have to think this because I can't bear the thought that something terrible happened to her and she ran for her life, like most people with her ethnic appearance.

As I was watching her, she abruptly and deliberately stopped. She meticulously rolled out her bamboo mat onto the dirt. She sat, lotus style, back straight and opened her mouth. I thought she was going to sing and was overcome with the hope that I could bask in her voice. Instead, she emitted short chirping sounds. Soon birds cautiously circled the energy above her head. These birds were nothing like I had ever seen before. They were twice the size of English pigeons, almost as large as our seagulls. The birds had red wings, green necks, blue trim around their rather short beaks. Their colors were even accentuated with small dabs of red at the tips of their wings. Victoria was again surrounded with color. I think that maybe she didn't wear her colorful headdress because it might disorient the birds… which in turn attracted more vibrancy and larger easels were needed. And for that adornment, she gave people around her hope. It emanated in her glow. It encompassed her head like circular ripples in water. The circles built upon each other, until the ripples were the entire body or water, or, more appropriate put 'the air above her head'. The colors followed her and flowed out of her. Her aura could be seen from space, pardon my dramatization. Life followed her.

We sat at a bamboo table in the hot sun. She placed

the misshapen piece of fruit on the table. The heat did not bother her. I gave the owner a small, shiny European coin. He knew it was European currency and quickly brought us clean water to drink.

Goats wandered in herds through the dirt paths which seem to pose as streets. Victoria walked over to the herder and graced him with her smile. He bowed. She showed him the apple. He smiled a huge toothless smile and nodded. She knelt and placed the apple in front of a soft furred, baby white goat. It was so small it could hardly keep up with the herd. Its mother instinctively head butted Victoria's hand away from the baby's mouth. As the gangly, unstable herbivore devoured the delicacy, it was obvious that even the goat was stricken with gratitude. The shepherd waited until the animal finished chomping, then he picked up the baby and handed it to Victoria. Its' legs and hooves dangled and it looked uncomfortable in the shepherd's arms. Victoria leaned forward for the shepherd to transfer the animal to her. Their shoulders touched. Victoria slid her arms under the goat's belly, pulling it lovingly into her own body. Then the oddest thing happened; she looked at me for approval. I was the recipient of her spirit filled smile.

"Yes, Yes," I yelled. "We will have a wonderful roast tonight." My mouth watered thinking about the succulent little mutton. I don't know if she understood my English. I will never know if she understood me. She stared at me with her smile of perfection, enjoying my enthusiasm. I stood to thank the shepherd, just as Victoria knelt onto the dirt. She carefully placed the soft, white furred equine next to its' very nervous looking mother. The little animal jumped wildly about, kicking its' back legs straight out behind him. The mother goat nudged and licked its offspring. The shepherd picked up the baby and with outstretched arms he implored Victoria to take the gift. The baby goat's fate hung in the balance. The mother goat let out painful baying noises that come from creatures right before their last breath, or once they know death is upon them.

"Two," Victoria said, raising two fingers. I did not know she spoke any English at all. Her pronunciation was as perfect as I expected from her curved red lips. Victoria would not take the baby from its mother. The shepherd looked at the mother goat and the baby dangling in his arms. His herd was small. He did not want to part with two goats. Victoria saw his dilemma. She shook her head, placed her hands in the prayer position and nodded at him. He beamed back at her and fell to his knees. She returned to the table where I still sat, having witnessed all of this compassion and gratitude over one small apple.

When my hand touched hers she did not recoil, instead her turquoise eyes burned into mine. I could feel how close I was to possessing her exuberance of life.

Journal ledger, December, 1470

I must return to Isabel. I am losing track of my days.

Many of the Portuguese men have chosen to stay in this paradise. It is just as well. Our supplies are short and the only ones we can gather from here will not preserve well; goats, mangoes, tortoises for meat, heavily distilled liquor, and gifts for our country; brightly colored beads made of bone, shoes constructed out of bamboo husk, and approximately one hundred tortoises for the queen's amusement. She will be able to add a unique attraction to the castle's zoo. Our return trip will be in haste. We must sail quickly to avoid starvation. The ship is lighter for this voyage. She has had a good rest and respects the time we gave her, basking in the Indian Ocean. Hopefully the Atlantic will be good to her. We must depart before the rains become treacherous. We should have left a month ago.

Journal ledger, February, 1471

The voyage was arduous. I am in Isabel's white canopy bed. I expected my dog to be lying at my feet. He did not survive my absence. My grief for him is weighing heavily on my lungs and I feel as if I can't breathe. My head is unclear and I fear pneumonia has set in. But I know I returned with pride. Our voyage was successful. We found an unnamed land. I was able to give the land's longitudinal and latitudinal coordinates to King Ferdinand and I returned with a new found exuberance for life. I have seen true beauty within the Indian Island chain. It is only measured by the dreariness and bleakness *of the strife within this country. In Portugal, life is divided by wealth and power. People starve on the streets. We kick them if they are in our way. Seeing the commonality of the Island people made me realize that Isabel is right, "Life should be better. No one should have to live in fear." Yet her husband, King Ferdinand, commands that fear and doles out tiny bits of rations to starving people only when he has had too much wine. The grapes grow in abundance here in Portugal, not as abundantly as in my mother Italy, but enough to keep the wealthy angry and heavy. Drink is not good for us Europeans. It causes unnecessary fights, duels, theft. I already miss my nights in the Islands. More drink became more dance. Days and nights flowed into each other. Mornings were not fearful and nights were not long. It was a place of oneness, that very few people will ever understand. Yes, I am resigned to not reporting the islands' extreme beauty to our king. I could never go to my grave in good conscience knowing that I had ruined a land of peaceful souls. Isabel will be proud of me for protecting the beauty. I am tired. My ink well is dry. I must sleep.*

Only earthly minutes had passed while Antonio read his journal. He was able to clearly remember his Seychellois life with Victoria, as well as his life in Lisbon with Isabel, but that was all at the present moment. Glimpses of love and its brightly colored beauty flowed through his "veins" directing him to a point of understanding. Like following a rainbow to a pot of gold, Antonio was able to follow the brilliant colors to a place of understanding.

Antonio and Tiberius began to ascend a white marble staircase up to the Hall of Records. "Housed in this building is every soul's 'chart,' Tiberious said, "Do you remember? A 'chart' is much like a personal journal. Each soul's journal details every earthly lesson which needs to be learned before it can graduate to the next stratosphere. It's as if each earthly incarnation is another level of education. Like graduating from high school to college, each soul must qualify and be accepted to attend a higher level of learning. Much like taking the S.A.T.s, each soul must test into its next level of education. Souls do this by following their charts. If a particular lesson has not been learned, such as 'patience,' has not been learned, then that soul needs to write a guide for its' next earthly life that will teach 'patience.' The soul may choose to learn this lesson by putting itself in the position of being a parent to a challenged child, or by caring for the elderly, or by any number of earthly situations which cause a soul to calmly wait and believe that all is for a reason. The soul may choose to learn this lesson over and over again in its next earthly life in order to make sure the lesson is learned to its fullest extent. This is why people make the same mistakes over and over again, in order to make sure the knowledge is embedded into their cerebral, spiritual and cellular memory."

"Yes, I remember," Antonio said. "After the lesson of 'patience' is learned another stepping stone to enlightenment is reached. The soul can progress to a more difficult lesson, such as 'love' or 'altruism'.

"Hey," called out a voice. "You floated right past me." Antonio turned to look at the voice. It came from a curmudgeonly man with a long, unkempt, Grizzly Adams style beard. Antonio stood in amazement. It was his spirit guide. Antonio hugged Pat as tightly as possible.

"Pat, you have never been here before when I crossed over. Why now?" Antonio asked.

"You were never at my level before. Now that you have learned how to love, you have progressed. I was your master. Now you will have the choice of whether to incarnate again with me, or go it on your own."

"Wow. So that was my lesson in my last earthly life? Learning how to love?"

"Yep," said Pat.

"Now I know why I saved this lesson for so long. It hurts even in the after-life. The other lessons where just learned and tucked away. This "love" lesson is very painful and it is following me."

"You need to embrace the pain," said Pat. "The pain of love is the only pain worth keeping. No longer will you be able to lead an empty existence. You have experienced true love and it will guard you from any selfish lessons in the future. You will now be able to choose whether you incarnate again or not. Your soul is no longer bound to return to earth time and time again in order to learn lessons. Now your fate is up to you."

"If I choose to incarnate again, will you and Tiberius come with me?"

"Yes," said Pat. "But we will be more closely aligned with your life choices. I will still be your Master and Spirit Guide and Tiberius will still be your evidence of unconditional love, but we will be intertwined in your life very early on, and you will have to watch Tiberius die again." Antonio winced. That was one lesson he had already learned too deeply and he didn't want to experience again. Yet, he did not want to return to earth without Tiberius.

"The group of souls with which you have karmic balances to clear up is short," said Pat. "Your immediate group of souls with whom you choose to be a part of your next earthly incarnation will be very wise and very useful. This is because you have spent the last thousand years with them. Everything around you will seem familiar."

"Do I have any more lessons to learn?"

"Let's find your chart and we can see for ourselves," said Pat.

The three of them continued into the Hall of Records and began searching for Antonio's chart. The tall shelves resembled those in The Library of

Congress. They seemed to stretch up into an entirely different stratosphere. The energy coming off them was palpable. The three souls could feel a tingling sensation. They vibrated with the knowing that eternal knowledge surrounded them. Their reverberations triggered their silvery auras to glow.

"Imagine all the answers hidden here," Antonio said.

"The original energy cells divided and multiplied and evolved until life flowed from them. You are one source of that same energy. You are that one original life. You already know where you came from and where you are going. It is all happening right now, in this very instance, therefore, you already know all the answers," Pat said.

"So, if I had done something differently in a past life I might be with Isabel right now?" Antonio asked.

"Yes, of course, you know that," Pat said. "Be patient. Your knowing will flow freely within your light again. You will feel the answers without ever having to ask the questions," Pat said.

"If past, present and future exist at the same time, part of me is with her right now," Antonio said, half answering and half asking the question. "Like space-time-continuum."

Tiberious used his right paw to pull a book off the library shelf. It was a massive, atlas sized book, entitled <u>Light number 100-515-560</u>. It was his chart.

He began to read. *"In each life I will return as a gigantic white Bullmastiff. I will live a life filled with unconditional love, so as to be able to learn this difficult lesson early in my evolution. From that love, I will be strengthened and able to move quickly through the rest of my studies. I have chosen to give my life, so another may live. I have chosen to follow the course as a companion to someone in need of love. As an obedient servant to this person I have repeatedly chosen to return to earth time and time again as a dog. Sometimes it will be difficult to exist in this submissive state. I will rely on others for food and run the risk of being caged or mistreated. I may have to beg or steal in order to maintain food. I will be forced to rely on strangers' kindness, until Antonio finds me. In past lives I lived in China and was denigrated to the streets. I died young of starvation on the Chinese streets. Antonio also died young in China as an abandoned child. We unknowingly looked all over China for each other, but were never able to locate each other. Therefore, we both chose to leave after learning the lesson of "abandonment." We were able to leave the earth relatively at the same time and spend much time above constructing our next life. In our next life I am well loved by Antonio early. He bought me at an Italian street fair as a puppy. I traveled with him to Portugal, but he was too afraid that I could not swim, so when he left on his first sailing voyage he asked a friend to watch over me. The friend failed. He did not give me proper medical care and I died shortly after Antonio left port. In my next life Antonio will accompany me from birth through death. My soulful mother will incarnate as a dog and serve the role of my earthly mother, allowing me to receive and give unconditional love. We will live a beautiful life with Antonio, traveling the Northern California coastal lands together. A dear friend of mine will die, soon after we meet. Antonio will mourn her death under an awe inspiring Aspen tree. I will stay with him for a while to console him through this grief as part of my unconditional love training. But living without her will be draining and soon I will have to depart earth and wait for Antonio in this stratosphere. I will not depart until he has found true love on earth."*

Again, Tiberious used his right paw to pull another book down. It was titled simply <u>Light number 131-131-131</u>. It was Antonio's chart. Again, the space time continuum gave the illusion that only minutes had passed, yet an earthly year had gone by. Antonio learned that Isabel bore him a son, exactly nine months after his death in February 1470 in Zaragoza. King Ferdinand raised the son, Stephen Miguel de la Paz, as his own, and believed it to be his own. Antonio's son was heir to the throne of Portugal. He was raised as a prince. Prince Stephen eventually shared rule of Portugal with his half-sister,

Isabel II. Although it was believed that the two were true brother and sister.

Antonio saw that he had abandoned two sons, one from Isabel and one from Victoria, the beautiful Seychellois woman. He saw a past life in China in which the government had taken him from his loving parents because he was a girl. No more girls were allowed to be born in China. He, as a Chinese girl, had been put to death and his parents had not fought to save him for fear of losing their only son. This was the reason he was never able to find Tiberius. They both died too young in this life, at the hands of evil. He knew what it felt like to be abandoned, although his parents had had no choice. So for Antonio's next earthly life lesson he chose to learn what is was like to be the abandoner rather than abandonee. In China he was not loved. In Portugal he failed to love and abandoned two children, yet romantically loved Isabel intensely. He wrote this into chart before he incarnated into a European sailor; his most recent earthly body. He had to complete this lesson in order to learn how to forgive his former Chinese parents. He chose a life in which he had no choice but to abandon two sons, just as his Chinese parents had had no choice but to abandon him. It was this karmic balancing that taught him the true lesson he needed to learn; forgiveness. He finally forgave his Chinese parents and therefore did not need to reincarnate with them. Yet, he had created a new karmic imbalance with his two sons; he abandoned his Seychellois son and he and Isabel's second child, Stephen. He could only hope that the children were able to forgive him in order to restore karmic balance.

While reading his past chart, in his trip to the Hall of Records, he learned that this decision to abandon two sons almost prevented him from incarnating the last time. To not know how his sons were going to handle the need for forgiveness now weighed heavily upon his choice to reincarnate. He wanted to wait in the upper stratosphere for his sons, yet he knew that they may not come to this place. They may reincarnate immediately, or not reach as high a stratospheric level. He wanted to show them love and remove the betrayal from their lives which he had placed there. It would have been too painful for him at the earthly time to try to rectify this. So he chose to pay his karmic debt later, thereby guaranteeing him another life-time with Isabel. He was happy to find that the illegitimate son he bore with Isabel will be treated as King Ferdinand's son and eventually take the thrown. In his chart it showed that he had chosen to cut his life with Isabel short so that their son would live the life of a king, instead of an illegitimate boy who would be treated as an outcast. Antonio's chart also showed that he had had to leave Isabel in order to save her from being treated as an adulterer and to save his son from being treated as an outcast, bastard child. Had King Ferdinand known the truth about Antonio and Isabel's love, Isabel could have been put to death. That is why Antonio's life with Isabel was cut short, in order to save her a painful life and a grueling death.

But Antonio's true lesson was never being able to fully give his life to the woman he loved. He was never able to be Isabel's king. He was a secret, manifested in many ways, as he had been in his previous Chinese life and as the father to Victoria's child.

He saw that many men died because of his sailing adventures. So, in his next life, he would have to make amends with the fact that their loved ones blamed him. He understood, at this point in the Hall of Records, that his sons would forever feel his abandonment and he needed to find them in the next life-time. Abandonment and betrayal from a parent can be devastating. It is the type of extreme earthly pain that causes mental defects and suicides. He had to rectify this.

Antonio's one good lesson was that he learned how to love. This ultimate lesson ensures that he crosses over to a higher plane of understanding and growth... if he chooses.

In this most recent past life he had known that he could not go a day longer without returning to Isabel. It was at this point that he returned to Lisbon, and died in bed waiting for Isabel one night. He died quickly of exhaustion and pneumonia, much like Tiberius had died years before waiting for Antonio to return from his first voyage. Antonio's return trip to Lisbon from the Seychelles had been in haste and he had not cared for himself. All he cared for was returning to Isabel, before the King returned from the European mainland. In his haste he did not take the necessary precautions to care for himself or his crew and many lives were lost. When he arrived in Lisbon, he collapsed into Isabel's bed. She kissed him on the forehead and went to make a pot of tea. He spent a magical night in the serene bed with Isabel, then his health took a turn for the worse. He missed his dog terribly. He never saw his illegitimate son and did not get to embrace Isabel's precious daughter, and, in life, he knew nothing of Victoria's stomach growing bigger by the day.

February, 1471-written by Isabel

I am concluding my beloved Antonio's diary. He died in this bed with this journal next to him today, I fear I am not far off joining him, yet I fear more that I am with his child. My children will be heirs to the thrown. This is little consolation for a life without a mother. I must find a way to survive this pregnancy and make sure our children are raised properly, with love and validation.

Queen Isabel was breath-takingly beautiful. She had alabaster white skin and silky blond hair. Her facial expression was that of an old soul; solemn, refined, and seemingly all-knowing. Her high cheekbones, oddly plump lips and unbearably long eye-lashes were features that would only improve with age. It was her physical appearance that forced the arranged marriage with the king. She was not born into royalty; however her beauty and grace placed her there. At barely twenty-years-old she was content with her life, until she lost Antonio. Being young and full of hope she never felt the desperation of loving a man who was not her husband. Deep down she had always secretly believed that the King would die, and she, being the queen, would bestow the position of the Great Admiral of the Seas, on Antonio. She had a plan for her life with Antonio. She dreamt of ruling a country with a man she loved. Mostly she dreamt of being able to wake up in his arms everyday. The nights they spent together were magical, filled with laughter and teasing. They talked and talked for hours, always listening intently to each other. Isabel sometimes thought it odd that she truly wanted to hear everything Antonio had to say. His words were like food for her soul. She survived on them. His hands fit perfectly around her waist. As she talked he held her waist tightly, holding her up higher and higher with each sentence. They had no need to prove anything to each other by speaking louder than the other. In fact, they both wanted to listen more than talk. They wanted to hear about the other's life. Not their present life of adultery, but rather their real lives and real selves. Antonio knew that Isabel was not born a queen. He knew she was born a peasant. And she knew he was not born a Great Admiral of the Seas. She knew he was basically an exiled convict from Italy. Years before her arranged marriage to the king, Isabel and Antonio found each other on a Portuguese beach. As teenagers they played hide and seek in a Lisbon lighthouse. They loved placing bets on who could find the most worthy treasures on their dives. After each dive they returned with their arms full to the lighthouse, where no one could see them. They dumped armfuls of oysters, lobsters, mussels, abalone, and various ocean relics onto the sandy lighthouse floor. They debated if part of an old anchor counted as more than two lobsters. Eventually they had enough booty to create a chess set. Mussel shells were white pawns. Oyster shells were black pawns. They broke an abalone shell in half to create two queens. The white queen had the brightest pink hue. The black queen was bluish grey. Rooks and bishops were various lobster claws. Isabel and Antonio devoured the lobster meat, which they shared in abundance with Antonio's huge, white dog. The dog licked the sand from the crustacean and daintily ate the claws. The lovers assigned the leftovers

to either the white or black figurines. Dead baby seahorses were the knight figurines and sand-dollars were
the kings. They knew sand-dollars shouldn't be kings
because they were so pure and white, like queens, but
the sand-dollars were the biggest chess pieces and
kings didn't move a lot, so they chose the biggest, least
defensive, ocean items as kings. They used these items
from the ocean instead of sea-shells because early on
they agreed that sea-shells belonged on the beach, not
locked away somewhere to gather dust. Antonio drew
black and white squares with the darker and lighter
shades of sand from the beach. The playing squares
were perfect. Not one square was larger or smaller
that any other. The rule was that the loser of each
game had to set up the next game. Isabel was more
of a sore loser than Antonio was and occasionally she
got mad if she lost. Sometimes she would storm away
from the chess board. Once she even knocked over all
the pieces in anger. After realizing that she had ruined
his perfectly made squares she felt so badly that she
cried. She spent hours piecing in back together. After
that, each game, win or lose, Antonio reset the board.
She told him not to and rushed to help him. He held
her down and threatened to tickle her all day if she
didn't let him set up the board. He always placed her
queen on the sandy board first. She yelled that he
was letting her win after that. In reality they were
perfectly matched. He did let her win occasionally

when she was grumpy and she let him win on the days that she had to return to her parents.

They played for hours and hours on their home-made chess board. Antonio's dog lazily rolled in the sand, napping through the long chess games, never leaving Antonio's side. Hours turned to days and soon Isabel's teenage years were over. It was then that her parents accepted the extravagant offer from the ruling royal family to arrange a marriage with King Ferdinand. Antonio's heart sunk, but did not break, nor did Isabel's. The two knew that they would always be together. It was at this point in their life that Antonio and his dog began spending more time on boats, as Isabel was forced into her life of luxury. Luxury did not turn to boredom as expected because Isabel knew that Antonio was close by. When she looked in the mirror at her regal clothes and tightly pinned hair, she smiled, knowing that Antonio would love her appearance. Whenever she stood in the royal palace looking in the mirror she saw herself through his eyes and she waited patiently for the king to go on another trip.

The king was quite pleased to have a wife who did not complain about his long absences and she was quite pleased when he left. In reality, it was the perfect arranged marriage.

Isabel had her own bedroom which she designed in a way that would accommodate Antonio's visits. They could no longer sneak to the lighthouse. She was the queen. Even dressed in peasant clothes her beauty was visible. She made sure her room was on the ground floor and had many tall windows and doors which opened to the rose garden. The room was decorated with long, white flowing curtains, a sand colored chaise lounge, a hope chest, a piano, two night stands, and a lantern in every window. Her favorite piece of furniture was a mirrored make-up table. Like the mahogany bed it was adorned with sea-shell carvings. The top left drawer was filled with scented oils and candles for the lanterns. All the oils and candles were scented with lavender from the garden outside her window. The top right drawer was filled with broken baby seahorses, cracked lobster claws, two perfect sand dollars, and numerous chipped oyster and mussel shells. Whatever remained of their childhood chess set lived in the top right drawer.

All the roses in the garden didn't matter. As often as they could meet, Antonio arrived with armfuls of white roses, purple lilacs, baby's breath and lavender stalks. The two lovers talked and laughed while Isabel slowly plucked the lavender from the stalks. She crushed each flower in a wooden spice bowl. She emptied the lavender crumbs into their pillow cases. They often talked so late into the night that as the sun came up. They grabbed onto each other tightly, afraid that time was running out for love making. When they were together it was always in private. This gave them the freedom to never let go of each other. Even if one said something slightly contrite to the other, their few sharp words were resolved before their hands and feet could have time to disentangle from each others'. There was an unspoken deep trust between them. Unbeknownst to Isabel this trust came from lifetime after lifetime together.

On the few mornings that they awoke in the same bed, she was happy all day. Those days were untouchable days; days when nothing could sway her. The first thing she saw on those days was a white, porcelain pitcher in a matching washing bowl. It was always over-flowing with the wild dahlias, roses, lilacs and baby's breath that Antonio brought her. The flowers were never from her garden. He brought her wild flowers from the meadow near the lighthouse. They weren't white or purple, like the ones in her garden. They were brilliant orange, yellow, magenta wildflowers with white lilacs and long lavender stalks. The flowers bunches from Antonio were unruly. They overflowed and entangled the porcelain pitcher. They smelled free and salty from growing so close to the ocean.

When she moved to get out of bed, he instinctively pulled her closer. All night he held her tightly, wherever they slept. Even in his sleep he never let go of her, especially when they slept on the lighthouse dirt floor. Subconsciously he watched over her as they both slept. Sometimes his protectiveness was so instinctual that he rolled on top of her and wrapped her underneath him. When she rolled away from him, his hand reached for her thigh. His hand was huge and warm. She crawled back into bed. The next thing she saw was Antonio's long eye-lashes and strong arms. She smelled the lavender pillows. On those days, she remained level headed and even keeled all day, as if strength had somehow been pumped into her veins all night. His protectiveness during their sleeping hours gave her a constant feeling of safety. When he wrapped around her, it was as if she could finally allow herself to fall into a deep coma. In their sleep, her strength and grace grew. She awoke refreshed and self-assured. When they slept back to back, her buttocks molded into his lower back. They were one perfect picturesque, white marble sculpture which could never be altered by even the sharpest chisel and mallet. Every edge, every contour, every piece was perfect. Even they did not fully understand that the sculpture could never be broken.

When they had to part from each other it didn't faze either of them. Their sculpture was perfection and they both knew if would be exactly the same as soon as they were back together.

Time caught them. Isabel lay in the bed clutching Antonio's journal. She thought she could survive without him, at least long enough to raise his child. Days went by before she could get out of bed. It was cold. The white pitcher of flowers began to smell moldy. The long, willowy stems dangled lifelessly. All the while she held her baby daughter tightly to her chest. The green dancing beads above her head turned grey. It was a slow crumbling. At first she noticed that she couldn't form complete sentences, so she stopped talking. Her only words were whispered into baby Izzy's ears. "Know that you are loved."

She could no longer go out in public. She felt in danger at all times. It was as if her brain stopped working. Blood stopped flowing freely through her veins. Her alabaster skin went from smooth, glistening satin to grayish blue. Her hands and feet were numb and cold. Nights without Antonio caused her to be confused. She walked from one room to another without remembering why she had entered each room. She took long baths, then, as soon as she was dry and had habitually put lotion on her body, she drew another bath.

Each morning she awoke covered in sweat. She could remember what it was like to awake in Antonio's arms after long nights of being cocooned into safety, yet, since she knew it would never happen again, she didn't see a need to get dressed. She dreaded the nights. She knew the night terrors would come and she was deathly afraid that they would sneak into baby

Izzy's basinet. She became almost afraid to hold her own daughter for fear of transferring darkness into the child's light.

Isabel spent all her energy nesting for the next baby. She knew it was a boy. Contrary to her fear of infecting Isabel II, she moved baby Izzy into her bed and wrapped the basinet in blue silk.

Food was the largest worry she had. Every bite was anguish. She ate only for the baby's sake. She forced herself to think of Antonio walking out of the ocean, filled with life and carrying lobster. He had nourished her. Now she must nourish his child. Her own body felt no need for nourishment.

At night, in bed, she played games with baby Izzy. They stacked blocks and played paddy-cake with their hands. She sang to her baby girl as much as possible, hoping that her child would remember her voice. Mostly she let baby Izzy build tiny castles with the mussel and oyster shells. The sand-dollars were the baby's favorite. They were so perfectly white and round.

Eventually Isabel called her mother to the royal grounds. Her mother gasped at her daughter's appearance. The sunken eyes showed every bit of emptiness encompassing Isabel's soul. It became understood that Isabel simply was not strong enough to survive without Antonio.

Isabel gave birth to a 3.6 kilogram baby boy. Isabel

was more amazed than anyone else. She thought that something would unquestionably be wrong with a child formed with such sadness. "Life finds a way," she whispered in the baby boy's ear. King Ferdinand paced the halls as the midwives rushed about with clean water and towels.

"Let me see them," King Ferdinand pleaded. Finally, Isabel agreed. As the king entered her bedroom she lovingly placed the baby in his arms.

"Please take care of him," she said. "Never let him be apart from his sister, Please Ferdinand."

"Nooo, Isabel. No. You will be fine," he said, staring into what he thought to be his own son's eyes. He sat down on the white chaise lounge. Baby Izzy, now fourteen months old, climbed into his lap.

Isabel watched the three until she saw true happiness on the King's face. "You are a great ruler and a great father, my love," she said to him as she closed her eyes.

Isabel did not look down at her body while her soul ascended. Her spirit gracefully bent to cut the grey cord connecting her body to her soul. She tugged and tugged at the cord. It was thicker and stronger than she expected. Suddenly her tugging and struggling released with a jolt. Antonio had cut the silver, ethereal, umbilical cord for her. Her spirit launched upward with a jolt. She looked down to see Antonio floating beneath her. As she tried to maneuver her awkward spirit in his direction he raised his hand and motioned for her to stop. He pointed upward into the next stratosphere. She was desperate to be with him. She writhed in his direction.

"Iz, Go up!" he commanded. "I will be there soon." She was confused. She didn't understand why he didn't rush to her. "Please," he said, "trust me. Just Go!" She trusted his request. As she peacefully floated upward she watched him fly down into their bedroom. He kissed his son on the baby's forehead. King Ferdinand noticed the drapes moving and felt a soft breeze. Antonio's spirit wrapped itself around the three living beings huddled on the chaise lounge. Antonio enveloped them in love and held them, in a safe cocoon, until they all fell asleep together on the white chaise lounge. They were unaware that Isabel was gone. Isabel stared down at them, not wanting to leave her children, but knowing that soon enough Stephano would show similarities to Antonio and both children would be in danger. She knew she had to wait for them on the other side.

Antonio flew quickly upward. He caught Isabel's hand on his way up and dragged her quickly with him. She burst into smile as soon as he touched her and laughed harder and harder as he flew faster and faster upward. "Wait," she yelled, barely able to get the words out through her laughter.

"No. No more waiting. I'm taking you home now,"

he said flying faster. He was an entire body length ahead of her as they whisked through the clouds.

"Wait, let's play in the clouds. These are the same clouds we danced on in our dreams," Isabel said.

Their hands barely touched. He could hold her full weight with one finger. He pretended not to hear her and flew faster.

They landed in front of a white, wooden beach cottage. Miles of brilliant flowers surrounded the house. "Welcome home my love," he said.

Tiberious stood in the open front door, wiggling wildly. He jumped over the jasmine vines encircling the front porch and ran to Isabel. They rolled on the ground. Tibbs licking her face, Isabel kissing his white, velveteen head.

"Thank you…for taking care of him Tibbs. I wish I could have remembered that you would be here," she said. "I wish I could have remembered that 'here' even existed."

"Thank you for taking care of him down there," Tibbs said. "He had a happy life with you."

Pat swooped in, plucking a daisy from the garden. He handed it to Isabel. "Oh Pat," she said, wrapping her arms around him. "Were you with me?"

"Not this past time my love," Pat said, "but next time I will be there for all of you."

Isabel looked at Antonio. "I don't want another life. Let's just wait here for our children and stay here forever." Everyone and everything went silent. Antonio decided to enjoy the moment without telling her that they had to go back down to earth at least one more time to finish their lessons and complete their karmic balance.

For hundreds of years their bodies danced as one. The music never stopped playing. There was no need for sleep or food. They emerged from this half a millennium as seemingly one soul.

Isabel was bent over an abundantly flowing purple lilac bush. Her appearance was the same as it had been on earth, when she was complete and self assured, before Antonio's death.

"It is time," Antonio said to her.

"Noooooo," Isabel protested. She knew this day had been coming and her soul had decided long ago to resist it. "No Antonio. We don't have to descend to earth again. We learned our lessons of selfless love. We sacrificed a life together to save our children. We are not bound to keep learning. We are fine here," she turned back to the lilac bush.

"Iz, we may have completed our education and are able to move on, but our children did not come back to us. It has been many lifetimes and they still have not found us here. They are waiting for something.

We need to give it to them. We hold the key to our childrens' education. For them to move on, we must give them the key."

"They may have moved on without us. They may be brilliant balls of light floating over us. We don't know, Antonio. We don't know. And I can't go back. You don't know what it was like there without you. You don't know how hard life will be if we aren't together."

"Then we will make sure we find each other."

"No one can be sure of that. No matter what we write in our charts," Isabel said. "Anything can go wrong. A war could break out and you will die. I can't live there without you again."

"I will go down first," Antonio said. "I will build us a beautiful home so it is ready for you when you arrive. It will look just like this home." He gestured to the white, wooden beach cottage. Flowers swirled around the roof. Purple lilacs adorned the front door. Hummingbirds darted around their heads.

"Iz, I must find your daughter and care for her until you find us. It is my fault that she had to grow up without a mother," Antonio said.

Isabel looked at him resolutely. "Then I will find your lost son. The one you never knew. The one you fathered out of our loneliness. You left him on an island in haste to return to me. I will find him and make sure his soul is peaceful."

Pat listened intently to their conversation. He had

been waiting centuries for this day. His hand rested on Tiberious's velveteen ears. The two knew that this was an endeavor that everyone had to embark on together. They were eternally bound to each other and none of them could move on to the next level of soulful growth without all of them setting their karmic affairs in balance. After hours of silence, Pat said, "It is time that we go to the hall of records. It is time that we reread and rewrite our charts."

As they once again ascended the white marble staircase Pat reminded them, "Remember, we cannot read each other's future charts. You will not be able to see what the other writes."

Again Isabel protested. "This is not wise. If we don't find each other I might not survive. I might not recover from this life and will spiral downward."

The four of them kept walking.

Antonio pulled Pat aside. "I want to be enlightened on earth. I know the risks. I also know that this soul has earned the right to this request. I have learned abandonment, love, compassion, famine, death, altruism and eternal knowledge."

"You are right," Pat said, "You have earned this right. You have also earned the right to not have to go back to earth for another lesson. Your earthly education is complete. I highly recommend that you not pursue this voyage. Very few have every survived a life of enlightenment. The world is simply too painful,

Antonio. It is highly likely that you will commit suicide or be put to death. The human mind cannot handle the knowledge of unending suffering that exists on that planet. I advise you to move on. Wrap yourself up into a ball of light and release your energy into the universe for once and for all."

"There is the possibility of a life on earth filled with love. I must take this chance," Antonio said to Pat.

Isabel pulled her <u>Light Number Book</u> <u>121-121</u> from the library shelf. She learned that in an earlier life she had been shunned from her clan and forced to survive alone in the rainforest. She did not flip through any more of the pages and become absorbed in her past lives. She knew they were sad. She simply looked at the "chapter guide" which outlined the lessons all souls need to learn to move on. Chapter One-*Survival of the Species*. She put a check mark next to this chapter signaling completion. She had completed 'chapter one' by climbing out of primordial ooze and procreating, adding to life. Chapter Two-*Abandonment and Betrayal*. She had survived abandonment and betrayal from her clan and had also abandoned her daughter, Isabel II. Therefore her soul knew what it was like to both be abandoned and to abandon. She put a check next to 'chapter two', signaling completion. She continued down the list of chapters/soulful lessons and realized that these lessons could only be learned by reincarnating time and time again. Earth was like a university of soulful lessons. Each soul needed to complete each chapter in order to complete its education. After completion, the soul could choose to be released as pure energy back into the universe. At this point it would be a ball of light, filled with complete love and understanding.

The last chapter in her <u>Light Book</u> was titled; *Found Love on Earth*. She did not put a check mark next to this lesson. She knew that even finding love on earth with Antonio was not enough since their lives had time and time again been cut short. She took a deep breath and stared off into the distance. She did not want to return to earth for another lesson. To Isabel, the lessons represented painful learning.

"The universe hates a void," Pat said to her. She looked gracefully at him.

"But I don't want to go," she said.

"You cannot move on without finishing your lessons," Pat said. "The universe will become stagnant and life cannot find a way to grow without death and sometimes pain. The lessons must be completed."

Isabel picked up a pen and began writing her next life's chart. "It is my mission in this incarnation to find and fulfill love on earth. I must care for my children and Antonio. My instincts will be heightened and I will live a life in search of love. The unconditional love of dogs and children will be my building blocks to finding ultimate love. If I am enlightened enough to remember that I am looking for Antonio, subconsciously my hobby will be to explore lighthouses in every port of the world in search of him."

"Can I see what you wrote?" Tibb's asked Isabel.

"You know that is not allowed," Pat said. "You know that we must all choose our own fates and be responsible for our own decisions."

"I don't want to live without them," Tibbs said. "How will I find them?"

"Let your instincts and love guide you," Pat said.

Tiberious knew his past lives. He didn't need to read them again. Tibbs too picked up a pen and started writing. He wrote, "I will remain a dog in this upcoming incarnation. I will wait for twenty earthly years in this stratosphere after Antonio leaves. I will serve as a conduit of unconditional love to bind Isabel and Antonio. I can only hope that our time together has been enough that when they see me on earth they know that I am there to enhance and strengthen their chosen earthly lessons. I cannot choose their lessons. I cannot make them love me. I can only be there. My lesson is to be present for the ones I love, at any cost. I am incarnating as a conduit for <u>Light Numbers 121-121</u> and <u>131-131</u>. I will become whatever I need to become and do whatever I need to do in order to bring other souls higher in their evolution. I will do my best to take them where they are supposed to go, through the karmic tradition of our past lives."

Antonio pulled his <u>Light Number Book</u> <u>131-131-131</u> from the library shelf. He reread his past lives, outlining all he had learned. He read his lengthy past charts. "In this life I will live in a cave" one sentence read. "There will be hostile tribes living in nearby caves. Isabel is with me. Everyday I have to venture into the dark night to slay animals in order to feed my clan. We are so bound to this damp, dark cave that we draw on the walls to maintain our sanity. At first the drawings are for our own benefit. Then we realize that because of the cave's environment and remoteness that our drawings will endure for future civilizations to find. So we draw the animals living at that time and we draw the recipes for our ailments. We draw detailed instructions on how to create weapons. The earth warms and our water source disappears. I, as the leader of the clan, am forced to venture out of the cave and find water. I am deep in the southern most tip of the largest continent. I find a hole filled with water. I jump into the water hole to drink and retrieve water for my clan. I cannot get out. My skin shrivels. Isabel is forced to leave the cave in search of me. She finds the hole, and, like me, dives in for water. She finds my rotting corpse in the water. She too cannot climb out. The entire clan suffers the same fate. Our animals and children, desperate for water and to be with us, all jump into the watering hole. They all suffer the same dying fate because of my initial ignorance of entering the watering hole. Thousands of lifetimes later, our bones are found and used in scientific research. Because of the watering hole's conditions our bones are more preserved than any previous clan living in this time period. In this life, I will add to humans' understanding of prehistoric life."

Antonio went on to read other lives, all ending brutally or sadly. It was one life in particular that affected him the most. He read about a disturbing past life which defied all present knowledge of space-time-continuum. It read: "In one life I live in Bangladesh, before it is ever known by that title, so I must be traveling back in time to create this life, or forward in time. The life will teach me one lesson. I will see an impoverished, crippled man dying in the dirt. People will kick and beat him. As I try to help him he will look up at me, and in his eyes I will see the universe. I will understand that this impoverished, cripple chose enlightenment. He chose the fast track to transcendence by adding more painful circumstances to his chart than ever imaginable. He made himself crippled to feel the pain of being ridiculed, outcast and dependent on others. He chose to live in an unforgiving land. He was enlightened which caused increased sensitivity to all of his and the world's pain. I will kneel and beg him to share his knowledge with me. When I ask him what I can do to help him and try to carry him to a safe place, removed from the street and gawking onlookers, he will beg me to leave him to die. He will tell me that he chose this life of pain in order to learn the most lessons possible in the shortest amount of time in order to move on. He will tell me that he learned to love himself. I will not understand. He will tell me that this is his last life on earth with a huge smile on his heavily wrinkled, dark, bloody face. He will tell me that he saw the worst of human nature in this life and yet, placed himself in this position in order to provide any giving soul the ability to complete the earthly lesson of compassion. 'I forgive all,' he will say to me. He will die bleeding in my hands. Even more ominously, he will tell me that this time period will provide every soul's last earthly incarnation. So, it must be a time in the future, a time when the world is ending."

Antonio picked up his pen.

Antonio simply wrote, "I will incarnate again, this time with full enlightenment and knowledge of this book and all other charts. I will incarnate into life knowing that it could be torturous suffering because I will be completely aware of the earth's entire suffering. I do so in search of love on earth. I have faith that we are at a point of cellular, auric, and instinctual memory and that will aid my ability to find Isabel. I engage in this endeavor to prove the hypothesis that our soul's have genetic building blocks, just like our human bodies, and that these blocks can be decoded.

As human DNA can be decoded to prevent physical disease, soulful DNA can be decoded to end human suffering. The only way to engage in this endeavor is with the mental faculties of full enlightenment. Therefore, I will able to access more brain power than other humans. My brain's increased capacity is a result of more functional synapses than other humans have to experience. Along with added knowledge and increased problem solving skills, my brain's increased synapses enhance my ability to feel empathy and compassion. This will create added knowledge and sensitivity to the world around me and all of its suffering. As a result, I will look older than my actual earthly years. I will feel more pain than other people. I will feel and understand more than in any of my other previous lives. I will use a lighthouse as a beacon to draw Isabel back to me. I can only hope that her instinctual, cellular memories will be heightened enough to remember that the lighthouse is a safe place for her. I can only hope that instinctively she will know to go to the lighthouse. When she smells the salty ocean air, she will hopefully remember our love. I will plant lilacs to lure her to me. I will create an environment full of her favorite things and will wait for her to find it. This will be my last incarnation."

Reading his chart reminded him that now and at the point of his death, Antonio was able to access his past lives. He saw then that Isabel was pregnant and that Victoria raised one of his son's alone. Therefore, he had abandoned two sons, one from Isabel and one from Victoria, the beautiful Seychellois woman.

It was over five hundred years ago that he learned this. Yet, everything he learned was saved in his soul, not his brain. When in the upper stratosphere he did not simply see his past life in China in which the government had taken him from his loving parents because he was a girl. His soul remembered it and accepted it, without the need for vengeance or even forgiveness. It simply existed as it was. As a molecular being he accepted that no more girls were allowed to be born in China, so he, as a Chinese girl, had been put to death and his parents had not fought to save him for fear of losing their only son. He knew what it felt like to be abandoned, although his parents had had no choice. So he had chosen a life where he had no choice but to abandon two sons whom he did not even know existed. At this point he internalized all these facts and lessons. They did not rattle around in his brain. These earthly lessons were internalized into his being. But his true lesson was loving unconditionally and yet never being able to fully give his life to the woman he loved. He was never able to be Isabel's king. He was a secret, manifested in many ways. He saw that many men died because of his sailing adventures. So, in his next life, he would have the choice to make amends with the fact that their loved ones blamed him. He understood, at this point in the Hall of Records; that his son would forever feel his abandonment and he needed to rectify this in the next life-time in order to save his child from the terrible perils of betrayal. These perils could haunt a soul forever and lead to lifetimes of seeking escapes, through drug use or suicide. He had to fix this. Antonio's saving grace was that he had learned how to selflessly love, and that a life filled with love is the ultimate reward for already learning how to live and accept everything, unconditionally. Lessons learned on University Earth were painful and seeking eternal enlightenment would put his soul to the ultimate test. The reward would be concreting the sacredness of love. The antithesis of which would be a lifetime of loneliness and suffering.

They all put their pens down and closed their Light Books. They each meticulously placed the books back in the allotted places on the library shelves. Their books were thicker than the books adjacent to them. The spines of their books looked old and worn. The covers were soft, supple, burgundy leather. All the books in the Hall of Records had gold tassels marking the last page written upon. Antonio noticed that his tassel was dangling near the last chapter in his Light

Book. He tried desperately to see where Isabel's tassel was in relation to the number of pages in her book.

Pat laughed. "What ya doing there," he chided Antonio.

"Oh just looking around," Antonio said nonchalantly.

"You know you can't see where she will end up, "Pat said. "All souls have been created piece by piece, atom by atom, molecule by molecule. All of us have different weaknesses and strengths. You, for instance, are prone to pneumonia. This might be due to the fact that when you evolved, the earth's dank environment caused your earthly body to freeze to death. You couldn't handle some environmental factor that other's could. On the other hand, you have survived many physical and soulful obstacles. Your fate is yours and yours alone. You can only affect Isabel's fate by loving her and making her strong. You must learn what she needs from her. I cannot give the answers, nor can the Light Books. Survival of the fittest, my friend. The most developed brains learn to compensate for physical weakness. The least developed souls compensate through brutality. The physically strong bodies and brains are at an advantage and thereby strengthen their souls. Their spirits will soar fastest."

"Pat, is he trying to read my book again?" Isabel chided.

"I just want to help!" Antonio joked.

Tibbs rolled his eyes.

Pat dusted off the books and sprinkled some kind of magic fairy dust.

"What is that," Isabel asked.

"It's just a way of signaling that you are ready to go," Pat said. Isabel took a deep breath.

"Our biggest obstacle is going to be remembering," Antonio said to all four of them. "Our conscious minds will not remember any of this. We will have to rely on our cellular memories and our instincts."

"Our children hold these genetic, cellular memories. We will know who we are when we find our children," Isabel said. "Cellular, instinctual, soulful memories will lead us to each other."

"Don't forget your auras," Pat reminded. "Your colors and energies will bind you to each other. And I might throw in a little help if you two get too lost."

"This doesn't always work, you know," said Isabel. "Souls always want to find each other. They search endlessly for each other, only to end up lonely and vacant. It is the main cause of suffering on earth. What if we don't find each other?"

"She's right," said Pat. "This will not be easy."

"Stay true to your path," Antonio said. "I will do the same. Don't loose yourself to nonsense and don't hurt your soul."

"Our souls must stay pure to stay on our paths," Isabel said. "We must always remember who we are."

"You won't be able to 'remember' all of this," Pat said, looking at Antonio with a knowing glance. Pat was not able to tell Isabel or Tibbs that Antonio had chosen all knowing omnipotence in this incarnation. He simply said, "If you lose your way, this may be a wasted life."

"No," Antonio said, adamantly. "I already lost our past life together. We can't fail again." Blue and green breezes swirled around his soulful body. Isabel noticed the colors.

"I will try to stay pure white, so your colors stand out," she said.

"You can't," Pat said. "If you are on your correct path, your energy will be vibrant colors."

Isabel twirled into a rosy hue of purple. "I will dance," she said. "The dancing will release my energy and you will see me."

"That's a good idea," said Pat. "Dance happily through life so you stand out amongst others. That will give us a better hope of finding each other."

"I will go down ten years before you," Antonio said confidently to Isabel. "That way I can get things ready for you. You know; build us a house, start building our life. So when you arrive it is ready for you. You will have the same beautiful mahogany bed. When you place your hand on my human heart you will know that it is only alive and beating because of you."

"Don't do everything," Isabel said. "I want to make

the quilts and comforters for our bed. I want to plant our garden with white roses and have a say in our house."

"I will be on the ocean waiting for you," Antonio said.

"How will I know how to find you?" Isabel said.

"Stay true to your path. Follow your instincts, and when all else fails; just look for the light, my love. We always find each other in the light."

Spring 1475, Northern California, Tomales Bay

A rubbery, reddish Aspen twig swayed in the wind. The four inch tall seedling fought for its life in the dry, sandy North American earth. One rock or one foot could stomp out the emerging tree's life.

BOOK TWO

Five hundred and twenty-four years later

1999, Northern California,
United States of America

CHAPTER ONE

just weird enough

He wasn't running away. It was just supposed to be one night at a badly remodeled Ramada Inn in Antioch, California, or some nearby town with a stench of placated permanence. Convenience store after convenience store flashed past him as he drove east on Highway 24. Sleep would be difficult due to the three cups of gas station coffee twisting in his head. The hotel clerk offered no dining options and his dogs had been in the car too long to consider sharing their kibble. He climbed back into the car. He couldn't drive back home. She would still be there, waiting in their house for their dreams to continue as planned. Maybe they should never have moved in together. Maybe he should have taken that job. It just didn't seem right at the time. What if he just kept going? What if he never went back? He really never had to.

He had done this before, but never this drastically. His previous escapes were comprised of football, beer, a lazy-boy and a remote control. Not this extreme, literal disappearance from his only known physical connections. His previous road trips always had destinations, or at least time limits. They were timely drug binges of self-loathing and escape, equally weighted in importance. If he had two days off he would travel for one, stay at a motel, binge on whatever he could get his hands on, and then turn around and return to Morgan. This time he had saved up all his vacation days at the San Francisco Fire Department.

The conflicting emotions and inevitable decisions caused his breaths to shorten subsequently causing a mild anxiety attack. He needed to breathe. His head bumped the steering wheel as he tried to place it between his knees. The hotel parking lot got darker and blacker. Desperation was setting in quickly and his immediate options appeared bleak for food and a comfortable place to sleep. He didn't like this motel or the front desk clerk. She seemed rude and nosy. He could hungrily scale the chipping pink staircase to his motel room three times in order to sneak in all three dogs, or find the ever present twenty-four hour Wal-Mart, where there was the possibility of pretzels, hopeful liquor options, squeezable cheese and rubberized cupcakes. This could get him through the night. He knew this town. He had passed through many of them driving to and from college. No history. No emotion. He always chose the long route from Northern California to UC Santa Barbara, driving through the middle of the state, past produce stands, modern windmills and lots of *conserve-water-for-local farmers* makeshift billboards. This route was easier for David than the partially coastal and scenic Highway 1 or the frequented Highway 5, nicknamed The Grapevine for the miles and miles of three foot tall wooden posts, which for three months of the year were appropriately adorned with grapevines. He needed to avoid all that traffic. This way he got to feel what it would be like to escape to a rural community, one in which Mom-and-Pop shops could provide immense obscurity without the opportunity costs of loneliness. His present personal plight seemed amplified by the surroundings. Mimi-mall after stucco mini-mall. "Oh how badly these structures will age," David mumbled out loud. He opted for the motel bed.

Morning came more quickly and less painfully, than expected and a night of stomach-shrinking hunger allowed a semi-calm numbness to settle into David's body. Usually, his lonely three-dog-nights in hotels were torturously restless, but he had learned the routine; feed the dogs, eat massive amounts of junk food, drink and binge, take a hot shower, be thankful for a clean bed, watch infomercials until the television went fuzzy, wake up somewhere new. It was amazing how routines could mask problems, or at least contribute to avoidance tendencies. He almost forgot that his fiancé was more than likely wondering where he was and that he had to decide what to do with the rest of his life. However, the more pressing problem was a lack of nicotine. He and the oldest Bulldog, Delilah, descended the stairs into the empty parking lot. Delilah's daughter, Boo, stayed snuggled under the hotel pillows. Boo was a majestic, all white Bulldog who seemed to understand everything David said. He had never taken her to obedience school because she never needed it. She was Delilah's first born puppy, out of six. As soon as she popped out, wrapped in placenta and green tinged blood, David's hands were there to catch her and remove her from her placental sack. Boo wasn't breathing when she was born. David performed CPS on her until her gums went from grey to pink and her chest rose and fell on its own. David literally breathed life into this precious puppy, hence he couldn't help choosing her as his favorite. He loved the other two dogs dearly, but Boo was the one he thought about the most. He missed her when he was at the firehouse. He had petitioned the fire department time and time again to allow him to bring her to work with him. He was hopeful that this time the petition would be accepted.

Delilah daintily tiptoed around the oil spot next to their car and anxiously leapt into the driver's seat, knowing that stale French fries lurked somewhere within the upholstery.

David returned from the convenience store slightly more awake, juggling a cigarette and a soda. The hotel looked different in the cold, hard light of day and the moisture off the asphalt caused an odd glow on the pavement. A rusted, green station wagon, with wood panels had moved into the parking space adjacent to his. Sleeping bags, an old wooden truck, overstuffed suitcases and a Rottweiler were all tied to various parts of the car. The dog appeared quite friendly, and gave David a head tilting, thoughtful smile as he and Delilah maneuvered around the station-wagon. A man's butt crack, loosely encased in baggy jeans protruded from the back seat. His head popped up like a groundhog from a hole and an enormously sincere smile swept across his Grizzly Adams face. "That's my Muffin," he exclaimed.

"What?" said David, with a crinkled brow. The man did not frighten or even startle David in the least. He simply confused him. If he had bought a muffin he would be happy to give it to this curmudgeon of a man.

"That dog! That's my Muffin. I had one that looked just like this." The man was already on all fours kissing Delilah's face.

"You had a Bulldog?" asked David. "That's

amazing. I have a Rottweiler upstairs and another Bulldog. Wanna see them?"

"After I'm finished with this little love muffin," he cooed at Delilah. He couldn't take his eyes or hands off the bulldog. "You know, these are very special dogs. They appear rough and strong, but under those wrinkles are some real fragile creatures. My Muffin…she died at eight. That's about the usual life span. The vet says that every day after eight is a gift. I think every single day is a gift. Once you've loved one of these things you never want anything else. The Rottweiler helps with the protection, but it isn't the same." Delilah's head rested gently on his knee. She had fallen asleep standing up. "Ha, look at that. They luv ya so damn much." Delilah was a people oriented dog who usually never left David's side, let alone fell asleep on a stranger. She didn't even seem to notice the new Rottweiler. David astoundingly stared at the unusual man's interaction with Delilah. And the guy had a dog! Delilah was never that friendly to people with other dogs.

It seemed weird that they had the same breed of dogs, seeing as how people are supposed to resemble their dogs and all that. He wondered if in any slight way he resembled this round little lumber jack. "I'm David," he said with an extended hand.

The gesture was reciprocated. "Nice to meet you David. You can call me Pat."

"Pat," David repeated as if to make it sink in. Such an innocuous name. David felt absolutely no emotion about the name. It didn't represent the era in which he was born or the age of his parents. No past or present. Just "Pat."

Pat looked at David just squarely enough in the eyes as to not frighten him. After all, they were perfect strangers. The two men and the two dogs sauntered up the stairs, in search of other canine playmates.

After fawning over David's dogs, like grandparents with grandchildren, they settled in the hall out front of David's room for their morning cigarettes. David leaned on an oddly twisted guard rail over looking the parking lot. It was a bad imitation of wrought iron, painted fake rust or "rustic". Whatever the color, it was now smeared over the front of his pants. Neither of them said anything about it.

Children ran past them, as fast as if they had just heard a recess bell ring, taking the corner so quickly that they gleefully skidded into the two men. The dogs went crazy. The kids started knocking on the hotel room windows to tease the dogs into further chaos. Pat continued chatting away. He never even so much as turned to notice them. David's admonishments to the children went unheeded and David became slightly agitated. More children arrived, until a flurry of children running circles around the hotel became a blur. The dogs were beside themselves, barking and lunging at the windows. The men continued to chat away in their own little world.

"You want a soda?" Pat asked, motioning to the refrigerator-like contraption in the corner with neon lights flashing SODATOPIA and blinking orange buttons.

"Sure. Just let me go get some change," David said pulling a plastic rectangular room key from his back pocket.

"Don't worry about it. Regular Coke right?" There was no *kerplunk* or *jingle* when the change went into the machine. It was more like a *swoosh* and suddenly two Cokes appeared.

"Thanks. So Pat, what do you do?"

"I spent three years wandering around the forest, "Pat said. A shriek of exhilaration from an unknown child came from above. The elevator doors opened and out poured a bevy of adolescent boys, skateboards in hands. They plowed past the two new friends, pushing their way toward the soda machine, as if they didn't even see the men. David jumped aside. Pat moved slowly, vaporously through the crowd. As they walked back to the room skateboards thundered past them. Boo, the younger Bulldog, greeted them at the door, convulsively wiggling as only a truly spoiled fifty-pound lap dog can do. The men exchanged their understanding for Boo's love of life with a simple glance. Boo had all white fur and the deepest set wrinkles ever seen on a Bulldog. Her body was svelte and beautiful. She danced gracefully through life. Her blue collar glowed against her white fur.

"She's always this happy," David said. "Even when I was in L.A. during the riots, back in '92, some gang member put a shotgun to my car window. Boo though it was a big toy. She jumped at the window. The guy ran away. I guess you can say she saved my life. This all happened down in Beverly Hills. Well, just on the edge. It's one of the reasons I left L.A. One near-death experience was enough for us," he said hugging Boo.

"Makes ya think about things, doesn't it?" Pat said.

"Made me think that no one knows what the fuck is up anymore. I mean, those cops knew what was coming and they just let it happen. For God's sakes, I was just driving down the street. The same street I drove down almost every day, and all of a sudden there was a fax machine flying past my windshield. They were looting Radio Shack. The thought they had some right or something. I don't know…," David's voice trailed off. It was obvious that this discussion both scared and saddened him. "Sorry to go off like that," he said.

"Don't worry about it," Pat said. "You know, *term limits* could have prevented all of this." Before David could even consider engaging in the political conversation he was sucked in. It turned serious, and yet respectful. It was rare for David to meet a stranger that wasn't immediately at least slightly annoying. He usually would have backed out at the first inkling of politics, religion, relationships, or even opinion, however this man seemed safe. David didn't feel trapped. He knew he could cut the discussion abruptly short whenever he so chose.

"I disagree with term limits in a democracy; however I fear our society and the people got too out of control. Twenty years with the same mayor in Los Angeles was too much for people. I bet Rodney King has an answer. Maybe we should just give them a little hope to hold on to. Hope for change," said Pat. Pat was the perfect Master, sent to send David on his own quest for pure altruism. Pat was given a child abandoned five hundred years ago, in search of connection, in search of finalizing the earthly bond of his cellular genetics.

"We all need something to hold on to," David said. His eyes sheepishly shifted to the strip-mall across the street; familiar stores, identical products, predictable processed tasting foods. David hated to admit the guilty comfort he found there. "We are just holding on to the wrong things."

"Hey, you're the one who had a shotgun put to your head. You tell me what needs to be changed. I'm not here to help you figure anything out. You already know all the answers. Everybody does." Pat's voice was strong and commanding. A strange feeling of inferiority combined with curiosity came over David. It was odd, but the confusion seemed somehow enlightening. Usually when he met someone his instinct was first to assess that particular someone, and then recoil. It wasn't that he meant to judge people, or that he didn't like new people, it was just that they all seemed to take such a toll on him. He was physically fatigued after meeting new people. There had been enough losses in his life. And more people could mean more loss, but he felt instinctually drawn to this man. The fact that the guy even liked his dogs helped. He began to hope that Pat did not want to recoil from him. For the first time in a long time David did not want to be alone, or maybe he just didn't want to be without Pat.

"Aren't you going to answer that?" asked Pat.

"My sister is the only one who knows where I am. It's either her or the front desk complaining about the dogs." David was ignoring the ringing phone for fear of Pat leaving the room. Pat understood and sauntered to the window, as if to check on his car.

"Hello,...Yeah,...Jenny, you wont believe this. These's this guy here, and, ...see, I don't want to ruin this. I want him to be my friend," David whispered into the phone.

David" Solace! It's only 9 a.m. and you're already drunk, or are you still drunk? Whatever! Do you want me to come get you and your little friend?"

"Jen, you would love this guy, but I don't want to scare him away. Gotta go." David hung up the phone.

"Pat, you seem like a guy who knows what's up. Could I ask your advice on something?

"Not now. I gotta get going. You know David, you may still be here tomorrow, right here in this hotel room, but your life might not always be where you left it," Pat said. "I gotta fix that oil leak. I'm staying right next door. You gonna be here when I'm done? "I'm not sure," Dave was still trying to sort out Pat's last instruction. "Maybe I should give you my number or something before you go?" he said.

Pat fiddled with his watch. "This damn thing always runs ahead. I know it's time for me to go. You got the right time?" The watch fell to the floor as Pat fumbled with the clasp. "I'm gonna run to my room and get a screwdriver. Back in flash." He pulled out the rectangular, plastic room key, and making sure to not let the dogs get out, Pat vanished.

David heard a nearby door open with a resounding *pop*. "I'll see you soon, David," Pat called from somewhere that seemed farther away than the hotel hallway. David's eyes darted to the ceiling. He thought Pat had planned to return immediately. "Oh well," he said with a deep sigh. "We can use the sleep can't we girls? " David and the dogs dropped onto the pillows. The stress associated with conflict avoidance had caught up with him. It had been a tiresome night, and a bit of a strange morning. There was something about this man, something strangely familiar and completely non-threatening. The deep purple glow around Pat seemed to linger. David thought Pat resembled his grandfather, or was it is farther? Or maybe the first dog he had as a child? David drifted off to sleep. Images of his boy hood friends and his bedroom with Noah's Ark sheets and pairs of animals walking across the walls filled his head. There was warmth. There was comfort. There was Pat. A bearded figure loomed over David. Pat had been a part of David's dreams for as long as he could remember. The same shadow had appeared in most every subconscious mental scene David had ever had. Daydreams, nightmares, fantasies, white lies, and every ounce of his free-flowing stream of conscious possessed a unifying force. There was a common denominator, if only a shadow. David bolted upright, unsure whether he had drifted off or not, but positive that Pat had always been that comforting figure in the distance. He grabbed the phone and punched "O" for an operator.

"Hello," David said to the heavily accented hotel operator, "I'm in room 501. What room is just to the left of me?"

"Five. OOOOOOOh Two," she reluctantly responded.

"Will you please connect me?" The phone rang continuously, emptily. David ran to the window. No station-wagon. Not even an oil spot. The operator came back on the line. "I'm sorry. No one in that room"

"Okay, well, who is staying in that room?"

"You don't know?"

"I forgot his last name, but he is a good friend of mine. Pat. Yes, his name is Pat."

"Okay, hold on, "the operator said. " No sir. Sorry."

"What do you mean 'No'?" David said slightly raising his voice. "Can I leave a message for the man in room 502?"

"No sir, no man in 502. That room empty. Nobody sleep there."

David looked down at the broken watch and slowly hung up the phone. "Thank you,' he said as he replaced the phone onto the receiver.

CHAPTER TWO

love, protection or a vodka tonic

The drive went by quickly. Spots on the windshield and the rearview mirror distorted into convoluted hallucinations. Dead bugs resembled Pat's beard, and, in the glow of oncoming headlights, smudged debris fused into animals crossing the road. Imaginary hitchhikers even made their way onto the asphalt. David kept seeing Pat's face. Sometimes it was hazy. Occasionally it was clear. Mostly it was just familiar.

David didn't understand how he slept through the entire day. The day was gone and he was forced to drive at night. He meshed into an unknown, esoteric world. It had taken twenty-six years for David to create the reality that provided cohesion for his life. Now it faded as quickly as night fell. His two year, passionately charged, seemingly permanent relationship was in upheaval and a curmudgeonly angle provided him with life-altering insights while drinking soda pop. Reality, as he knew it was gone. He felt as if he had drunk way too much coffee, yet he craved caffeine. This wasn't simple anxiety. Anxiety would have been a welcomed relief to this confusion. Anxiety attacks at least have beginnings, middles and ends. This plaguing confusion could be eternal. He could become one of those burnt looking Californians, searching for the meaning of life via some good ole' Humboldt homegrown. He felt a growing void, an emptiness that had already started eating away at his insides in a much more painful way than even his worst anxiety attack.

One thing was certain; David was slowly losing his mind. Grayish blue lines flowed downward through his neck, making it hard to swallow.

Gas station coffee seemed to calm him. It was an instant fix. A constant. The result was predictable. The coffee coated the grayish pain. "Ten on seven and a coffee," David said to the cashier. He could have just swiped his credit card at the pump, but he craved human interaction. David lingered around the blackened coffee machine, over-sugaring and creaming his coffee.

He browsed through a few magazines then focused

on the San Francisco Chronicle's headlines. It showed a republican politician with a wide open mouth. "Hey, can you believe this guy?" David said to the cashier. She knew David was speaking to her. She saw a lot of his type; actually, there were a lot of his type living in the neighborhood. They never seemed to want to go home.

"You haven't started pumping your gas yet," she said.

"Oh, yeah," he muttered, putting his coffee to his lips. David went to the car and cupped is hands around his face and placed his outside palms on the rear tinted window, to get a close look at the dogs. He saw that the dogs were sleeping. It had been a long, trying trip for them. Like children, they needed stability, not hotel beds and rusty tap water. Gas stations usually meant treats. They weren't even excited that beef jerky could be forthcoming. David inserted the nozzle and returned to the cashier.

"I guess I should probably stock up on peanut butter cups and beef jerky. Maybe even some sunflower seeds. And I'll need some apple juice to wash those down. Got a looooong drive ahead of me," he said with the hope that the cashier would respond to this with more interest that she had to his newspaper headline reference.

There was no reply from the middle-aged woman behind the counter. Her glasses were attached to her head with a faux pearl chain and her sensible applied make-up gave the air of acceptance of her place in world. She seemed to be someone whose opinion wouldn't be worthless. David presumed she owned the station.

"Are you married?" he asked, dropping a twenty dollar bill on the counter.

Slightly squinting, she peered over her glasses, skeptical to engage in this conversation. "Used to be," she said.

"Is it that bad? I mean, maybe it's something we are all supposed to do. I mean, I just don't get it. She should have called my sister to see where I went. She should check with my friends. How does *she* know if I'm ever gonna come home? Maybe I don't wanna come home," David said, as if the cashier knew who **She** was.

"Uh huh. Maybe **SHE** doesn't give a shit. Here's you change." His mouth dropped. David was at first embarrassed by her lack of interest, then, as the heavy glass door swung behind him, he became annoyed.

"She doesn't own this place," he muttered to himself. "Her husband probably left her for somebody younger, somebody 'who gave a shit.' She doesn't even care enough to comb her hair. I bet there are things living in that rat's nest." His sarcasm entertained him until he could be with his dogs. Delilah opened one eye. The other would open only if and when the beef jerky surfaced.

David crinkled the bag. "Look what I have for you girls." They perked up and he doled out treats as he pulled away. The car jumped. David dropped the treats. The dogs leapt to the windows for an answer. It was as if something had grabbed David, or rather the entire car, from behind. He sat frozen. Only his eyes moved as he searched up and down for signs of Pat. No Pat. The coast was clear. He moved his foot from the brake, back onto the gas. Again the car jerked, or rather lurched. David was terrified. Then came a pounding. Then a voice.

"Stop the damn car you space case."

"What?" David practically whispered.

"Put on your brake and roll down your window. You still have the pump in your gas tank," the cashier said. David exhaled. "You have to back up so I can get it out." She spoke to him as if she were talking to a child.

The dogs didn't seem concerned that a stranger was sticking her face in their window. They sniffed the bag. Beef Jerky was more important than any of this commotion. David reached over a grabbed a piece from Delilah's stash. He gnawed at it like one of the dogs, all the while cursing at the helpful cashier and slowly backing up. He had no intention of checking what damage he had done.

"It's all her fault. Isn't it Delilah? She didn't have to be a bitch about it. Let's blow this pace." He lit a cigarette. It seemed odd to him that he could actually do such a stupid thing. "I just need to blow off some steam. How 'bout we stop at the dog park on the way home? It's not much out of the way and it'd be good for us," David said to Delilah.

The dog park was a strip of grass in the Haite-Ashbury district of San Francisco. Nine to fivers usually arrived between six and eight p.m. complete with Frisbees and tennis shoes. Doggie happy hour commenced quickly. There was a group of regulars. Although the owners were welcoming, the popular dogs, who usually dominated all the slobber covered tennis balls, shunned most any new dog over the age of three. Puppies were always welcomed. It was easier to break into the popular dog group than it was the popular group of teenagers in high school; however this social climbing is only necessary in the life of city dogs with working owners. The fact is; this small park was a flea-infested mud-pit which satisfied only the busiest and most dedicated dog-lovers. Anyone who had the time to drive elsewhere did so. David convinced himself that this activity helped to properly socialize his dogs. The truth is; it was easy to score drugs.

Coffee and cigarettes seemed to be the only thing that even remotely made him feel better the past couple of days, so it seemed reasonable to carry on in the same medicinal fashion, only it was time for something more effective. It was just so much easier than going back home. A sip of coffee, a drag off a smoke, a hit of a joint, a gulp of a pill; all produced a specific effect. It all helped David forget what he was running away from. It's easy to know what will happen next when taking drugs. Walking through a door, on the other hand, is an unknown. Anything can be on the other side.

David did not even know what exactly he was running away from. For some reason he just knew he had to run. David had no idea what he would encounter when he went home to Morgan. He needed to get up enough confidence and courage to return to her. The thought of her produced a shock wave through his body followed quickly by an intense calmness. She was a big part of the reality he was losing. She was stable and loving, and knew what was right about the world, but she wasn't with him. She seemed to be in a distant land, far away, over a big golden bridge. Here on this strip of mud, where beads and colors still decorated passersby in hues of purple and bright green, there was an illusion of peace.

People didn't have these colors in David's regular world. He was a San Francisco firefighter. The colors were blood red, lost grey, safety orange, crime-scene yellow and, unfortunately, mostly death black. This was the world David had chosen. The women in his professional world tucked their clothes neatly into their tight waisted pants and handed out daily evaluations. David never knew what the evaluations would say. The Haite-Ashbury was different. It was a constant. It always produced drugs with pretty colors; sky blue, sunset pink, fertile green, brilliant white. The real world could turn to black at any time. It was confusing and anxiety filled compared to other colorful worlds. Some firefighters could handle the anxiety and nightmares that went with the job.

David kneeled behind a large oak tree. He stuck out his open palm to the strange shadow emerging from the bushes. Four yellow, chipped pills fell into David's hand. The dealer never considered that David could be begging.

"Twenty bucks."

"Ludes or ecstasy?" David asked.

"Ludes dude."

"Cool. Got any green?"

"Make it thirty."

"Deal," David said quickly reaching in his pocket.

"Deal."

Before he knew it David was driving happily across the Golden Gate Bridge and into San Rafael, an area of Marin County. It was easier than he thought to make the return home. He gave this credit to his personal strength and not the Quaaludes. Delilah started whining. It wasn't an urgent whine. It had more aggravation to it. After all, her trip to the dog park had been less than exhilarating seeing as how she never got to get out of the car, and she knew that if she caused enough fuss she might weasel one more park stop out of him. She smelled the Marin wetlands.

It was early fall. Red, orange and yellow hues graced all but one tree. Delilah pushed her left paw down as hard as she could into the arm rest on the car window. She knew if she bounced around enough she would find the button that magically made the window go down. She moved her weight back and forth on the armrest until it worked. Delilah stuck her head, brisket and front legs as far out the window as she could. Her paws flapped in the wind. Her jowls were pinned into her cheeks. Her bottom teeth protruded more than usual. Other drivers smiled and pointed at her.

She knew David had been Antonio's son in a past life. Delilah was born with this knowing. She knew David was the son Antonio never knew about and never cared for. She knew it was her mission to care for him now. She knew all the running in the world wouldn't help him find a father lost in a past life, but she stayed with him on his journey to keep him safe. As soon as David parked the van, Delilah jumped out the window and broke into a full stride. She galloped sideways, as Bulldogs do, looking clumsy, awkward and happy. Her tongue lolled to one side.

A single aspen tree greeted hikers to this hidden

natural habitat. Its leaves were the color of perfectly ripe sweet corn and when the wind blew the leaves simulated the light sound of early rain. Delilah could sit under this tree for hours. It used to be closer to the coast. She could still hear the same waves Antonio had sailed the boats through. She remembered the smell and texture of boat's wooden decks under her long, narrow feet. She remembered the boat's white sails in contrast to her brightly colored scarves. In this life, Delilah didn't care about toys or water or playing with other dogs. She was there only to help David, but as the winds blew the salty water scents drew her back to her knowing. She longed for Antonio. She had been on this earth five years and still had no trace of him. Maybe he hadn't reincarnated with her? But then what would be the point of running all over this crazy planet with Antonio's long lost son, she thought. She knew she couldn't outlive David. She had tried so hard to in their past life, but, thankfully, rarely do mothers outlive their children. Being a firefighter was dangerous and accidents tragically took many of them too soon. Either David was meant to die young and Delilah would guide him up to Antonio, or Delilah still needed to find Antonio in order to connect her two boys. She could smell him in the salty air. This was the first time she could feel him nearby. Delilah sat in front of the aspen tree like Buddha in front of his temple. The other dogs and David admired the regal Bulldog from a distance. She sat unknowingly without want or need, blending with the universal energy. Her head rose high, facing the wind head on, waiting for Antonio's scent to blow in from the seaside.

The Aspen tree she protectively sat in front of was technically titled Populous Tremuloides. The trembling of the tree excited Delilah with more scents. It frightened David with its' fragility. It seemed so fragile, and yet a single grove of Aspen trees in Colorado are the world's largest and perhaps oldest living organism. They live for hundreds and hundreds of years, unless mankind destroys them. The trees have the physical ability to view past, present and future lives. Their roots grow towards each other, as groups of karmic souls reincarnate together. The numerous Aspen roots fuse into one root system and continue to expand as one living entity, the same way humans eventually blend into one universal connectedness. One grove of aspens can dominate a plateau or mountainside. Each aspen grove has its own distinct hue of yellow, orange, green and red. This color fingerprint helps define not only individual trees, but also individual organisms. They are like families with lots of children and all the kids have the same eyes and hair color, but differently shaped noses. The families are bound by similar auras, as the trees are bound by distinctive hues.

David didn't like this single tree. He did understand

why its' branches twisted in such a strange way. A breeze blew softly, causing the leaves to whisper and David to shiver.

"Time to go Delilah," Delilah reluctantly sauntered towards him, wistfully looking back at her resting spot. "Come on Delilah," he commanded. "Faster please!"

The ludes stated really kicking in. That small window of drug-induced confidence was closing. It no longer seemed like going home was such a good idea. A few shots of tequila should do the trick. This meant going to his favorite tequila bar. Morgan actually liked this place so maybe, David thought, she would be happy to meet him there. A coupe of margaritas and a beautiful view of the bay could solve anything. It seemed like the right thing to do. He would just call her when he got seated.

Guaymas restaurant and bar was located on a small peninsula in Tiburon, CA. It was named after a Mexican city near La Paz, Mexico. This had always been one of David and Morgan's favorite places; hence David used it as his girlfriend's nickname.

They had vacationed at a Club Med in La Paz and, daring to venture out of the manicured resort surroundings, had taxied into the city of Guaymas. They were the only tourists who did so. The others seemed so envious, asking questions about the *real* price of liquor and food. They felt stronger than any of their fellow vacationers. But that was a life-time ago, or maybe just last year. He remembered Morgan's white, sweetheart neckline sitting across the table from him in the filthy third-world country restaurant. Somehow she managed to leave without a speck of dust on her white dress. They were, he thought, untouchable. "Disaster Proof" was the term he used to describe their relationship. He heard it on a television show years ago about a couple who had lost their only son. That couple made it. They were truly "disaster proof". For some reason David felt deep in his gut that he was "disaster proof". Not the relationship, just him.

The call to Morgan was easier after the Herradura tequila shots. She arrived undaunted. I'm glad you didn't try to drive home after drinking. Thank you for calling," she said.

"Hi my Guaymas," he said to her affectionately, "will you do a shot with me?"

"How about a kiss first?" she asked firmly.

He reached up and pulled her face to his.

"One shot and then you come home with me, okay baby?" she said.

"Three," he negotiated with a mischievous grin. His life of running and the constant external validation of being a firefighter had given him the *je ne se qua* of a perpetually wealthy bachelor instead of someone lost at sea.

"Two. And I don't kill you when we get home."

Her smile was more intoxicating than any amount of liquor.

"Deal, my beautiful Guaymas." He knew he didn't have to barter anymore. She crumbled at his smile. Things felt right for him, or at least familiar. "But I know you wanna do three," he teased. "I already can't drive. Will you put the dogs in your car?" he asked without meeting her eyes.

"No. We're too close to the main road to be moving them around like that. I'll drive your car home. You can get up nice and early tomorrow so we can get my car before work."

"You're a doll for putting up with me," David said.

"I know! Now give me one of those drinks before I remember what a shit you can be."

"Ah, ah, ah, ah, ah," he said waiving his index finger. "You know the rules."

"No, you don't deserve it today," she said.

"Oh come on. Just tell me what's underneath those blue jeans."

"The beige, lace teddy. Okay?"

"Cheers!" he said, raising his glass.

"You're buying me dinner tonight. You know that don't you?"

"Anything you want my love. Anything you want." The past two days seemed to melt away. His time with Morgan was bittersweet. It was ripe avocado green surrounded by bands of red. Reality, or rather a drunken version of reality, was back.

They snuggled closely together under their down comforter, Delilah snoring at their feet. Delilah snoring the same beautiful aura of blue in every lifetime. The blue surrounded the couple's bed and lulled them into comfort. As Morgan had done for Antonio over a hundred years ago.

"Tell me you love me," David said.

"David Solace, I love you more than life."

She could not have answered more perfectly. He knew she loved him, and he her. It was all most people could ever want out of life. He lay there with her in his arms, blond hair tousling over his chest, thinking how far and how fast he could run from this agony.

Chapter Three

cellular memories

Sebastian Carpricio's family was one of the oldest in the fishing import export business. It was rumored that hundreds of years before the family had been exiled from Italy to Portugal, but had kept the Italian name and heritage. At the early age of twenty-two Sebastian ran the oyster and abalone company. He learned to dive for abalone off his native coast of Lisbon as a child. He was too young to use S.C.U.B.A. gear so he went with a snorkel and net in the early mornings and brought up more abalone than his father's biggest boats. Sebastian was mesmerized by the abalones' colors. The hues of blue and pinkish grey were seemingly made perfect by the streaks of silver. As both a child and adult Sebastian could stare at the shells for hours. He placed his two index fingers in front of the open shell, as he slowly separated his fingers he could see how the lines of energy still connected. The foggy energy between his fingers was the same color as abalone meat and the inside of abalone shells. Each shell was different, as was the fogginess between Sebastian's fingers each time he focused on the string of energy connecting them. The farther he moved his index fingers apart and tightly squinted his eyes the more he could see and feel the colors. And the more the world made sense to him.

Not much of Sebastian's life made sense to him, because he could feel and understand too much. Everything touched him. His mother died tragically of pneumonia and dehydration one day when his father was out to sea. The family lived in Lisbon at this time. Sebastian sat by her side, swearing to never leave her, not knowing what to do to save her, deep down knowing that nothing would save her.

He could see energy in the pink stringy fog between his index fingers. He sat for hours as a child staring at the shells, squinting his eyes until her face came into view. Sometimes it was his mother's face; sometimes it was Isabel's face. They were both always there. They both always loved him and he never felt alone when he squinted at the abalone shells. Their colors brought him back to a place of understanding.

As he grew up and took over the fishing empire

he, as most men in their twenties do, felt the need to expand. He needed to see the world. So he took the family's largest fishing vessel and took off in search of something, anything, which could lead him to Isabel. Not knowing where he was going, but knowing exactly what he was looking for, he hunted for signs of her existence. Although he had chosen enlightenment on earth, that painful all-knowingness did not guarantee him all the knowledge he needed to find her. He was the type of man that had enough confidence and strength to embark into the unknown, mostly because he knew who he was. He knew who and where he came from. His roots gave him wings. He wasn't a lost soul trying to piece together pieces of his life. He was a man moving forward, except for an occasional tinge and flash of green light. These green flashes made him feel empty and full at the same time. He would never admit to anyone that the flashes were what kept him moving forward, exploring, diving deeper and deeper into the ocean and life.

What he found was thousands of miles away; an American bay filled with oysters. As he placed his index fingers and thumbs adjacent to the open oysters, like guns firing at each other, he squinted hard, creasing the deep crows' feet around his entrancing turquoise eyes. He slowly separated his fingers. Bands of green emanated from the oysters. The American oysters had everything the European abalones had; blue, pink, and silver accents to show him his way home, plus the crustaceans had slimy green hopeful growth inside them. He knew he had found a second home as he stared at the oysters. He knew he could make a living with oysters as well as he had done with abalone. So he called his father and grandfather in Lisbon and explained that he was buying a dock and office in the United States, "In a wonderful, lucrative place," as he put it. "Tomales Bay, situated just below Bodega Bay and within a couple of miles of San Francisco." He explained that he would import abalone from Portugal and farm oysters locally. He told his ancestors that all the businesses in Bodega Bay would buy from him. And they did.

Sebastian quickly stopped enjoying the trips to and from Lisbon, whether by sea or plane. He couldn't find it in his soul to leave the Pacific coast and return to the Atlantic. He didn't know why, but every morning he dug his feet into the sand, stared hard at the oysters and waited for something magical to happen.

CHAPTER FOUR

a watered down version of life

There was a brutal honesty about Morgan O'Neill. At dinner parties the conversations seemed confining to her. She didn't much care about people's careers. Their families and love lives were much more revealing, hence she routinely asked questions that made people, including David, wince. It wasn't that she meant to startle or intrude. She simply was genuinely interested in what composed the characters that decorated her life. These slightly intrusive questions were Morgan's means to her ends. "So I hear you're starting the search for your biological parents," she asked a perfect stranger one day at a dinner party in San Francisco. The person ran off.

"So, George, I hear you are going through another

divorce. How's it going?" George talked to her for hours. She pretended to listen so convincingly that he followed her around for hours, talking compulsively and nonsensically the entire time. She finally acknowledged him with eye contact, "So, you're an attorney. I'm shocked. How do you find time for this hectic life?" That egged on more of his delusional rambling. Finally, she sent him to get her a drink.

For almost unexplainable reasons these types of questions fueled Morgan and led her to believe that she was a confidant for the person next to her, who, of course, needed her desperately. For even more unexplainable reasons people were immediately drawn to Morgan O'Neill and immediately thankful that they could have just met the best friend they would ever have. Some people regarded her as a snoop and ran quickly away from her. Her questions made questionable people, who felt the need to hide something, run from her. Maybe they were just afraid she would try to help. Maybe they had never analyzed their own lives enough to answer her. She never understood this. Knowledge was power, but only power to help heal, as far as she was concerned. She had a healing light blue energy about her. This energy was only tapped into when she was silent. At other times she talked so much and asked so many questions that she became lost in her quest for knowledge. The outcome of helpfulness was sometimes overshadowed by intrusion and people sometimes became nervous around her, as if she was looking too deeply inside them. She wanted their secrets. Very few people she talked to even knew their own secrets. They carried them deep inside where only their dreams, or Morgan, could retrieve them.

Other people immediately regarded her as someone "who really gets them." They would bear their souls to her and then walk tearfully away, shaking their heads in disbelief that a stranger could be so much like themselves. An elderly man once asked her if she could analyze dreams. She asked him to tell her his dreams. He said, "I dreamt of a beautiful library that held all the answers to my life, but the books were all glued shut."

"You are not reaching you're full potential. Practice lucid dreaming. Dream of opening books. Make your body float above the books and watch them open instead of prying them open with your fingers," she said to the old man.

"I am old. I should have the answers," he said.

"Somewhere you are young," she said to him. She made people feel strong and less alone in the world. She helped them to understand that everyone is connected, but the people and their problems exhausted her. She snuck out of parties early without ever saying "good-byes," then she called the hostess the next day and thanked her or him.

First impressions were Morgan's strong point. She didn't strive for this. In fact, judging from the dozen or so outfits that were discarded onto the floor before she found something she deemed suitable to wear; it was obvious that she was indecisive. She strove for something that didn't make her completely self conscious about one slight flaw or another. She settled on a black velvet pant suit that evening. She always settled for something regal and conservative. Her power was in her poise and grace.

She and David frantically rushed around the kitchen, occasionally brushing against each other, as they prepared for their dinner party. David wanted to serve spaghetti, second only to pizza as the staple food of not-so recently graduated college students. Morgan insisted on lasagna. Cooking was not one of her strengths. She did it when she had to, and she did it well. She just didn't like to cook much.

"Please David, let's at least give the illusion of knowing what we're ding in the kitchen," she pleaded.

"Did say *delusion?*" he joked.

"Okay, come one. Help me slice the vegetables."

"I bet we could think of other things to do with this," he said holding up a carrot. Morgan ignored him. This type of humor was childish to her. She'd experienced amateur sexual innuendo from her many high school and college boyfriends. She was David's "first." Not his first girlfriend or first sexual encounter, but first *everything*. Before Morgan, David never altered his life for anyone except himself. She knew he loved her. She also knew that he had never really loved before, so she laughed at his jokes and humored him through his still collegiate social skills. There was a beauty to his naiveté. When there was a knock at the door, he barked. There wasn't any insecurity with the bark. He just thought it was funny to be one of the dogs. His bark was deep and throaty, almost indistinguishable from the real dogs. Afterwards he didn't look around to see who had heard him. Morgan was sure he did this even when he was alone.

"Just slice that up for the salad," Morgan said. David reached for a packet of mushrooms.

"No, the carrot," Morgan said. "If you want me to sauté the mushrooms as an appetizer I will, but please don't add them to the salad or lasagna. You know I hate mushrooms."

Oh yeah, "David said, "how about we throw them out all together? And instead we use these." Morgan didn't take her gaze off the cutting board.

"Use what?" she said.

"These."

"These *what?*"

"These flowers that some dark, handsome, mystery man must have left for you." David held out a bouquet of red roses for her.

"She took the flowers. He picked up two half-full

glasses of white wine and handed her one. They clicked glasses.

"You're welcome. Now what are you dawdling around for? We have guests arriving any minute," he said.

"You know Honey, my throat is starting to hurt a little bit," Morgan said. "Let's not make it a late night."

"I'll get some aspirin for you," David said.

"No, I think vitamin C would be better. I'll get it."

"You work on that lasagna of yours. I'll be right back," David insisted. He headed for the bathroom, wine glass in hand and a one-hitter in his pocket. His drug of choice for the night was pot. He remained in the bathroom until long after the grassy aroma faded and a few of his friends arrived. Morgan's voice filtered down the hallway as she greeted his friend, reminding David of the vitamin C mission.

"There you are," Morgan said as David peeked around the corner. "I was beginning to worry about you."

"Yeah, I'm not feeling so well."

"We won't entertain late. Let's just get it over with. Our neighbors, Jaime and Regan, and some of your college buddies are here. They look a little out of it," Morgan whispered. "I wonder what they're on tonight."

"Hard to tell," David said.

A joint was circulating the living room when

David and Morgan entered. It was passed David's way. Quickly Morgan noticed that one guest had brought a child, a toddler. Morgan looked at David. He didn't really notice. Morgan quickly walked over to the little toddler. She was a girl with unkempt hair and a blank look on her face. Morgan picked up the child and walked out of the room. The child didn't squirm or even look for its' parent. Morgan sat in the kitchen with the child, feeding her spaghetti. Neither of them said anything. Morgan twirled the noodles on the fork. They both laughed. Eventually the parent sauntered in. "There you are," the parent said to his daughter, smiling.

"People are smoking pot at this dinner party," Morgan said.

"Yeah, pretty good weed," the father said.

"Get your daughter out of here," Morgan calmly said. The man looked at Morgan like she was crazy. "And brush her hair."

"Hey, it's all good. It's just weed," the dad said.

"Get out," Morgan said. The dad picked up the baby and huffily left. Morgan actually hoped she had offended him.

David watched the dad quickly carry his daughter down the steps. "Where is Darin going?" David asked Morgan.

"I don't want kids around drugs in our house, David," she said sternly. A guest passed a joint to David.

"No thanks man," David said with a slight wave of his hand. "I quit a few months ago."

"I'm very proud of him," Morgan said to their guest. "Quitting smoking pot was one of the hardest things I ever gave up."

"I thought about getting hypnotized to quit," their neighbor, Jaime, said.

"I wouldn't," Morgan replied. "Then your subconscious would have to find something to replace it. Who knows what you might start doing. It's better to figure out why you're smoking. If you can do that, you won't turn to something else."

"Like sex," David interjected.

"Well, things could be worse," Morgan responded, wrapping her arms tightly around his waist. Jaime took a hit off the joint. She had a nice, tight figure which she maintained by running up and down the San Francisco streets, including doing laps in front of Morgan and David's apartment every morning. She was originally a Jewish girl from Long Island, but her five-foot-eight-inch frame led her to the West Coast. Jaime bartended in the local watering hole and was getting her herbalogy credentials at the local school. Her life existed solely within a six-block radius. It seemed she had already traveled so far that she no longer had the energy to go much farther. She acclimated by adding the requisite piercings and tattoos. And substituted drugs for culture. Morgan immediately felt empathy for her. Morgan knew what it was like to move, to want to change, to want to grow, only to be thrown back into the same situations. The names, faces and places changed. The patterns remained the same. From one school to the next and one man to the next, Morgan knew that Jaime had to make some serious changes before she could sleep peacefully.

"I think it's great that you're studying herbs," Morgan said.

"Yeah, it's very healing," Jaime said, taking another hit off the joint. The room became smoky. The sofas and coffee tables, survivors of various garage sales and assorted roommates, seemed as oddly mismatched as the assorted guests. Monday night football was muted on the television and an over-amplified stereo distorted James Taylor's soothing voice. If there was such a thing as a lost generation it was certainly alive and well at this dinner party. David's college friends all complained about the inconveniences of living at home. Regan circulated the room in search of a man that would bestow attention upon her. And David diligently prepared the dinner.

"What do you recommend for a constant sore throat?" Morgan asked.

"Maybe echinacea," replied Jaime, "it seems to be the answer to cold-related symptoms."

"I take it every morning."

David sneaked up behind Morgan and wrapped his hand around her neck. "Lots of warmth and closing the window at night," he said, cradling Morgan's neck in his large, calloused fire-fighter hands.

"That feels good," she said, clasping her hand over his. "I can almost feel the pain going away." Jaime stood and watched as Morgan melted into David's arms.

"Dinner is served," David said.

They filed into a cubby-hole at the rear of the tiny kitchen. A round table covered with a white tablecloth proudly displayed the flowers David bought. Swiveling office chairs and coolers substituted for dining room chairs. David dominated the conversation, asking questions about his friends' careers, while Morgan filled in the gaps with intrusive comments about their guests' various love lives. The wine bottles all emptied quickly and people moved on to beer or hard booze, or whatever their favorite poison was. Not a crumb was left when people adjourned to the living room for another round of smoking. Morgan and David remained in the kitchen preparing desserts. The ice cream was so frozen that Morgan put it into the microwave to melt.

"I still find it funny that you microwave ice-cream," David said.

"Only for seven seconds."

"Why don't you eat ice-cream," Morgan asked. "I know you told me, but I can't remember."

"It reminds me of when I got sick as a kid," David responded. "I had one of those ice-cream cups that came with the school lunches. I started choking. My throat closed up and I turned all blue. I guess I had the flu and couldn't tolerate the lactose or something.

My mom came to pick me up. I guess I seemed fine by the time she got there. There was some big sale at Macy's that she couldn't miss. So when she picked me up we *had* to go shopping. All I remember is puking in the shoe department. My head felt like it was going to burn up. Dad said I had a temperature of a hundred and three when he came home.

I'll never forget the look on the salesman's face when chocolate ice-cream spewed all over the white, high heeled Candies."

"Why did your mom take you shopping if you were sick?"

"It was some big sale." David started stacking the dirty plates, one on top of the other, without removing the silver wear. I guess she didn't know I was that sick."

"They sent you home from school!"

"Mom said Macy's department store was on the way home. She tells everyone that story. It's become kind of a family joke." David moved onto hand drying the glasses. Morgan stepped in front of him as he reached to put them in the sink. She wrapped her arms around him and buried her face in his chest. He kept his arms out-stretched with a glass in each hand.

"Your family has a weird sense of humor."

"Yeah. The best one is that Mom wanted Grandma, Dad's mom, to like her so much that she convinced Grandma that they have the same birthday. I guess it started as some kind of misunderstanding, then Mom just went along with it. We joke that she gets two birthdays each year."

"What did you guys do for her birthdays last year?"

"Dinners. Then I came home to you, remember?"

"Remember? I've never met your mother!" she said, slightly agitated.

"Okay. Okay. This week we will all have dinner together. I promise."

"Is this something I should be looking forward to or dreading?"

"Let's talk about it later. Right now, let's get rid of our guests and go to bed."

"Anytime you're ready sweetheart," Morgan said.

They walked hand in hand down the wood hallway. An ominous layer of grey smoke crawled out the door covering the ceiling. The girls were seemingly passed out on the floor with there heads on sofa cushions while the guys took up the sofas. Their heads were tilted back and their mouths drooped open. One had the remote control in his hand. David took the remote from his old college roommate's listless hand and placed it on the coffee table. Morgan covered up the girls.

"And we were feeling guilty for going to bed," Morgan joked. The answering machine flashed a series of green lights signaling unanswered calls and week old messages. Morgan mentally counted the number of green flashes. Each flash was a message from someone. Each someone could be the thing that took away the tiny spot of emptiness within her soul.

"The machine is full," she said.

"It always is. Isn't it?"

"I guess I never noticed how infrequently I check it anymore. No wonder everybody thinks I'm a flake," she said.

"People just think you are busy."

"Let's listen." Morgan longed for one message, one green flashing light to make her feel whole.

"Noooooo. We'll do it in the morning." David grasped her hand led her to the bedroom. Her eyes stayed on the machine, watching the flashing lights she sighed and hit the *delete* button.

"No need to think about it," Morgan said. "I don't want to wake up to a lot of stuff that I missed. Let's start our day fresh," she said. David smiled.

"Speaking of fresh…." David veered her attention to the flowers next to the bed.

"More flowers," she said.

"I know that you love to see flowers when you wake up. Isn't that what you said?"

"Yes, but you already gave me flowers tonight."

"I wanted you to have some for the bedroom and some for the kitchen. You said it makes your day better when you fill the house with flowers."

They climbed under the covers both tugging a bit at the top comforter. "I guess this isn't really big enough for two. It's probably time I bought a bigger one," said Morgan. The worn, burgundy cotton was worn through the edges. Morgan had used safety pins to put it back together. Feathers poked though. The dogs jumped up, claiming what little bit of blanket was still available.

"Yeah, we gotta get a new one." David looked at his toes as they peaked out of the bottom. "This reminds me of childhood. I grew up so fast that I didn't fit into my bed all of a sudden. One day I just woke up and didn't fit."

"I never got used to my feet hanging over the edge," David said. "Ever since that movie, *Carri*, when the hand comes out of the grave. Right up out of the dirt and grabs the person with flowers. I think it was Amy Irving. I swear that movie changed my childhood. I couldn't sleep if even a finger hung over the edge of my bed."

"I finally got used to it," David said.

"Okay, Okay. I'll buy a king size," Morgan said.

"It's okay. I got used to it."

"Oh, why did I have to think about that movie? Now I'm going to have nightmares," Morgan said.

"Try not to think about it. Just wake me up and I'll hold you if you can't sleep."

"You too," Morgan said.

"I won't," David said. "I don't have nightmares.

"Never?"

"No. Never. I don't even dream. I just wake up with a clean slate," David said.

"Everybody dreams," Morgan said.

"I swear. I don't have dreams," David said.

"Of course you do. You just don't remember them. We all dream. We probably all dream of the same things over and over. It's when we can connect those dreams to whatever they need to be connected to that they make sense. Then they change our lives," Morgan said.

"Okay, so maybe tonight I will dream," David said.

Morgan stared at the ceiling listening to David's breaths deepen. The dogs joined him until Morgan was completely alone, still staring up, as if the ceiling or the sky held an answer for her. She started muttering slightly some of the prayers she used to as a child, thanking her grandparents for being there, saying goodnight to her stuffed animals and long since dead cat.

Angels of Love
Our Guardians dear
To whom your love commits us here

Ever this day
Please be by my grandma and my cat's side
To light to Love
To guard and guide

She changed the words "grandma" and "cat" to whomever she was thinking about each time she said the ablution. Morgan knew she needed to talk to someone with more answers.

"No, my mother isn't here yet," David said.

Morgan sat up. "What? David, are you awake?" She held her breath and silently laughed. "Oh, so you don't dream, huh?"

"I don't want to do that this time Mr. Foster," David mumbled. Morgan noticed beads of sweat on David's forehead and suddenly a huge erection. He moved the blankets between his legs and rhythmically rocked himself back to sleep.

CHAPTER FIVE

everything is exponential

"Hey Honey, let's get away this weekend. Let's go some place we've never been before," David suggested.

"Like where?" Morgan asked.

"What about Bodega Bay? It's only an hour away and everyone says it is beautiful."

Their relationship had been loving, but rocky. There was just a level they could not find. That level of true love. But their karmic seed was full-filled and they were substantially, passively happy together.

They loaded all three dogs into the van, again.

"Let's take a detour through the wine country," David said.

"Then the dogs have to sit in the car while we drink," Morgan said.

"We won't **drink,**" David said. "We will just sample."

"Oh please, you know that people sit at those wine bars for hours. The last time we went up to Copalla vineyards we didn't leave for four hours. That's not fair to the dogs," Morgan said. She looked back lovingly at Delilah, Daisy and Boo. They were peacefully sleeping in the shape of horseshoes on their individual sheepskin beds. Morgan wished she could be that happy. Instead she was filled with dread that this trip was a really bad idea. Already, David and she couldn't even decide which route to take.

"Okay," Morgan said, "if we drive up through Petaluma instead of the coast we can come close to a couple of vineyards."

"No, it's okay. You're right. The dogs will get restless if we stop and don't let them out to run. It's better just to drive to the beach."

Morgan was relieved to hear this. She knew how sensitive Boo was. Boo was the baby and when she got nervous she trembled with anxiety and glued herself to Morgan's leg. Morgan was always afraid Boo would have a heart attack. Bulldogs were so physically sensitive that their emotions and stress took a hard toll on their lives.

They drove north up Highway One. David drove so fast that Morgan held onto the door handle for stability. The Pacific Coast highway was windy. The dogs' beds slid around in the back of the van, like people on a boat afloat on tumultuous waters. David didn't really know where he was going and refused to ask for directions. He decided to just drive as close to the ocean as possible to keep his bearings headed north.

Morgan tried to intently read a book on dog friendly beaches and dog friendly Bed & Breakfast Inns. She was getting car-sick trying to focus on the words. "There's a beach that let's dogs run free just a little north of here," she said. The dogs heard her. Their ears perked up. David didn't respond.

"Turn right here," she said. "It will wind us around to a town called Tomales, and then we drive through some windy roads and are at this dog beach."

David listened to Morgan's suggestion without looking at her or acknowledging her.

As they entered the town of Tomales, David said, "Now entering Tomales." The town had a church and historical center. A sign noted that the historical center was open Saturday afternoon from 1-4 p.m.

There was a hotel called *The William Tell Inn* and an arrow pointing left, directing driver's to the beach. "Now leaving Tomales," David said. He followed the street sign toward the beach.

There was no beach in sight. Rolling green hills littered with sheep and an occasional patch of wild flowers was all they saw for miles. "I think we are lost," David said.

Morgan looked around anxiously for signs of water or sand. She cracked the window. The dogs jumped up. They could smell the freedom of the salty beach air. That smell meant open space to run and play. Large stones, similar to Stonehenge, appeared on the rolling green hills. They drove past a Coast Guard Training center and suddenly, abruptly, came to a T-intersection filled with real estate offices.

"This doesn't look like the beach," David said.

"Just a little farther," Morgan said. "The book says there is a dog friendly beach just up here."

"We aren't near the beach," David said. He did a U-turn. He spun the car around so quickly that Boo went flying into Daisy, the Rottweiler. Daisy prevented Boo from hitting the metal wall.

For the first time, Morgan freaked out. "David TURN AROUND. You are going the wrong way!"

They drove back through the green rolling hills, back through the small town of Tomales and back to the T intersection surrounded by real estate offices. This time David drove south at the intersection, instead of north. They drove in tense silence.

"Look," David said, "there's the beach." His U turn had them heading south. It was a small oyster bay. The beach's covering was layered oyster, mussel and clam shells instead of sand. Centuries of waning and waxing tides had crushed the shellfish into regurgitated, sharp, ground ocean fragments. This area was abundant with marine life dining on crustacean innards. Seemingly the emptied shells had forever washed up onto the beach after having their rubbery innards devoured by larger marine life. Otters were the prime beneficiaries of the shell's inner delicacies; therefore the waters were decorated with the adorable, fuzzy, slippery creatures. The otters floated on their backs and cracked the shells open on their stomachs, picking away at the insides with their sharp claws. The brown otters popped up and down in the serene waters. This drew tourists to the area, complete with cameras and hiking boots, to gawk at the otters.

A seafood restaurant sat adjacent to the beach. Morgan saw a busboy come out from the back of the restaurant with a bucket. The employee emptied a bucket of empty shells directly onto the beach.

"The dogs can't walk on that. It will split their paws. David please turn around. The book says that there is a really nice dog friendly beach a half mile north of here." He kept driving. "DAVID. I swear to god. I'm sick of this. You have no idea where you are going." Morgan's instincts kicked into gear. She could feel something she had never felt before. For once in her life, she felt like she knew where she was going. "DAVID!" The dogs cowered in the back. "DAVID, right up here is a B & B; TURN AROUND in the parking lot."

David pulled into the restaurant parking lot. There

was a small, five room hotel above the restaurant. "Let's stay here," he said. "There is obviously great food and we can get a room for the night." Morgan looked at him in bewilderment. David barely acknowledged her stare. "I'm going in to get a room." David left the van. The black and white sign read *Tomales Bay Inn* in a tasteful oxford font.

Morgan sat quietly with her head in her hands. Her heart beat so fast that she could hear it. Her annoyed energy pulsated through her body into her brain. The dogs felt her energy and bounced up and down in the back of the van. They whined to get out. Morgan composed herself and picked up their three leashes. She crawled into the back of the van and clasped a leash on each dog. She had forgotten to bring the double leash, which allowed her to walk two dogs with one tether. Morgan opened the van door. Daisy jumped out, pulling Morgan with her. Delilah and Boo stood tentatively at the open van door. Delilah quivered a bit, not wanting to get out.

"It's okay Dee," Morgan said, coaxing her out. Finally Morgan had to lift Boo out of the van while trying to hold on to all the leashes.

All three dogs and Morgan walked slowly around the edge of the seemingly dangerous shell beach. They walked on the sidewalk, veering slightly off the pavement to pee. When they were all finished, the dogs immediately headed back to the van. They wanted the security of their beds and confined walls. Even the salty ocean breeze wasn't enough to make them want to run free at this beach. They sensed danger. Morgan helped load them up into the van and waited for David to return.

Morgan and the dogs fell asleep in the van waiting for him.

David jerked the van door open. All four of the girls in the car, canine and human, jumped. He waved the plastic room key. "Let's go see our room," he said. "They wanted a fifty dollar security deposit for each dog, so I told them we only had one dog."

"Well, I'm sure we can pass Daisy off as Boo," Morgan said, sarcastically. "They look so much alike." Morgan had resorted to sarcasm in lieu of anger. She felt trapped. Even here in this beautiful marine setting she wanted to scream or run or something. Inside she shook with anxiety. She didn't know why she was so unsettled. She just felt that she had to get away. "Well, why don't you go ahead and take Daisy to the room. The Bulldogs and I are going to drive to the dog friendly beach."

"Whatever," David said. He unloaded Daisy. Gave Delilah and Boo a kiss on the head and grabbed his bag.

Morgan turned the car around and headed back up the coast toward the dog friendly beach. She drove, for the third time, through the T-intersection filled with real estate offices. She turned left at the sign directing her toward the beach and again was overcome with energy while she drove through the rolling, sheep filled hills, past the Stonehenge like black granite rocks and finally to a small general store sitting on top of a cliff. She pulled into the small parking lot. The dogs were both hanging out the passenger window. At a small General Store, she saw bundles of firewood for sale for five dollars with a sign that read *Honor System* next to a wooden box. There were weathered book shelves which read, "Please barrow and please return. Add to our collection or keep what you like." It was here that she saw the ocean. She breathed in freedom. The dogs smiled at her, knowing that they would get something that made them happy.

She decided to go inside to get out of the car and indulge herself by looking at the weathered books for barrow. Morgan's soul leapt as she saw her favorite books staring back at her. She pulled Richard Bach's <u>One</u> and <u>Illusions</u> off the shelf. An old, brown leather book with a gold tassel fell off the shelf. Morgan picked it up and placed back on the shelf. Behind those books were <u>Big Rock Candy Mountain</u> and <u>Angle of Repose</u> written by Wallace Stegner. Morgan could barely balance the four books already in her arms when she saw a short collection of Grace Paley works next to Isabelle Allende's entire collection of published novels. The theme of 'magical realism' continued with many books by Gabrielle Garcia Marquez placed next to Allende's. The last book on the top of shelf was <u>One Hundred Years of Solitude</u>. Morgan grimaced. It reminded her of a life not lived with the person you love. She felt her stomach churn.

Morgan felt greedy wanting to barrow so many books. She knew there was no way she could read them in one night. She just wanted to play her favorite game with the books. Morgan liked to ask a question, then flip open any book to any page and see if it answered the question. She had read all these books in the past. They had answered many questions and made her feel fulfilled. Right now she needed that fulfillment and all the answers she could find.

The general store door was propped open with a log. She poked her head in the door. The store was filled with beachy items. Hanging on the door were perfectly shaped sand-dollars turned into necklaces held together by chains made out of shells. "Hello," she said into the emptiness. "Hello?"

A huge white dog sauntered to the door. He looked at her and his ears perked up. If there is ever a way to see pure joy, it was in this dog's eyes. He walked deliberately to Morgan, careful not to scare her. He placed one paw on her foot, so she couldn't move. He pinned his head and body against her leg and extended his other paw up for her to shake. When Morgan reached down to take his paw, the world stopped spinning. Her nausea went away. She knelt down and cradled his head to her chest. Without knowing why, tears rolled down Morgan's face. She caressed his velveteen ears. They seemed like the softest thing she had ever touched. The books tumbled to the floor. Tibbs breathed in her scent.

"Tibbs, come inside." a girl's voice called. Tibbs closed his eyes and nestled into Morgan. Morgan's eyes were closed also. When she opened them a beautiful, young girl stood over them. The girl could not have been more than twelve or thirteen. "I'm sorry," the girl said. "He usually listens better."

"It's okay," Morgan said, wiping away the tears. "He is beautiful."

"Yeah, he's one in a million," the girl said, noticing the books all over the floor.

"Oh, sorry," Morgan said. "I wanted to ask if I could barrow these." Morgan looked at the floor without letting go of Tibbs. "Now I see that I took too many. I will put them back."

"No, it's okay. Nobody ever reads them. I think I've read those a hundred times. You picked my favorites. There's not much to do here except listen to the ocean."

"Oh," Morgan uttered. She couldn't take her eyes off the girl or her hands off Tibbs. "I'm Morgan."

"I'm Elizabeth. Lizzy Carpricio."

From the car Delilah saw Tibbs attached to Morgan's leg. Delilah leapt out the car window and ran to them. She barreled full force into Morgan and Tibbs, knocking them over. Delilah and Tibbs danced around each other, licking each others' faces and circling each other with excitement. They stopped for a moment for Delilah to clean Tibb's ears. Delilah softly licked him, like a mother chimpanzee grooming her baby.

Morgan and Elizabeth laughed together at the dogs. The girls' laughs each had a small, happy chirping sound at the end of each breath. They sounded the same. Morgan was so happy she snorted and Elizabeth laughed at her. In her embarrassment, Morgan laughed even harder and Elizabeth let out a similar snort. This made Morgan laugh louder. Elizabeth blushed with embarrassment and laughed louder. "I guess they like each other," Elizabeth said about the dogs.

The dogs started stepping all over the dropped books. Morgan and Elizabeth rushed to pick them up. Instinctually, Morgan held out her arms as Elizabeth loaded the books into Morgan's outstretched arms.

"Please, take all of them," Lizzy said.

"Really?"

"Definitely," Lizzy said.

"I will return them," Morgan promised.

"Don't worry about it. I've read them all a hundred times. You should get that adorable Bulldog down to the beach before sunset. She will love it," Lizzy said.

"Hey, would you mind taking Tibbs? He loves the beach and he knows his own way home. You don't have to drive him back. Besides, my dad is down there. Tibbs can come home with him."

"Really?" Morgan said, again. "It would be my pleasure." She looked down at Tibbs wiggling next to her. His eyes were pleading with Morgan to take him. His eyes were pleading with Morgan to never let him out of her sight or life again.

"Okay, well, Bye, ummm, it was nice meeting you," Lizzy said.

Morgan did not want to leave her. The thought of leaving her new friend made Morgan's stomach drop into a pain she hadn't felt before. Morgan instinctively reached out to hug her. Lizzy touched Morgan's shoulder as she gave Morgan two, graceful European air kisses on each cheek.

"I will take good care of him," Morgan said looking down at Tibbs. Morgan walked to the white van and opened the door. Tibbs and Delilah jumped in without hesitation. Boo immediately started licking Tibb's face. They both had rabbit-like, beautifully soft, white velveteen fur. Tibbs meticulously cleaned Boo's wrinkles one by one as they drove down the short cliff to the beach. Morgan drove the van onto the sand in order to avoid the parking lot. She didn't want the dogs jumping out of the van near any cars, although the beach parking lot was empty.

All three dogs charged out of the van toward the water.

About a quarter mile up the beach, Sebastian Capricio was busy making a bonfire to stay warm when he felt his heart skip a beat. He looked and saw Tibbs playing with his family and Isabel/Morgan walking peacefully on the sand. Tears started streaming down his face. "That a way Tibbs. That a way, good boy. I always knew you would find her," he said to himself. Sebastian stood crying and staring at Tibbs and Delilah in the water and Morgan walking across the beach.

Morgan kicked off her simple white flip-flop sandals and followed behind the dogs, noticing that the sun was going down and a cold breeze was coming in, she pulled up her sweatshirt hood and tucked her long, blond hair in to keep her warm. About a quarter mile down the beach she saw a bonfire. Every instinct in her body compelled her to head that direction for warmth. Every cell in her body pulled her in that direction.

Morgan dug her toes into the sand for traction and ran straight forward toward the dogs and the water. She sat at the tide's edge watching the sun go down. The sky went from pinkish magenta, with a magnificent purple streak, to the ever-mythical green splash just as the sun disappeared into the water. Morgan watched the green flash when the sun hit the water. It was something she had only read about. She sat in awe of the beauty before her.

Sebastian almost fainted as the green light flashed. The hairs on his arms stood up. His neck tingled. A cool ocean wind blew onto the sand, but Sebastian felt sharp warmth well up inside him. He had watched the sun set from this vantage point for years and never seen or felt the green flash as deeply as he did this time, especially with Morgan sitting meditation style right in front of the sunset and the dogs. It was everything he had dreamt about and waited for all of this life. The energy was so strong that he became light-headed. He collapsed into his beach chair; as every lifetime together, every promise, every plan, every child together, and every future together raced through his conscious mind. He didn't want to go frighten her. He tried to will Tibbs to bring her to him. He thought the fire might work.

Fog rolled off the water onto the beach. The chill pulled Morgan out of her awe stricken trance. She realized she better get back to the van before it got dark. She whistled for the dogs. The bounded toward her, wet and sand covered. Tibbs sat down in front of her, begging her with his eyes to not go. "I have to go boy," she said. "You can come with us. I will drive you back to the General Store." She made a motion with her arm and started running to the van. Delilah and Boo ran next to her. Tibbs whined and took off, sprinting toward the bonfire and Sebastian.

"It's okay Dee," Morgan said to the dogs, "That's probably his owner by the fire." Morgan had an intense desire to follow Tibbs and make sure he was okay, but Elizabeth had told her that he would be fine and Morgan was worried about the incoming darkness. She and the two Bulldogs reached the van. She toweled the sand off them and fluffed up their dog beds.

Tibbs reached Sebastian at the bonfire. "I know. I know," Sebastian said to Tibbs. Sebastian was frantic with confusion. *I don't want to scare her.* Tibbs stepped behind Sebastian and head butted him. "Okay. Okay. I will go. You're right. I have to catch her." Finally Sebastian snapped out of his trance and started running toward Morgan.

Morgan slowly pulled the van out of the parking lot.

Sebastian and Tibbs were sprinting toward the departing van.

"My shoes," Morgan said out loud. "Shoot." She pressed on the brakes and stopped the car. She looked in her rearview mirror. The beach was black except for the tiny red glow of the fire. "I will never find them in the dark," she said to the dogs. The dogs sat upright, ears perched high on their heads. Delilah whined to turn around. Morgan continued driving.

Tibbs caught up to the rear of the van. "Run next

to her, so she can see you!" Sebastian yelled to his faithful companion.

Tibbs knew he had to get her to stop. He knew that his job, his life's work was to be a conduit for the two star-crossed lovers. Plus, Tibbs just wanted Morgan back. He wanted to feel the way he did when he pressed against her leg and her hand stroked his velveteen ears. He started running faster and faster. Morgan did not see him. He made a last ditch decision to throw himself in front of the car. He didn't care if she hit him. He would do anything to bring them together.

He knew he had to make her see him, then dart in front of the car. She would know that the thumping noise was him. Without hesitation he ran as fast as he could in front of the van. Morgan smiled and waved at him. He closed his eyes and took a deep breath, then he literally threw himself in front of the oncoming van.

Morgan's eyes hadn't left Tibbs since she saw him running. She was conscious of his every move. She veered and ran into the curb. She rolled down her window and saw Tibbs lying in the street.

She dashed to him. She hadn't heard a thump and she didn't think she hit anything. Tibbs lay in the street unmoving. "Nooooooo," she screamed. She ran to him. She checked his pulse. She checked his heart and breathing. Everything seemed fine, but he was unconscious and Morgan presumed him to be dead.

Delilah jumped out the van window again and ran to help. Delilah licked and licked Tibb's face. He didn't move. Morgan started CPR. "Come on Tibbs, come on," she cried. She ran back to van and grabbed a dog blanket. She wrapped his listless body in it. She hugged him close, rocking back and forth in the street crying.

When she looked up, Sebastian was standing over them, tears streaming down his face.

"Oh my god. I'm so sorry. I should've stopped when I saw him. I thought he was just running home. The girl in the store told me he knew his way home. We have to get him to a vet…," she rambled on.

Sebastian kneeled next to her. He placed a hand on Tibb's head. Tibb's tongue was purple and flopped to one side. "He was running home. It's not your fault."

Morgan transferred the lifeless blanket to Sebastian. They both sat crying in the street. Delilah frantically licked at Tibb's ear. Delilah jumped up and down with anxiety. Sebastian carried Tibb's body to the grassy area in front of the General Store. "I am going to rush him to the vet," Sebastian said. "Just stay with him while I grab my car keys." Tibbs lay on the grass. The blanket flopped open and his stomach slightly lifted. Then his ribs slightly expanded. Delilah licked him faster and faster. Morgan placed her mouth around Tibbs mouth and blew as hard as she could.

She watched his rib cage rise and fall. She continued administering CPR.

Sebastian returned with the car keys and knelt to pick up the listless blanket. Sebastian cradled Tibbs in his arms. Morgan looked longingly at the majestic white beast in Sebastian's arms. Overcome with anguish, Morgan lovingly placed her hand on Sebastian's arm. A shock of energy ignited. The hair on the back of Morgan's next stood up and goose bumps tingled on both she and Sebastian's arms. The electricity increased with a jolt. Delilah jumped straight up into the air. Morgan and Sebastian felt as if lightning had hit them. Tibbs shot out of Sebastian's arms and landed on the ground in an electrocuted heap. Their tear filled eyes froze…and instantly Tibbs lifted his head. Sebastian and Morgan stared at him in amazement. Tibb's lifeless body twitched for a moment, and then Tibbs stood up. Happily wiggling his entire body, he looked directly at them. His eyes were clear, healthy and filled with joy.

Morgan collapsed to her knees and hugged Tibbs so tightly he couldn't move. Her touch was magical to him.

Barely audibly, Sebastian whispered, "You healed him."

"I swear I didn't hit him. I was watching him run next to me and then he was just gone. I swear I was watching him. I don't know if he darted under the car or what happened."

"It doesn't matter," Sebastian said. "We are all here. All together. All fine."

Delilah was frantically licking Tibb's ears. Morgan held on to him for dear life. Sebastian stared, quietly with complete understanding of what Tibbs had done for him.

Tibb's and Sebastian's eyes were glued to each others' while the girls fawned over Tibbs. They gazed at each other, knowingly, lovingly, until they could both breathe again. "You're one hell of a wing man," Sebastian whispered to Tibbs. Tibbs nodded in acknowledgement.

Morgan was still shaking as she continued to hug Tibbs tighter and tighter. Tibbs attempted to absorb her anxiety by nuzzling his nose into her neck. This caused Morgan to start crying again. Tibbs shot Sebastian a look. Sebastian immediately took off his long, sleeved flannel shirt and wrapped it around Morgan's shoulders.

To his own bewilderment, Sebastian wrapped his arms around Morgan to comfort her. When he touched her his life flashed through what was left of his conscious mind. Feeling her body next to his was overwhelming. He tried hard to remain calm and comfort her. Every cell in his body was quickly slipping into emotional sub consciousness. Her body was convulsing and freezing. Every ounce of Sebastian's being needed to comfort her.

His mouth was dry. He couldn't get words to form. Here *she* was, right here in his arms and he couldn't tell her all that he knew. He couldn't tell her that Tibbs ran in front of her car to bring them together or that if they stayed together every thing would be fine; more than 'fine'. It would be perfect. In that instance he remembered what it was like to have a perfect life. For so long, his nights had been long while the years flew by waiting for her and looking for her.

The beach fog got thicker and colder. The only thing Sebastian could see was the lighthouse flashing in the distance and its straight, seemless light stretched directly across the ocean to where they knelt; wrapped around each other for the first time in over two decades. He took deep breathes and tried to compose himself. He had to be the strong one. That was the gift he had chosen for this life. Full knowledge came with the price of feeling too much. He held her, forced to control and contain his uncontrollable emotions.

"Hey," he said with an attempt to laugh, "Let's go grill Tibbs a steak. I think he earned it." Morgan tried to wipe away her tears without him seeing. It didn't work. Sebastian took the sleeve of his shirt and dabbed Morgan's tears away. They sat silently. He took her face in his hands and continued to clean the salty tears away. He dared not look in her eyes for fear of crumbling. Morgan did not pull away. She was too shaken up to speak.

"So," Sebastian said breaking the silence, "how 'bout that steak?" He looked at Tibbs to divert the energy. "You want a steak don't you boy?" Tibbs nuzzled deeper into Morgan. Tibbs was clearly not going to let go of her. "Come on, let's go inside. I will grill us all some steaks, even you Delilah."

Morgan's face slowly slipped into a soft smile. "I could eat," she said.

Sebastian was euphoric that she wasn't leaving. He jumped to his feet. "Okay, let's go, chop chop. It's getting cold out here." He scooped forty-pound Delilah into his massively large arms like she was a baby. "I will carry this one inside. I think Tibbs wants to walk with you."

Morgan took hold of Tibbs collar. "I'm not letting go of you near the street," she said shaking a scolding finger at him. She dragged Tibbs to the van with her to get Boo. All five of them walked into the General Store.

Sebastian didn't hesitate with anything. He quickly pulled steaks from the refrigerator and lit the barbeque. He was afraid that any down time would give her an excuse to leave. He pulled corn, tomatoes, basil, and apples out of the produce bins. Buffalo mozzarella cheese, red wine vinegar and olive oil were already on the cooking island.

Morgan was amazed, "Do you live here?" she asked.

"No, no, I live down the street. We own the store. I mean my family and I. My daughter runs the place when she isn't in school. Here is where all the good food is." He placed a make-shift beach table in the center of store and threw a decorative beach towel on it as a substitute table cloth.

All three dogs squeezed onto Tibb's fleece bed. They huddled as close as possible to each other, spun a few circles around each other and collapsed into one sleeping pile. Within minutes they were snoring. Delilah and Tibbs occasionally opened one eye to make sure everything was okay.

Morgan noticed freezer after freezer filled with oysters, mussels, clams, abalone, and lobsters. "Ohhh, your daughter Elizabeth," she said.

Sebastian whirled around in amazement. "Do you know Lizzy?" he asked wondering if Morgan had met her own daughter.

"I met her earlier. I stopped here to look at the books." Her voice got softer, "that's when I met Tibbs and I took him to the beach with me. It was such an irresponsible thing to do. I'm so sorry. I should never have put someone else's dog in my car. I'm so sorry." Morgan felt entirely responsible for almost killing a dog. She looked at the floor and took a deep breath. She wasn't hoping for forgiveness. When she looked down she noticed that she was still barefoot. She realized that she was a barefoot mess with a tear stained face and sand covered clothes. Sebastian was going about preparing the meal.

"I should go. You two need to rest," Morgan said. Sebastian almost fainted. He couldn't stand the thought of her leaving. Tibbs whined.

Sebastian stopped everything he was doing and looked at Morgan. Her hair was perfect. Her face and skin were perfectly flawless. She wasn't wearing a wedding ring. He thought that life had been good to her and he was relieved that they had a chance.

"Really, I should go," she repeated. "It's late. And I'm a mess." The words sounded shallow and meaningless even to her. She looked down at her bare feet and started laughing.

Sebastian walked closer to her and looked at her bare feet. Then he looked at his own bare feet and started laughing with her. Their laughter was contagious. It continued without rhythm or reason. They stood face to face looking at what a mess they both were and laughing hysterically at themselves. He reached his hands behind his back. With each hand he took a white flip-flop sandal out of each of his back jean pockets. She laughed even harder. He tapped his knee, signaling her to put her foot on it. She did so and he slipped the flip flop onto first her right, then her left foot. She blushed.

"You should stay," he said, with her foot still on his knee.

"How did you know these were mine? I mean, they could've been anybody's."

"I just picked them up to put in the lost and found bucket. Dumb luck I guess." He turned back to the food preparation and tried to make light of the fact that he knew they were hers the instant he saw them in the sand and that the feel of the sandals in his back pockets had warmed his heart.

Elizabeth walked in, with her arms filled with lilac bunches. "Those are gorgeous," Morgan said.

"Oh 'Hi', glad to see you are still here," Elizabeth replied. She began separating the lilacs into bunches. Morgan instinctively helped her. They worked methodically together. Elizabeth manicured the lilacs, then handed the bunches to Morgan who wound tan twine around the bottoms and trimmed the stems. Elizabeth opened a crate of preserve jars. Morgan mechanically filled each one with water. Elizabeth placed the lilac bunches in the jars. Jar by jar, Elizabeth and Morgan decorated the room with the lilacs.

"It's beautiful," Morgan said, deeply inhaling.

"Dinner is served," Sebastian said. He placed three steaks on the dog blanket. The dogs elegantly devoured them. Morgan looked at the red and white striped beach towel covering the table. It looked like a work of art. Bright, complimentary colors filled the table. The tomatoes were bright red and sliced minutely thin on top of the deep green basil leaves and white buffalo mozzarella drenched with olive oil.

Sebastian pulled out the chairs for the girls. Once seated, Morgan noticed a handful of fresh basil on the table. Without asking or hesitating, she took the basil to the sink and washed it. She shook it dry and twisted the basil leaves like licorice sticks until they broke into pieces on top of the tomatoes. Neither Elizabeth nor Morgan noticed that Morgan felt completely at home. Sebastian simply smiled and raised his glass of white bordeaux for a toast.

"To Tibbs," he said.

"To Tibbs," Elizabeth and Morgan said simultaneously with identical monotone voices. Only Sebastian knew that they were both tone deaf.

They all ate at the same pace, unthinkingly eating off each others' plates when they felt like it and refilling each others' drinks.

Morgan paid special attention to Elizabeth. It was impossible for Morgan to not wonder where her mother was. She was dying to ask. At any other dinner gathering this would have been a wonderful source of conversation. This time Morgan didn't feel the need to question things. At this table, the puzzle pieces seemingly fit together. There were no painfully obvious, ironic geneticists who didn't care to find their biological parents. There were no bizarre strangers smoking pot in her living room. This dinner party of three was stable. For the first time Morgan could remember, silence was not awkward.

Morgan stood up and started clearing the plates from the table. Sebastian and Elizabeth looked at each other and laughed. Morgan noticed what she was doing and laughed also. Sebastian stood up and took the plates from her hands, "Let me get this," he said jokingly. He took the dishes to the sink. Morgan washed them, while Elizabeth dried them. Sebastian put the clean plates away. They moved their new assembly line back to the table. Elizabeth put away the spices. Sebastian and Morgan each held one end of the decorative beach towel. They folded the towel together without missing a beat. The seams and edges lined up perfectly. Sebastian put away the folding table.

They all went outside to sit in the over-sized Adirondack chairs. The fog was thicker. As Sebastian and Elizabeth relaxed into the beach chairs, Morgan said, "I really should get going." Sebastian instantly felt cold and clammy. If he didn't know better he would've thought he was having a heart attack.

"We have an extra room. You and the dogs will be very comfortable here," Sebastian offered. "The roads here are very dark and windy. Plus the fog is bad. Please, stay here and be safe."

Morgan tried to think of any excuse she could to not leave. She had no doubt that she would be comfortable here. For the first time tonight she thought about David, her guilt got the best of her. "I can't," she said. "I have someone waiting for me. I have to go." Sebastian's heart sank so deep into his throat that he felt himself choke. Elizabeth saw the pain on her Sebastian's face.

"You will come back, won't you?" Elizabeth said.

Morgan looked at the young teenager's exquisite face. Morgan studied the girl's timeless beauty. Finally Morgan couldn't help herself, "Elizabeth?" she began.

"Yes, *Morgan*," Elizabeth laughingly, interrupted. The name only made the girl more beautiful to Morgan. Sebastian watched Morgan gaze at the girl whom she did not remember was her daughter in many previous lives.

Morgan lost her graces and blurted out, "where is your mother? No, no. It's none of my business. I just, just really want to know." Morgan realized that she simply couldn't bare the idea of this girl not having a mother.

"I adopted Lizzy when her mother died," Sebastian said. "They lived here, on this beach and it would not have been right for Lizzy to lose her family and her home. It was a car crash. Lizzy was only six. That's when I moved my family business from Europe to here. Before her, I traveled a lot. She gave me a reason to settle down. Stay stable. You know, build a home and all that."

"I am very sorry about your mother," Morgan said.

She reached out and hugged Elizabeth. "I will be back. I have to return your books."

Elizabeth smiled and reciprocated the hug. She held onto Morgan as tightly as she could. Sebastian knew that hugging Morgan was the closest thing Elizabeth had felt to home and true love since her biological mother in this lifetime had died.

"If you must leave, I insist on driving you. These roads are treacherous at night," Sebastian said.

"I'm only going down the coast a bit, through Tomales to some little hotel," Morgan said. "Actually, I don't live here. I'm on a road trip. My hobby is lighthouses. I heard there was one around here?"

Sebastian pointed north. Morgan saw the blinking light, beckoning to her. "Oh great. I will come back to see the lighthouse when I return your books. Thank you for a wonderful dinner."

"Please let me drive you," said Sebastian.

"I'm fine," she said. She was digging deeper and deeper inside her soul to not leave.

"Maybe I could come back tomorrow?"

"Tomorrow is perfect," Sebastian said.

He stopped sweating. "Just one thing," he said. "Just wait one sec." Sebastian said, holding up a finger to convince her to wait. He ran into the store and came out with an armful of lilacs. "Please take these. Put them next to your bed, so you are happy when you wake up," he said.

Morgan's heart skipped and she lost her breath. She couldn't speak. She looked directly at him. Their eyes finally met. Their gaze locked upon each other. Elizabeth stared at them, entranced with their intensity. There was no nervous laughter or uneasiness. For once, nothing was awkward. Tibbs nudged Delilah, signaling her that life was finally going to be okay. After a full few minutes of silence, Morgan blushed and graciously took the flowers. She placed them next to the books on the front seat of the van and loaded up the dogs.

Sebastian did not dare scare her off with an emotional good-bye. "See ya tomorrow beautiful girl from nowhere," he said.

"Yeah, tomorrow," she kissed Tibb's head. "No stunts tomorrow Tibbs."

Morgan drove away. In the past few hours, the van had been figuratively converted from a counselor's arguing office to a flower shop/library. Life was manageable again. For the first time, Morgan truly had something to look forward to. She picked up one of the lilac bunches, as she inhaled its intoxicating scent the road had an abrupt turn. Her car careened out of control.

Sebastian felt a pain shoot in his stomach and an earth shattering breaking of his heart. Since he wasn't physically with Morgan/Isabel, he didn't know exactly what it meant. Apparently his fully knowing enlightened state only worked in the presence of people. He realized that this is why he couldn't find her for all these years. Even a fully enlightened individual could not at first find love unless it was right in front of him. All the years of this lifetime he had pined over her existence and searched to the ends of the earth, when she was, in reality, living only an hour away from him… and now she was gone. The pain in his chest got worse. He could not eat or sleep. He knew the pain had to do with *her*. In his soul, he knew something was terribly wrong and that she would never return. He and Tibbs paced desperately all night. Sebastian began to shrink into nothingness. He shivered uncontrollably and lost consciousness. Elizabeth wrapped him in a warm, cashmere blanket and made numerous untouched cups of ginger and lavender tea. Sebastian stared in a stupor, unable to even look at the gorgeous ocean because it reminded him of his Isabel. The nightmares came. They came and they came and they came until they stayed inside Sebastian's soul and mind even during the day, taunting him of their night time return. In the nightmares, Isabel was covered in blood and lost forever. Just as painful to him, the nightmares showed another man at her side, comforting her and keeping her from returning to Sebastian. Yet, the night terrors were his only connection to her. It was the only time he could feel what she was feeling and her unbearable freezing cold physical pain kept him alive, while at the same time, it prevented him from living. He preferred to live in a coma-like state to stay close to her, to possibly catch a glimpse of her in a dream. His head jerked uncontrollably back and forth. He repeatedly collapsed onto his desk then bolted upright as his body twitched with exhaustion. He could not sleep or eat, or function. All he was capable of was chastising himself for allowing her to leave. If he closed his eyes, if he even blinked, his entire being remembered the pain of the cold nightmares. The warmth of holding her was too painful to remember. The nightmares took over his life, as he sank into an abyss of life without his Isabel.

David waited up for her until about three a.m. when he fell prey to his own exhaustion. As the sun came up, David's eyes opened and he noticed she had not come back to the hotel. At nine a.m. David went to the hotel desk-clerk. The two of them called the local sheriff department.

A Search & Rescue crew drove down the winding Pacific Coast Highway. Less than two miles from the *Tomales Bay Inn* they found a van partially submerged van waters edge. Morgan was unconscious and blue from hypothermia. The dogs were fearfully shaking and cowering in the back. The dogs' feet were also submerged in water. They were alive and also hypothermic. The paramedics arrived and removed all the victims. All three were wrapped in heat blankets. David vigorously rubbed Delilah and Boo while he watched Morgan be put onto a stretcher. The cocaine in his system allowed him to feel nothing, except the usual adrenaline rush he got when the fire bell rang. Seeing Morgan on a stretcher was to David like seeing any other victim being put into an ambulance. He had seen it so many times, with so many drugs in his body, that his brain didn't register the tragedy. The tide began rolling in quickly and the waves increased on the rocky shore while the paramedics worked feverishly on Morgan.

David averted his eyes from Morgan for a second to see the van completely fill with ocean water. Luckily, the van's dive from the road to the ocean was stopped by a large boulder sitting, unmovable for centuries, at the water's edge. David called a tow truck.

Morgan was rushed to the hospital, barely breathing and purple, but still with a faint pulse.

Leaving Sebastian and Elizabeth the night before had been so disorienting that she couldn't concentrate on anything. She had reached for the lilacs to smell and feel stability and beauty. Burying her nose in the familiar flowers and inhaling their comfort only made her more scared, scared that she may never feel complete again. Her confusion of leaving what she instinctively knew to be her proper life path caused her to panic and veer off the unfamiliar road.

David and the traumatized dogs waited for the tow truck, while Morgan was rushed to the hospital.

Morgan lay in a cold hospital bed in Petaluma, California, wondering if her dogs were alive. She remembered everything that had happened. She also remembered that she had promised Elizabeth she would return to the general store. She reached for the phone to call Elizabeth. Her purse was empty. The contents were strewn all over the van floor, encased in water, never to be seen again. She cried at the thought of never smelling the lilacs again. She reached for the hospital phone and attempted to dial 411 for the general store's phone number. The phone didn't work. It was only allowed to receive incoming calls. Morgan became slightly frantic. Her heart raced and she felt captive in the hospital bed. She ripped the I.V. tubing from her arm and removed the oxygen tube from her nose. All the monitors went off. A nurse rushed in at the protective sound of the loud monitors, signaling distress.

"I need to make a phone call," Morgan said frantically to the nurse.

"You need to keep your I.V. in," the nurse said replacing a needle and catheter in Morgan's hand.

"You were dehydrated and have a concussion. The doctor will be in shortly."

"No, I need to make a call now," Morgan said. Somehow she knew Elizabeth would be scared today. Somehow she knew Tibbs and Sebastian were frantic and desperate. For the first time in her life, she knew what it was like to have someone worry about her. Even worse, she was deathly worried about Elizabeth. She began hyperventilating and quickly became groggy and unfocussed.

"I put a narcotic sedative push in your I.V. You need to sleep."

"No, please, please," Morgan begged, as she dropped into a deep sleep. In the Lorazapam and Morphine induced sleep she felt Tibbs laying next to her. She felt his warm body and his velveteen ears. Her feet were cold and Tibbs sensed this, so he positioned himself perfectly on her calves and toes to warm them. In her sleep she felt Tibbs nestle his head into the curve of her knee. This gave her the strength to know she had to heal.

In her hallucinogenic sleep, Pat appeared. He instructed her that it was not her time to die and that she would find true love. He placed his healing hand on her head. Her head pain ceased. Her concussion calmed and normal blood flow was established to her brain. She awoke feeling slightly alive. The hope fueled her.

David and the doctor entered the hospital room. "You are going to be fine," the doctor said. "A couple more days of R&R in here and you can go home."

"David, where are Dee and Boo? Are they okay?"

"They are at the vet. Dee suffered a small stroke. She needs to be monitored and Boo was purple. She almost died of exhaustion from trying to stay above the water. They are going to pull through. The vet bill will be outrageous," David said.

"Delilah needs love. Go be with her. I am fine. She needs you. She made a new friend at the beach yesterday. He is a gorgeous white Bullmastiff. She was happier than I've ever seen her. The Bullmastiff almost died." Morgan's words sounded like rambling to David. He didn't hear her.

"The vet will watch her," David said.

"No, she needs us." Morgan again started pulling the tubes off her body and attempted to get out of bed. The doctor and David restrained her. "No, no, David you have to call the general store at Dillon Beach. Morgan fell trying to get to the phone, again.

"A few days, Ms. O'Neil. Give your self time to heal," the doctor said as he left the room.

Morgan closed her eyes. David waited next to her bed until he heard her breathing deepen. When she became conscious of David leaving the room she said, "Please go sit with Delilah."

"Okay," he lied to comfort her.

Once he left the room, Morgan opened her eyes and called the veterinary hospital. She requested that Delilah and Boo be housed together. The technician tried to tell Morgan that only one dog was allowed per kennel, however the technician quickly learned that Morgan would not take 'no' for an answer.

A few days later Morgan checked herself out of the hospital. She took a taxi to the veterinary hospital, called David and they soon all returned to their San Francisco apartment to recover together. Morgan didn't leave the bed for days. She didn't allow the television to be turned on for fear of having their peace disrupted by some news story which would disturb her sleep by exposing her brain to the horrors of the world. Delilah and Boo only left the bed to go outside. David was on a three day, twenty-four hour a day shift. So Morgan and the dogs all had time to heal, alone. During this time of healing Morgan fully realized that the beauty inside her would not exist without that one night at the beach. She knew Tibbs, Elizabeth and Sebastian felt the soulful awakening of their time together. "Maybe that's all we get," she said to Delilah. "We had everything for one night. That is more than most people ever get in their whole life." Delilah's deep almond eyes watered as Morgan spoke. "Seriously Dee, we can't go back and ruin the best thing we ever had. What if we went back and they were too busy to spend time with us? We would lose all this joy inside us. I couldn't take it, Dee. And they are all happy at their beach. We should just leave it as it is…perfect memories. Perfect memories can make a happy life. I can't take that away from them, or from us. It's better this way," Morgan said to Delilah.

Daisy was the most confused and most in need of healing. She had not been in the accident or at the beautiful beach that evening. She didn't have the memories of Tibbs, the waves, the seagulls, the lilacs and the love which the others had now embedded into their three souls. Daisy didn't have the hope that the other three shared.

It was as if the beautiful embedded memories of love were enough to keep Morgan going. It was as if it really didn't happen. It seemed too perfect, to Morgan, for it to be real. The memory of feeling fulfilled seemed enough to nourish Morgan's soul forever. She didn't want to lose that by reaching out and trying to capture it again. She was alive. The dogs were alive. She had true love in her heart, cells, blood, fingertips and soul forever. She felt grateful every minute of every day for this experience. She wouldn't trade a near death car crash for anything. She knew she recovered quickly because of the few hours of bliss she felt at the beach. This was enough for her. The meal with Sebastian and Elizabeth seemed to good to be true. The unconditional love and near death experience she shared with Tibbs was almost too emotional and uplifting to recreate. She refused to be selfish and ask for more by contacting the general store. Morgan was convinced that she had touched their lives for the better and she didn't want to jeopardize a happiness that most souls never experience on earth.

That day she dared to leave her bed. She walked the dogs to park, sneakily picking a bunch of wild lilacs behind a chain link fence. She reached her small hands through the fence links over and over, each time returning with one or two lilac stems. The lilac flowers were white instead of lavender. The white ones always smelled stronger to her. It was odd, she thought, that white flowers could be called lilacs. Just like people, she thought, it didn't matter what color they were. They were al people. It took her an hour to collect enough for a full bunch of lilacs, during which she pontificated on why caucasian people couldn't be called black; just like white flowers were called 'lilacs' . She took the lilacs to a nearby faucet on the side of someone's home and rinsed the flowers. She then found an empty fast-food paper cup in the road. She filled it at the faucet. She realized that she couldn't squeeze her hand through the chain links without spilling the water, so she tied the dogs to the fence while she scaled it and poured the water over the bush. She insisted on doing this five more times as an offering to the bush for giving her the beautiful flowers. She promised the bush that when she was stronger and healthier she would bring it buckets of water and B12 vitamins in order to fortify it.

At home she placed the flowers in a white porcelain pitcher next to her bed. She tied bows made of tan hemp. They decoratively surrounded the pitcher. The brown, rustic twine complemented the perfectly sculpted, smooth pitcher curves. The white pitcher sat inside a smooth, large wash bowl. It was reminiscent of days when woman washed their hands and faces in the bowl, their faces reflecting back at them. This pitcher and bowl set was modern. There was not a chip on it. It was seemingly perfect. Morgan felt that perfection as she placed the pitcher full of flowers in the washbowl. The set was so moving to Morgan that she became engulfed in letting it into her own soul, or adding her own soul to the set. She wasn't aware of what was she was actually doing minute by minute. She moved on auto pilot. She went to the kitchen and got out her old paint set. She let her subconscious take over as she painted a beach scene directly onto the washbowl. She enhanced the bowl's beauty with sea-shell images, seahorses, and a perfectly round sand dollar on each side of the bowl. She painted four sand dollars in total. Each sand dollar had a navigational 'w', 'e', 'n', or 's' in the middle. She transformed the bowl into her personal compass. She so enjoyed the painting that she continued the stream of subconscious mental healing by painting the pitcher. She didn't bother to remove the water or the flowers as she painted a perfect lighthouse onto the white porcelain. As she stared at her wet work she felt there was something missing. She loved the work she had created, but knew she could make it better. She carefully rotated the flower filled pitcher, careful not to smudge the lighthouse, under the flowing faucet. It was at that point that Morgan felt possessed. She picked up a pencil and book and outlined perfect squares all over the back side of the pitcher. It looked like a mess. To anyone watching it would seem as if she was ruining the masterpiece. The lighthouse pitcher painting complemented with ocean items could have been displayed at any art show. Morgan appeared to be ruining it with lines of graffiti, taking away its' intrinsic and artistic value by adding black squares all over it. Even Morgan gasped at the one hundred and the forty four squares she adorned the former tasteful decoration with it. Morgan's gasp was different than that of a normal person who would have watched the pitcher be 'ruined.' An on-looker would have thought the artist was on lithium, filled with darkness and the desire to corrupt something. Morgan gasped at the bizarrely abhorrent chessboard she had painted. She gasped in wonder, in amusement, in pure joy at her creation of squares. She exhaled deeply, feeling more fulfillments in her soul than just five minutes before when she remembered the general store. Morgan looked at the white lilacs. She wanted more color. She looked at her paintbrushes, searching for the smallest and sharpest brush she could find. None would do. They were all frayed or bent or broken or hardened from not being cleaned after each use. Morgan went to the bathroom to find a box of Q-tips. She opened every paint she had. She started with orange. She dipped a Q-tip in orange paint, and lightly touched the orange paint to one miniscule lilac bloom. The entire flower bunch changed its' aura. A fully white arrangement became a droplet of colorful hopefulness. The possibilities were now endless. Next, Morgan chose blue. She again dipped a freshly clean Q-tip onto the color palette and dabbed the freshly blue tip onto another pure white bloom. The blue was the shade of the ocean on a calm, clean day. Her next choice was green. She dabbed the Q-tip onto the palette and this time she painted four white lilacs a rainforest green color. She found a way to create colorful life out of white purity. "First we give them sunlight to warm their souls and grow," she said to herself. The white lilacs came alive for her as she added sunflower yellow droplets to the entire bunch. The possibilities increased as Morgan smudged an orange Q-tip with the already used sunflower yellow, creating a brilliant, bright red. She took three steps back from the pitcher. "Brighter," she said. She added more sunflower yellow to the natural orange and the red became brighter. She found that by adding the slightest amounts of colors to other colors she could significantly alter her own mood and the aura of the pitcher. It amazed her that one Q-tip drop of green paint could change the entire room from what seemed like an ocean to a rainforest. With each drop of color painted onto a small white lilac bloom she found the possibility to create any emotion she chose. The orange sunrise spoke to her to awaken early and not miss a single minute of life. The purple and red sunset beckoned her to reward herself with a sunset at the end of each day. The green Q-tips tantalized her and called to her to fill every white lilac bloom with green dabs, so as always to remember how much green means growth. The green called out to her the most. Every time she painted a white bloom green she felt as if she was giving it life. Red dabs filled her with pure passion to keep painting. If she got tired, she simply dabbed a white lilac bloom with red paint and she was re-energized with the passion to create. When there were no more white blooms to paint, she stepped back and looked at what she had done. She immediately felt shameful for covering up all the white. She thought she should have left some to remind her of the purity of the original plant. She decided to go get more lilac bunches from the tree.

As she was leaving she noticed her wooden painter's palette. There were swatches of all colors and combinations of colors. She had smeared colors together and added fresh colors as she worked feverishly. The one area on the pallet that was not a mess, and that she had not meshed into other colors, was the large, egg shaped blue color swatch. She looked at the painted flowers. There were more blue flowers buds than any other color. Unknowingly and with no plan at all, the lilac bunch was a portrait of brilliant, blue life. All the other tubes of paint were seemingly used to accentuate the now blue, ocean masterpiece. She didn't even remember painting with blue. Yet, all the other colors she had dabbed with a Q-tip. The blue flowers were painted with her one, favorite brush; the one with the perfectly pointed tip and unfreyed edges. She didn't remember even picking up this brush. She didn't remember painting with the blue. The green was not a mixture of blue and yellow. It was green. The purple flowers were not a mixture of blue and red. They were purple paint. She had not made anything out of the blue paint. Blue, the most versatile and mixable color, other than white, was treated with respect and reverence. She had created a blue lilac masterpiece, set atop a lighthouse, chessboard and navigational sand dollars. She noticed that the only other time she used blue was to create the directional headings within the sand dollars. Blue was her perfection.

She didn't need to go get more lilacs. She didn't need more white. The pitcher and the wash basin's porcelain finish was enough. All she knew was that she needed more blue. "I'm not a painter," she said as she collapsed onto the bed. She stared at the lighthouse painted pitcher. It was beautiful. Her life was beautiful. Being around the people at the general store reminded her of how beautiful she really was.

Morgan drifted back to sleep, inhaling the strong lilac scent and feeling the small buds fill the room with life. Green light beads encircled her head and blue iridescence waved her toward the ocean.

Chapter Six

Dave Or David?

Neither of them slept well. They had shared the same bed for over a year, yet Morgan was meeting David's parents for the first time today. Or rather, Morgan was meeting David's mother. This introduction had been politely rescheduled no less than a dozen times over the past year, with alternating blame on all involved. Stories barely preceded Mrs. Gina solace. That was the problem; Morgan knew little about her, except that David spoke with her everyday and never repeated any of the conversations. It seemed she knew exactly when to call; right when Morgan was out of earshot or when they were just starting to fool around. It was, to Morgan, as if David and his mother spoke in their own secret code, and had their own secret life.

After an hour of changing from one outfit to the other and then back again, Morgan emerged from the bathroom in a darkly flowered chiffon dress. She felt as is she was in mourning, and the circles under her eyes didn't help to dispel the image.

"You look beautiful," lied David, sporting even darker rings under his eyes. "You know, I know my mother didn't sleep last night either."

"So I really do look like I didn't sleep? Great," Morgan said sarcastically. "Are you ready to go? Because if we don't leave now I'm going to change again."

They descended the apartment stairs, dogs in tow, into bleak, dreary, Bay Area fog. Delilah adamantly stopped on the bottom step, refusing to venture into the puddle in front of her. David picked her up with an agitated scoop of his arms and carried her to within feet of the van. Delilah seemed quite pleased with her early-in-the-day accomplishment of getting held and leapt happily into the van. Morgan trudged behind with Boo, who knew that after witnessing David's reaction to Delilah that she should dutifully walk through the puddle. Her white paws turned to brown and mud splattered her soft neck fur.

The drive to his parent's house seemed interminable to both of them. It was as if neither of them could catch their breath and conversation was stilted as they drove through Marin County and past Marin

Catholic school, a local parochial school that spanned grades eight through twelve.

"That's where I went to school," David said, breaking the tense silence between them. "Marin Catholic."

"Wasn't it in the news recently?" she asked.

"Not that I know of."

"Yeah, it was Marin Catholic. The priest was convicted."

"I don't think that was here," he said quickly.

"I think so. He got ten years in Folsom prison."

David turned the car into a convenience store and got out without saying a word. He returned with a newspaper, an orange juice, and a bundle of daisies wrapped in cellophane. He put the flowers in the back seat and opened his orange juice. Morgan surmised that the flowers weren't for her, even if she did have a terrible night and he knew it. At that point she understood that he was more nervous and dysfunctional than she was due to visiting his parents. He bought his mother flowers to break the ice at the beginning of their meeting. Morgan stared blankly at him, wondering what she could do to help. Morgan watched David settle into what she knew to be his normal morning routine. "I can't believe you," she finally said.

"Oops," he said, gulping down some juice, "do you want anything?" I wasn't thinking." He tapped his hand to his head to show how clueless he had been.

"Yeah, I would like my fiancé to stop worrying. A morning with your parents is sounding better by the minute," she said sarcastically.

"I'm sorry," he said. He face looked redder and sweatier than usual.

She could see that the situation was stressing him out too. "Don't worry about it," she said. Just don't leave me alone for too long today, okay? I'm glad you remembered the flowers."

They pulled into the driveway just in time to find his mother sneakily pulling the window curtain aside. A quick glimpse of her face appeared then disappeared. Morgan shot David a glance. He didn't reciprocate. They unloaded the Bulldogs and the obligatory flowers and marched past a decaying rose bush to the front door. They stood on the concrete porch, tapping their feet and staring up at the weathered awning. Morgan reached over and held David's hand. He allowed her to hold it without responding to her touch. She let go. Still no answer at the door. "Maybe that window isn't transparent," joked Morgan.

"What?" said David; still pretending to not know his mother had watched them pull into the driveway.

"Oh my goodness are you here already? I didn't see you pull up?" Gina Solace said as she swung the door open. A Golden Retriever darted past her. "Bailey! Get back here," she shrieked. But Bailey discovered Delilah and Boo, thankfully giving him a distraction from running amuck and even more thankfully giving the three people something to talk about.

"Dave, put the dogs out back," said his mom.

"Don't you have a pool?" asked Morgan.

"Yes. Dave make sure the pool gate is closed," said Gina.

"Bulldogs can't swim. I better go back with him," said Morgan.

"Oh they will be fine. He will close the gate," said Gina. Morgan had visions of her dogs floating bloated in the pool. She envisioned herself sinking with them and it felt like a better prospect for the evening that what was to come.

"I had one drown when I was little. I better go check," said Morgan. David was disappearing around the corner. Morgan quickly handed the flowers to Mrs. Solace and took off after David and the dogs. This was her introduction to David's mother.

The house was small, seemingly too small for a family, yet David was an only child. Sliding glass doors opened from the kitchen nook to the pool area so Morgan could keep an eye on the dogs while seated at the kitchen table. The pool view seemed to divert the tension, however suddenly Morgan became acutely aware of the silence surrounding them. Gina busied herself at the counter; chopping, dicing, and frying. David buried his face in the San Francisco Chronicle.

"Can I help you do something?" asked Morgan to Gina.

"David maybe you would like to help out in here, with me and your mother," said Morgan as she dared to enter Gina's kitchen. David didn't look up from his paper.

"Dave, come help slice up the mushrooms," yelled Gina. David put down the paper.

"Yeah, **Dave**," chided Morgan. "We need a man in the kitchen."

David began to slice and dice random foods. With his head bent and a protruding bottom lip David meticulously chopped the mushrooms then dropped them into the bowl of eggs. Morgan stared blankly at him, but decided it best, at the present moment, to not remind him that she absolutely hated mushrooms and wouldn't eat anything the little foul fungi have touched. It looked like she would be having toast for breakfast. David was already buried back in his newspaper.

"You must be Morgan," his father bellowed as he trudged his dirty, black rubber work boots across the living room's white shag carpet. He had just returned from work. Captain Dan Solace had been on the San Francisco fire department for over thirty years and his son had proudly and easily followed in his father's footsteps, contrary to the few available job openings within the department. Thanks to his father's position and his mother's minority status, David had no trouble becoming a civil servant. David described his father to Morgan as "one of the good ole boys." The phrase referred to a time when safety rules and codes didn't exist, or rather, weren't enforced. Firefighters regularly indulged in happy hours which lingered well into the morning hours, after all, they did work twenty-four hour shifts and it was only tax dollars they were sucking down, but the disability insurance and widows' pension plans became exorbitant and eventually the men ceased climbing on flame infested roofs with an extinguisher in one hand and a flask in the other, much to the imbibers' chagrins.

Thirty fire department years had been good to the captain. Morgan noticed that his over six foot tall physique resembled a young college athlete's and the grey around his temples enhanced his strikingly handsome facial structure. A curled, Irish moustache underscored his well-defined nose and big blue eyes, which showed no signs of dulling with age.

His son did not share these features. David had instead inherited his mother's darker complexion, deriving itself from her Central American heritage. She was short, by any standards, with dark puppy-dog eyes and a rather bulbous nose. Dan and Gina Solace stood in complete contrast to each other; genetically, physically, intellectually and morally.

Morgan outstretched her arm to greet David's father. "I'm Morgan. It's nice to finally meet you."

"Morgan," he exclaimed, "no wonder he's been hiding you. We wouldn't want a beauty like this to get out much. She might be discovered."

"Did you notice my hair Dan?" Gina interjected.

"Of course honey. It looks very healthy," the captain responded to his wife.

"It is. But oh my little ears. They get so cold now without their little blanket." Gina clasped her hands over her ears. "It's a bit too short isn't it Dave?" she asked.

"No Mom. It looks fine."

"I think it looks great," said Morgan. "Short is in style." Morgan shot David a look; as if to say that he should indulge his mother's insecurity instead of dismiss it. "Gina, could you point me in the direction of your restroom?'

"Around the corner," said David. This explanation was descriptive enough due to the confines of what Morgan observed to be a studio sized house. The living room and kitchen were each the size of sport utility vehicles, but with less décor. Their stark whiteness was numbing. A few oddly placed crystal vases decorated imitation marble tables and the immaculately polished fireplace had seemingly never warmed the room. Bailey's food dish, displayed prominently in the entry way, was neat and tidy, not a crumb dotted the serving mat beneath, unlike the Bulldogs' wet and food-stained eating area. The one bathroom, which David shared with his parents from the day he was born until the day he left for college, was immaculate. The wash cloths were folded so as to properly display the lace edges. No bottles, jars, cans, toothpaste tubes, or combs were on the counter. It was barren.

David's bedroom adjoined the bathroom from the rear. It looked suspiciously like a remodeled, but not expanded, closet. Morgan had before wondered if he had ever brought a girl to this house while his parents were away. Her mind was now clear. The bed was cot size. It would be difficult for even the most willing teenagers to enjoy themselves. There was no way for him to fit length-wise in the bed; forcing him to either sleep in an embryonic position or have his feet dangling over the end. No wonder he got used to his feet not being covered by a blanket, she thought.

A quick glance on the way back to the kitchen showed her that the master bedroom was the only room of average size. It had all the regular creature comforts; a king size bed, two dressers, a walk-in closet, armoire, television, and perfectly placed book tables on each side of the bed, complete with trashy romance novels on one side of the bed and travel books on the other side. There was no phone in the bedroom.

In fact, Morgan hadn't seen a phone anywhere. "Not the people to call in an emergency," thought Morgan.

When Morgan quietly returned to the kitchen, the family was seated with food on their plates. She helped herself to some toast and fruit. David's nose was still buried in the newspaper. Gina was busying herself with salting her eggs. Dan was intently studying a camping magazine.

"So," Morgan started, "David drove me past his high school on the way here. I never knew he went to Marin Catholic."

"He played football for Marin Catholic," said Dan.

"Oh yes," said Gina. "He was the quarterback."

"Yeah, he's told me a lot about his football days," said Morgan. "Did you hear about that priest from Marin Catholic?" the room fell silent. "It was in the news recently," Morgan continued. "Didn't he go to jail for molesting some of the students?"

"That was a different school," David said quickly.

"Dave, do you want some more eggs?" asked Gina, as she scratched the bottom of the skillet for remaining burnt chunks.

"*Dave*. Do you prefer Dave over **David**?" asked Morgan.

"I've always been Dave."

"I thought you liked *David*," sad Morgan.

"I just became *David*."

"You're friends all call you '*David*'."

"Only my new friends."

"I guess I started calling you **David** so as not to confuse you with my brother," said Morgan. "My brother goes by **Dave**."

"Oh yes, we love your brother, *David*. What a nice boy. Always so polite and helpful," said Gina. "It's so nice that the boys could share that house in college. Hard to find others who pay the rent on time."

"Yeah," agreed Morgan, in order to keep the conversation going. "It was just easier to call your son *David* to distinguish between the two of them. It was too hard for me to start calling my brother by a different name. Also, David said he liked it."

"Hummm" said his mother. "Well, you'll always be *Dave* to me." Suddenly a frantic yelp came from the backyard. Morgan ran out back to find Delilah hanging over the edge of the pool, staring down at Boo. The white Bulldog, Boo, stood at the bottom of the pool. Her whiteness blended in with the white pool paint, making her almost undetectable if it weren't for the few bubbles floating to the surface. . Before Morgan could dive in, Captain Dan was in the pool, Boo in his arms, swimming to the surface. He dropped her on her right side onto the cement. She was limp. He started compressions. Morgan immediately put her entire mouth over the Bulldog's mouth and nose and began CPR. Neither Dan nor Morgan looked at each other. They each did their job until Boo sputtered.

She exhaled water and flipped her body upright. She was none the worse for the wear and tear, thanks to her protective mother, Delilah. Morgan and Dan also exhaled deeply. They sent a knowing look of approval to each other, they both looked at Delilah.

Delilah, the protective Bulldog mother, was licking Boo's face.

"That's one hell of a dog you got there," Dan said, referring to Delilah.

"Thanks Dan," Morgan said with a tear in her eye. Morgan clutched the wiggling, wet dog to her chest. David petted Delilah's head and looked gratefully into her eyes. Morgan reached a hand over and to Delilah and stroked the dog's head. "I thought you closed the gate?" Morgan said to David. There was silence. David didn't look up at her. Gina was nowhere in sight. Dan went in search of a towel.

"Isn't she just the best mother in the whole, wide world," cooed Morgan into Delilah's face. "She saved her baby's life."

"Yes, she is," said David.

It was warm outside. Soft Santa Ana winds reminded Northern California residents how close they were to both the desert and the ocean. Morgan patted Boo with a towel until the dog was completely dry. The flowers wee in full bloom, deep burgundy bougainvillea draped over the awnings. The pool was kidney shaped and browning under the tiles. Delilah dangled her head over the pool's edge, carefully balancing on her two front paws while she lapped up chlorine water. She wrinkled her nose at the chemical flavor and walked away.

"Seems like she is okay," said David, looking at Boo.

"She'll be fine. It just brings back bad memories," said Morgan. Bees started dancing around the bougainvillea.

"So do those," said David.

"What? The bees?"

"It reminds me of when I was stung by a bee right here." David pointed to his arm. "I was sitting right under that bougainvillea. My whole head swelled up and I had to stay in intensive care for a couple of days. If I get stung again I will probably die. Unless, of course, I carry an Epi-pen wherever I go."

"Maybe we should keep one around?" Morgan said almost sarcastically.

"Yeah. But it looks wimpy," he said.

"If you'll die without it, I better get one. Do I need a prescription?"

"I can bring one home from the firehouse."

"Will you, please?"

"Yeah."

"Tomorrow?"

"Yeah."

"Thank you. Now let's go back inside WITH the dogs."

"My mom will have a fit with the wet dog in the house."

"They aren't wet anymore. And I think she will understand after a potential drowning."

"We better jut get back to the city," said David.

Dan and Gina waved "good-bye" from the patio, as the couple walked around the outside of the house, loaded the dogs in the car and drove back into the city.

CHAPTER SEVEN

just one, long, twisted trip

They did what they thought they were supposed to do. Married couples went to cultural events. Playing house properly meant they had to pretend they were married, even if it was only on a subconscious level. Morgan and David went to the theater in San Francisco. Phantom of the Opera was playing, starring some critically acclaimed Phantom. The traffic was heavy and the numerous one-way streets confused Morgan, even when David was driving. She felt safe in the pampered theater surroundings. The baroque balcony boxes had heavy green drapes, cascading almost down to the red and gold-carpeted aisles. Men with flashlights in tuxedo jackets ushered patrons to their seats, slightly stopping to flicker the lights on gold placards with letters and numbers. Her black satin dress sank into the red velvet seat. The guests wore everything from blue jeans to formal gowns. David wore black jeans, penny loafers and a suit jacket. He planned on wearing the entire suit, but it didn't fit when he finally got dressed. He always told Morgan than he looked forward to being in the same physical shape ten years after joining the fire department. Five years had passed and things weren't looking promising. Few firefighters achiever this goal, what with the low amount of exercise and excessive amount of idle time mandated by the job. Each firehouse was equipped with a fully functional gym, compliments of tax dollars, and with a fully accessorized kitchen. The kitchen's appeal won out. Firefighters became more accustomed to swapping recipes than comparing amounts bench-pressed, hence slower response times, and high deaths rates plagued older firehouses.

Morgan noticed David slumped in his chair, absorbing every note, seemingly glad to not have to talk. Morgan listened intently wondering if maybe she was missing something. The music rose and fell without warning. It was both disconcerting and invigorating to her.

As the curtain fell for intermission in became apparent to Morgan that she didn't know much about this mysterious phantom. She felt as if she was missing something. She and David had been too late, due to the confusing directions, for her to have time to read the program. As far as she could tell, the prima-donna of the musical had acquired her heavenly voice from a secret tutor who would bestow his wrath on anyone he felt the urge to and the poor, gifted pupil was forced into a life of constant practice n order to prevent harm from befalling others. Morgan didn't have a strong grasp of the story line. It was unclear how it was all to going to turn out. It seemed like a love story, but the phantom didn't possess the virtues of a typical hero. She opened her program. A masquerade ball was the opening scene of the upcoming act. Without reading the program, she thought, there would be no way to figure out who was who and what was what. She read further to make sense of it all. When she discovered that the phantom was really a musically talented carnival freak she smiled at the story's simplicity.

"Do you know what's going on?" Morgan asked David. His swallowed hard, thinking she knew he had done a line of cocaine in the bathroom during intermission.

"What do you mean?" he said, calmly.

"With the play," she said.

"Yeah."

"It helps if you read the program. Want mine?"

"I've got it. Reading will distract me from the beautiful music." He closed his eyes and slowly moved, inhaling every note.

When there was a lull in the music, he opened his eyes. "I'm going to stretch my legs. Do you wanna get a cocktail?"

"Sure."

They walked down a practically empty aisle to a wide, curved staircase leading directly to the bar. The bar was packed. There was not enough time left in intermission to serve all the customers. David insisted on ordering. Morgan found a smoky seat near the bathroom entrance. Handsomely dressed men milled around waiting for their dates, two drinks in hand. Morgan watched the couples lock arms. Their elbows became a pretzel center while their free hands held their drinks. They strolled away in sync with each other. It all seemed so understood and important. David handed Morgan a vodka tonic. She stood up and took hold of his arm. He awkwardly transferred his drink to his other hand. It seemed like they knew what they wee doing, she thought. They returned to their seats.

"Are you sure you don't want to know what's going on?" Morgan asked.

"I do know what's gong on," David replied.

"Sometimes I just sit and listen. The stories are just the background for the music. They get so messy. So I just sit and listen. It doesn't always make sense to me either," Morgan said.

"It makes sense to me," David said. "May I explain it to you?"

"Really? Okay, how dos the phantom kill so easily if he is really not a phantom?"

"He doesn't care."

"No, I mean literally. How does he pull it off?"

"He plans it out and kills."

"And what about the threatening letters? How does he get them to the old lady?" asked Morgan. "I guess the old lady is in on it and delivers the letters for him?"

"Yes!" David said.

"Is the phantom evil?"

"He's okay," David said. "His notes are a little off."

"What?"

"The *notes* are a little off. He sounds like he has a cold," David said.

Morgan could not appreciate the range of voice. "You know I can't hear that, David. I mean his character not his voice. Is he good or bad?" Morgan asked.

"He's okay," David said. The lights flashed and the curtain rose. A New Year's Eve masquerade ball ensued. There was pomp and circumstance, then some ominous phantom activity and ghostly threats. Morgan found it hard to take seriously after finding out the main character was a reclusive, escaped carnival freak. She wanted real ghostly stuff and super-natural activity, not simply insanity and agoraphobia. That was easy to come by in the world. Inevitably the phantom kidnaps the woman he loves and 'much to Morgan's chagrin' the hope of spiritual insight vanishes. The phantom is exposed as the human being that he truly is. His depraved notion of love is evident as he tortures the young man that this kidnapped woman loves. The woman kisses the phantom lovingly. His heart is touched and he releases the man.

David stretched and took a deep breath. The couple remained in their seats until most of the theater was empty, as they did at the termination of movies and airline flights. They did their best to avoid crowding or touching of any kind.

The underground parking garage was darker than ever after the already somber theater setting. Morgan tightly intertwined her arm in David's. They climbed into the white mini-van. As they pulled out of the structure onto the main downtown street a strange figure ran past the front of their car. David swerved. A seemingly homeless person, without shoes and with a crazed look I her eyes, stared at Morgan and David. She had stopped in the middle of the street. They both reached over and locked the van doors. Morgan noticed blood on the woman's face.

"David Stop! She's hurt."

"Hey," David yelled out the window, "are you okay?"

"The woman stared blankly at them.

"David pull over," Morgan said. The woman began

walking towards them. Morgan yanked up the door lock and stepped out of the car. David reached to grab her, but it was too late. Morgan was out in the street headed toward a bleeding person, running into danger instead of away from it as usual.

"Can we help you?" Morgan asked.

"Morgan, please," pleaded David, "get back in the car. Let me do this. I'll help her. This is what I'm trained to do. Please."

The woman got closer to the car. Morgan's initial shock was quelled as sh saw the fear, not anger, on the woman's face. The woman's facial features were soft hints of smudged baby blue eye shadow and smeared frosted pink lip stick. The makeup looked like something a younger woman would wear, thought Morgan. She was short with a plump stomach and thin legs. Long black, disheveled hair stuck to her tense, tired face in clumps. She was sweating. There was blood on her shoulder and hand, as well as her face. Her purse strap was broken. Her feet were muddy and black polyester pant dragged on the ground. There were tears in her yes. David jumped out of the car.

"Please, we can help you?" he aid to the woman. Morgan stared at him over the hood of the car. She thought she was ready and able to help this poor woman, instead she was frozen. David's training won out over Morgan's empathy. Morgan's mouth went dry.

"He'll be mad at me," the woman said. At this,

Morgan's fear was replaced with anger at the possibility of domestic violence.

"He can't hurt you here," Morgan said. "Come on. Get in the car and let's get you cleaned up. What happened to your shoes? Do you want to go find them?"

"I need to go to the police," the bleeding woman said.

"That's a very good idea," David said. Moran ushered the woman into the front passenger seat of the minivan. David returned to the driver's seat. Morgan positioned herself on the floor in the backseat, directly between them. They were all shaking. David checked the seatbelts and started driving. The woman's hands trembled as she showed the blood to Morgan.

"I fought for it," the woman said, holding up her broken purse strap. "He not taking my purse. I keep it around my neck. Not like the school girls. They keep on their shoulder. I win."

"What? Who?" Morgan asked.

"He pull me to the ground. That man. My shoes! Oh…he'll be so mad at me."

"Who?" asked Morgan.

"My husband. He tells me never take bus at night. Not n that place. He says 'not safe'."

"He's right," David said.

"The police station is right here," Morgan said. "Can we go in?"

"Yes, we need my husband."

"We'll have the police call him."

"No, we need my husband. I go to him first. He tell me what to do."

"I thought you said you wanted to go to the police," David said. "The sooner we go to the police, the better chance they have of catching the man who hurt you. Do you remember what he looks like?"

"I go to police with my husband."

"We're already here at the police station. Let's just go inside," Morgan tried.

"No." The car was silent. Morgan did not want to further upset this woman.

"Do you think you need medical attention?" David asked.

"Of course she does, David," Morgan said. "The police station just happened to be the closest place."

"Would you feel better if we went to the hospital?" David asked.

"I want to go home."

"Where is home?" Morgan asked.

"Over that way." She pointed towards a suburb of what is known in San Francisco as 'The Tenderloin' district. "Not far. Let's go to my husband." Morgan and David let out a deep sigh. "Then we go where he say," the bleeding woman said.

"Oh God, we're in Bonfire of the Vanities and there's no escape," Morgan said. "Ma'am, let's call your husband from the hospital." Morgan adopted the woman's broken English in the hope of better communication.

"No. He not hear good. Maybe not answer," the woman said.

"David turned the car around. "Are you hungry?" he asked. "Do you want something to drink? Maybe we should stop and clean you up a bit. Morgan there's a first aid kit in the back."

"Oh, you angels. Sent straight from heaven. Right here!" she motioned to turn right.

"Why do I think we should be starting a trail of crumbs right about now," Moran muttered under her breath.. She knew David heard her by the smirk on his face. The woman directed David to her hoe. It was a four unit flat. The entryway was littered with restaurant fliers. David parked in the middle of the street next to a car that was also wall papered with unwanted advertising.

"Maybe I should go first, so he doesn't get scared when he sees the blood," David said. The woman stared back at him blankly. "He maybe mad," she said.

"How bad is his temper?" David asked.

"He get mad when I don't listen."

"It'll be okay," David said. He stepped out of the car then looked back in through the window. "Ma'am," he said, "what's your name?"

"Dolores."

"It's nice to meet you Dolores. I'm David and this is my girlfriend Morgan."

"Oh, you not married. I think for sure you married. Now I see no rings. You should marry. You are angels."

"David walked to the door. Morgan leaned over Dolores to watch. David spoke loudly enough for Morgan to hear the conversation in case the situation became heated. A middle-eastern man dressed in an old white button-down shirt and brown pants opened the door. "Hi sir," David said, "I'm a friend of Dolores'. Well, not really a friend but see she's been a little, little bit hurt and my girlfriend and I wanted to bring her home to you." The man stared at him.

"What do you want?" the man said.

"I want to bring Dolores into the house," David said.

"Where is Dolores?"

"In the car?"

"Where?" the strange man repeated.

"The van," David said pointing to the white minivan. "She's right there."

"Why?"

"She had a little accident. She's okay."

"Oh," the husband grunted.

"Why don't you get her some clean clothes and we'll all go to he police station."

"Police Station! Why? Where is Dolores?" Dolores

noticed her husband becoming visibly agitated and got out of the car.

"We maybe should go with them," she yelled to her husband from the car.

"No police!" He stormed back into the house, leaving the door open behind him. Dolores and Morgan got out of the van. The three of them; David, Morgan and Dolores stood under the burnt-out light fixture. Morgan took hold of Dolores's hand.

"Why police?" He bellowed from inside the house.

"A man tried to steal your wife's purse. She was mugged," David yelled.

The husband stormed out of the house. His footsteps pounded their way to the van. "You went to the bus place didn't you?" He shouted into Dolores's face.

"Emile, we don't have money for taxi," Dolores said with a shaky voice.

"I give you money."

"I buy food," Dolores said.

"You no work there anymore! You quit! I told you 'quit'." Emile screamed at his wife.

"I have to work."

"Not there!" His face was red. He took a breath and looked at his aging wife. "Blood," he said. "There is blood. Where from?" His hands touched hers. Turning over her palms, running his fingers over her shoulders and through her hair, he became increasingly agitated. "No police. Hospital," he said.

David and Morgan breathed a sigh of relief. Dolores was going to be okay. She was home and home was sage to her. "To the hospital then," Morgan said with a sideways glance at David. Morgan knew that it never even crossed David's mind to leave Dolores at home without getting medical attention. That was what she loved about him. Morgan let go of Dolores's hand. Both of their palms were sweaty and sticky. They had been holding onto each other for dear life. The question was, "whose life?"

"No you have done enough. She will clean up then we go alone to hospital," the husband said.

"It's really okay," David said.

"No you angels go have you life together. Go home. Wait!!! I need you phone number. I call you. I clean school at night. I call you and thank you. I come clean you house," Dolores said. Morgan fumbled through her purse and finally came up with an old receipt. She scribbled their phone number and handed it to Dolores.

"Now go on," said Dolores. Morgan and David knew that the best they could do was smile and agree. They waived good-bye from the minivan.

Home seemed so far away to Morgan. It was twenty minutes before they even reached the Golden Gate and longer than that before either of them said a word.

"Is that what you do all day?" Morgan asked.

"What?"

"Solve problems like that. I mean, I know you don't fight too many fires on those eleven days a month that you work."

"We do a lot of saves like that," David said.

"It's so exhausting," Morgan said. "I never knew your job was so tiring."

"Are you hungry?" David asked.

"More tired than hungry. I could eat, but I'd rather just curl up in your arms."

"Yeah me too. I'm almost too tired to eat. I can't wait to crawl under the sheets with you. How about just a little snack?"

"Sure," Morgan said.

David pulled into a twenty-four-hour food mart type gas station combination place. "Back in a flash," he said. Morgan watched him walk past the counter and back to the secluded refrigerated section. She loved the way his pants hugged him in all the right places. His slightly pigeon-toed swagger made him look boyish and vulnerable to her.

"I better not," he said to Morgan as he climbed back into the minivan. "I starting to get a tummy," he said rubbing his stomach. She laughed at his mimicking of Dolores's broken English.

"Okay Mr. Fireman. Whatever you say" she said with a smile in her voice. The night had been hard on her and now she was ready to have it over with. They had done well together as a couple. Morgan was proud of her life with David.

The dogs wiggled happily at the door. Boo leapt into Morgan's arms and Delilah pawed at her leg. The Rottweiler waited on the sofa for David to come pet her. When David stroked her ear, Morgan noticed Daisy pull slightly away. The dogs looked a little shifty. "Is she alright?" Morgan said. "Maybe her ear is infected?"

"Sometimes she doesn't like to be disturbed," David said. "Just let her sleep."

"Maybe we should let her sleep in the bed with us tonight, to keep an eye on her?" Morgan said.

"Maybe we should just go to bed," David said, wrapping his big arms around Morgan. He kissed her, slightly clumsily. His lips barley moved when they kissed. Morgan thought this was due to his lack of experience with women. She found it endearing, however, at times she wanted more. More movement. More groping. More tongue. More anything. She felt like a high school girl with her braces locked on someone else's metal mouth. They continued kissing. They were standing and Morgan was becoming light-headed. She wondered where it was going. His hands hadn't moved. They were statues in a cold, frozen embrace. And yet he continued to press his lips to hers. She finally took his hand and led him to the bedroom. She didn't turn the lights on.

"Leave your dress on," he said, breaking the silence in the room.

"There's something underneath you might want to see," she said.

"I like your dress," he said. She kept the dress on. He barely touched her. She fell asleep in the dress, happy for the earlier vodka tonic.

Strange mumbling awakened her. She noticed David's hands and feet twitching. His eyes bounced in odd sleep behavior and his words became more and more coherent.

"That's right," he said. "Right there."

Apparently, thought Morgan, our evening didn't end very satisfyingly to him either, since he was having a sex dream.

"Yeah, just like that. We better hurry. Your mother's coming. Oh just stay there," he continued to mumble in his sleep. The sleep talking was getting more and more interesting to Morgan. David looked peaceful. Morgan got out of bed and changed into an over-sized white t-shirt. She crawled under the blankets and turned her back to him. She pressed her back to his for warmth.

"Good. You did good today," David said, still in his sleep. "Thank you Mr. Foster." This made Morgan sit up-right.

"David," Morgan said. She shook him. "David, who's Mr. Foster?"

David moaned a little. "What, honey?"

"Who's Mr. Foster? I know I've heard that name before."

"I don't know what you're talking about."

"You just said his name in your sleep."

"I don't know what you're talking about. Let's go back to sleep." David put his arms around her and held her so tightly she could barely breathe. When the alarm went off at seven a.m. he was still holding her. He buried his face in her neck for as long as he could before leaving the bed.

"You had a bad dream last night," she said. "Do you want to talk about it?"

"I don't dream," said David. He pulled a tight fitting blue and white t-shirt onto his huge shoulders. The letters SFFD covered is chest like a badge.

"Everybody dreams," she said.

"Not me. I've never had a dream in my life," David said.

"Yeah, you told me that before. That's weird and highly improbable."

"Well it's true," he said, curtly.

"Okay then, who is Mr. Foster?"

"What?" his voice was sharp. His eyes darted around the closet for pants. He pulled matching sweats on. He was now completely coved in firefighter propaganda and that meant that he was safe. His voice reflected confident safety. "I have no idea who Mr. Foster is," he said.

Her voice softened, "His name has been in the paper for years. He was indicted for child pornography? Ring a bell?"

David didn't look at her as he continued dressing. "Nope," he said.

A wave of sadness and empathy swept over Morgan. "Please, call me tonight from the house, okay?" she asked.

"If we get busy I'll just see you tomorrow morning."

"Please try to call."

"Okay," he said, closing the door perfectly, not too hard as to make a slam, not so soft as to wonder if it had closed. The door clicked perfectly, quietly closed, as if nothing had touched his inner being.

The phone never rang that night.

Chapter Eight

people do...

The effects of the ecstasy David had tossed down his throat while ducking into the food mart on duty the night before still lingered. It's a good thing traffic wasn't heavy as he and Morgan drove home from breakfast. He only had one day off. He was trying to work extra days in order to make time for a vacation with Morgan. The stress was getting to him. The constant, bloody, dramatic, adrenaline releasing, heart pounding work-related emergencies haunted what little sleep he had time for, and the drugs prevented napping.

He thought, "It might've kicked in while I was driving." Then she would've known. The dog almost gave it away. Morgan wasn't stupid or even naïve.

She would try to help him if she knew he was on drugs. And that was the last thing David thought he needed. His little drug escapes were the only thing that kept him sane. Other peoples' tragedies were removed enough that he could solve them. Ironic as it was, he thought his reality too difficult to change. He remembered a few nights ago; the way his heart beat faster and faster when he saw the blood on Dolores. It was as if he had just heard the alarm go off in the firehouse and his adrenaline had gone into over drove. That's why he had to take the ecstasy. Morgan would've smelled pot or booze. Anyway, he had to start finding some mind-altering alternative before they traveled to Europe together. It was an eleven-hour flight. Morgan wouldn't mind a few cocktails, but what would he do the rest of the time. Maybe he could convince her to indulge. He couldn't believe he had committed to this trip. They were supposed to spend a few days in Prague, then London for a week. He had never been to Europe. She had been a dozen times, including a semester of college in London. He was completely at her mercy. She had already started "helping" him pack. She had complete access to his suitcase and personal things. This loss of control was almost too much to bear. Back in their apartment, he slammed his suitcase closed and announced that he had to leave for work early. Morgan shrugged and drew a hot bath for herself.

He pulled into the firehouse. Tonight was his night to drive the rig. He had just been relocated, transferred, to a house near the airport. It wasn't a good neighborhood and he didn't know the streets. Unfamiliarity bred anxiety. The streets were narrow, winding and treacherous in his new district. He probably shouldn't have taken the ecstasy. It impaired his vision and with his new transfer he should be trying to make a good impression, or at least not completely screw up.

Some firefighters were sitting in cars out front of the house with their girlfriends. Others were smoking cigarettes on the back of the fire engines.

"Busy night tonight?" David asked the men.

"Never know down here, Solace," the captain replied.

The bell rang. "Come on kid," the captain said, "you're driving."

David jumped in the driver's seat and waited for the other firefighters to load up.

"What is this one?" he asked.

"Some lady's study stuck under a burning car," a firefighter said.

"No. She's next to a burning car," another one said.

"I think the car is about to go up," another one said, dramatically.

"Drive," the captain ordered to quiet the men's laughter.

The streets seemed even narrower than David remembered. He had to practically stop the rig in order to make turns.

"Damnit Solace where'd you learn to drive?" the captain bellowed at him. David and the captain were alone in the cab of the rig. The other men were perched behind him. He could hear the men's sighs of exasperation with each curve and corner he rounded. Oncoming traffic was a larger obstacle. For some reason people didn't pull over for flashing red lights as they were supposed to in this neighborhood. "Plow through it" the captain, "without touching it. You have enough room."

David didn't see how there was enough room to get by the oncoming car. He kept driving and nicked the car's rear bumper.

"Keep going Solace. They'll know where to find ya. Don't worry. They always know where to find ya," the captain said sarcastically.

Sweat poured from David's forehead and hands as he white-knuckled the steering wheel.

"Over there," one of the firemen shouted. David jerked the rig in the direction of the empty parking lot. A man was waving his hands wildly. When the man saw help heading his way he plopped into a torn, abandoned lazy boy reclining chair and proceeded to guzzle some whisky. The rig pulled up next to him.

"What's gong on?" the captain said.

"I called yous guys cuz a my wife. She's stuck under and the car and she lost her cigarette and we afraid it might catch un fire."

"What car?" the captain asked.

"That car right there." The unemployed man wearing old Levis said, pointing to a broken down Chevy that oddly enough, matched the lazy boy. "We like to sit out here in the fresh air on weekends. You know. Air ourselves out a vit. Anyhow, she's stuck and she can't get up." A large woman's fleshy red feet, bluish ankles, and lumpy calves protruded, like turkey drumsticks, about three feet from underneath the back bumper of the car.

"I stuck and I can't get up," the woman yelled from underneath the car, "and that damn fool husband-a-mine too stupid to get me out. I stuck! Help me up Daddy."

"Are you smoking under there, ma'am?" the captain asked.

"I was, but I dropped my smoke. That damn fool husband won't give me another. You got a smoke Daddy?" she said to the captain. At this remark the husband howled with laughter and lit up a cigarette for himself, making sure to take a long, loud drag.

"You can't even hold onto your first smoke," he taunted.

"What are you stuck on ma'am?" the captain asked perplexedly.

"I stuck," the woman said lifting her head and banging it one the bottom of the car. "See Daddy. Owww."

"She stuck and she can't get up," the husband said mocking her.

"Why don't you try to crawl out," A freshly smoldered cigarette rolled near the back truck tire. David watched from the rig as the captain smudged it out with his steel-toed boot.

"Cause she too damn fat That's why," the husband hooted."

"When I get out you betta run."

"Try to crawl out ma'am," the captain ordered. The woman tried to sit up and banged her head again.

"Ow! See! I stuck, Daddy. I can't get up. I stuck!" The husband hooted and hollered with laughter.

"I told you not to crawl under there," he yelled.

"I don't care why you crawled under there," the captain said. David saw that the captain accepted the absurdity of the situation. The woman was too drunk to reason with and lacked the necessary motor skills to crawl out from underneath the car. "Before we help you out you have to promise me that you won't crawl back under there, okay?" the captain said. At this comment, David laughed. He couldn't imagine why someone would crawl under the car, let alone be foolish enough to do it twice. David was really impressed that the captain even thought of this. He gave the captain a nod.

"Yeah, sure, Daddy. Get me outta here before it blows."

"Nothing is going to blow" the captain said. "Okay guys, Get Down Here." Four firefighters grabbed hold of her, two on each fleshy leg. They pulled. She moved a few inches.

"How much does she weigh?" the captain asked the husband. He was doubled over in laughter, spilling his whiskey all over the place. He was laughing too hard too get his words out. He held up three fingers followed by two zeros then fell hysterically back into his lazy boy.

"Three-hundred pounds of solid woman. Pull guys," bellowed the captain. They tugged her loose. She crawled to her knees, gravel and scrapes covering her body, and fixed her eyes on her husband. He darted away. It was hard to tell if her dress was disheveled from the incident or extended wear. Her head had a lump, but no blood.

"Okay, clean it up," the captain said. "No abandoned vehicles or furniture on public property. If these are yours I suggest you move them, or I will have them moved for you. And public intoxication is illegal."

"Thank you Daddy" the woman said. "I gonna bring you some nice fixin'. You and all the boys at the station." She was still on all fours. "Which way did he go?" She looked around, like a starving coyote fixating on his prey.

The captain didn't answer and apparently decided against filing a report. "Back to the rig," he said.

David repositioned himself in a proper driving stance. His hands were placed perfectly at ten and two. He was relieved that he go to witness this incident rather than fight a fire. The prospective drive back was threatening enough. He couldn't ask someone else to drive. That would seem wimpy. He took a deep breath and started the rig. The captain was smiling.

"One helluva stupid predicament," the captain said.

"Why couldn't she get out?" David asked.

"Too drunk. Tooooooooo damn drunk," the captain said.

The street curves came up sooner than David expected, followed by hills and double sided parked cars. The pavement was slippery due to the typical San Francisco mist. The rig seemed like a boat afloat in an unpredictable sea. It was just luck at this point, he thought, to make it back without hitting something or someone else. The firefighters and captain were all still laughing about the drunken couple in the lazy boy. David felt left out. He hadn't participated. Maybe he did get this job because of his dad, a fire-captain at a different fire house in the city. Other firefighters had been waiting months, even years, to get assigned to a house after passing the entrance exam. Maybe his dad had put in a good word for him, or maybe he got the job because of his mother's minority status. She was Central American. Maybe he should've taken the paramedics position. He just didn't feel ready. He was relieved to hear a voice on the radio. There was another incident only a couple of blocks away. He followed directions from the dispatcher. As he turned the corner, he saw flashing police sirens. A man ran past the rig with one cowboy boot in his hand.

"Stop!" the captain yelled at David. The rig came to a screeching, sliding halt. Police ran after the man. David watched in his side mirror as the police grabbed and tackled the man.

"Go get him. Man down," the captain said.

"What?" David said.

"Take you paramedic's bag, Solace. You're trained."

"The police were cutting the man's other boot off when David caught up to them. Dollar bills spilled over the top of the boot. Blood soaked through the leather toe. The police and David pried the boot off. The man yelled and winced and asked for whisky. A David turned the boot upside down; a pocket knife and a bag of cocaine fell out of the boot.

"Do I want to know what's going on here?" David asked the police.

"The guy jumped out of a second story window to avoid a raid," said one of the cops standing over the drug-addict.

"He needs medical attention," David said.

"Yeah, that's right. I need medical attention. You can't take me to no lock-up," the addict said. He grabbed David's neck and pulled David's face into his own. "You gotta listen to me man. I can't go to no station or lock-up. I just dosed. I will loose my shit."

David shook the guy off. "We got ourselves an acid freak here," David yelled out. "How long ago did you drop?" David asked the addict.

"About an hour. Maybe two. Maybe three. I think it was today," the addict said.

"Okay, he's just starting to peak. We've got a handful here. Are you noticing any numbness in your extremities?"

"Everything is numb, bro. No wait, I feel EVERYTHING." The addict's eyes rolled back into his head as it bounced onto the pavement.

"Seeing any colors?" David asked. The man didn't respond.

"Where are you right now?" David asked the addict. The man didn't respond.

Are you in a room or outside?" David prodded. The man's eyes darted around. No response.

"What color is my shirt?" David asked. The addict's eyes looked wild and unfocussed.

"Red. It's blood. You are bleeding all over me!" the acid freak screamed at David.

"He has slipped into paranoia," David said to the captain. "He could turn on any one of us now, especially if he did some of that white stuff from his boot combined with the LSD."

The other firefighters had gathered behind David to observe the scene. David felt their presence. David knew he had said too much. When he looked up, the captain was gazing right at him. It was a stern and cold, yet knowing gaze. There was something strange about it to David. The western acid freak was strapped to a stretcher. Paramedics took him away.

On the drive back the captain asked him how long it had been since David "messed around with that stuff."

"Not since college sir," he lied. David was still experiencing a bit of an ecstasy comedown and wasn't about to allow paranoia to slip in by telling the captain the truth. "It would just lead to more question," he thought "and I don't have a problem." He always used to tell himself that if he had to lie about 'using' that he had a problem. The captain and David didn't say a word the rest of the ride back to the house. The captain browsed through the sports pages and David concentrated on driving. The streets seemed even narrower when this little bit of paranoid anxiety set in. This made David want to crawl back into bed and pull the covers over his head, with Morgan next to him. She had smelled so good this morning, so pure. Their bizarre episode with Dolores made him feel closer to Morgan. Maybe Europe would be fun. He could hold her and talk to her and laugh with her as much as he wanted. Maybe he wouldn't have to hide things from her and lie to her. She never really had gotten angry with him. He called her as soon as he docked the fire engine in the garage.

"Hey," he said when she answered. "I knew you'd call" she said.

"So did I. You know I can't go a day without talking to you."

"What time is it? I was just taking a nap."

"I don't know," he said. "We had a long night and a rough morning. I haven't even slept yet."

"I need to get to the book store before it closes," Morgan said.

"I already bought Prague books. We need London books," David said. A guy behind him motioned for his attention. "Can you hold on a sec?" he said to Morgan. The firefighter waved David over towards the bathroom.

"What's up man?" David asked.

"Can we talk?" the firefighter asked.

"Sure, Jeff. What's up?"

"You want in on this? Jeff opened his palm displaying some pills.

"Let me get off the phone," David said. David returned to the phone cubical. Hs heart raced at the sight of drugs. "I'll call you back, okay?" he said to Morgan.

"Yeah," Morgan said, "if you want me to do any of your shopping you better call soon. I don't know what you need."

"Sock," David said quickly. "I need socks," he said and hung up the phone.

"I love you too," Morgan said into the dead phone line.

"Jeff was leaning on the cubical. He was David's age, but since he didn't go to college he'd been in the fire department long enough to hit his ten-year mark. He was wearing dark blue, stone washed 501s, clean white tennis shoes and a white t-shirt from some bar in Mexico. He was engaged to be married in six months. David liked his fiancé. She seemed nice enough whenever she came around the firehouse. She was a local girl, brownish hair, fair skinned with a little too much makeup and nicely painted nails. She always had questions for Jeff about how many groomsmen he wanted, or what color towels she should register for. She brought him chocolate chip cookies from her mom's bakery.

"You want in on this or not?" Jeff asked David with an outstretched hand full of pill.

"Maybe we should go outside," David said.

"Let's go to the workout room," Jeff said. David nodded. He knew it would be empty.

"How about passing me one of those now?" David said to Jeff as soon as they entered the dusty, abandoned, tax-paid-for gym.

"It's X," Jeff said.

David's mouth watered. "Perfect. I was just starting to feel a come down." David's desire for the high overcame any discretionary wisdom. "How many do you want to part with?"

"As many as you need, "Jeff said.

"Is it good?"

"It's not that strong. I make it like that you I can keep a steady buzz, " Jeff said.

"You make it like that?" David asked.

"Yeah. Right here in the house."

"Right where?" David asked.

"Right here in the back bathroom. Nobody ever goes in there. Besides most everybody n the house knows. We didn't say anything to you cuz you're a captain's kid, a legacy and all. We didn't know if you were cool. After that acid trip today I think you're pretty safe." Jeff laughed. "Now we all know you use."

"Does everybody know?" David asked.

"Everybody heard you ask the bloody guy how long ago he 'dosed dude'," said Jeff, kiddingly. He elbowed David in the ribs as a sign of camaraderie.

David breathed a deep sigh. It was almost relief. Fear of losing his job was overridden with the relief of not having to regularly hide his shaking hands and red eyes.

"What about the captain," asked David?

"He's the one who showed me this bathroom,"

Jeff said. They walked into a dark, stale smelling room that resembled a storage shed. There was a sink and a stained, porcelain bathtub filled with a tan colored paste. The counter looked like an abandoned chemistry lab. Empty pill containers and faded yellow powder was scattered all over. There were spider webs and dust and dirty dishrags. Brooms, mops and metal buckets with cleaning solution and mop ringers littered the room.

"What's that shit?" David asked, referring to the goo in the bathtub.

"Peanut butter," Jeff said.

"What in the hell for?" David asked.

"You know, peeeeeeeeanut butter," Jeff said emphasizing the word.

"Nooooooo," David said, almost speechless. He had heard that term referring to a type of meth, but he had never seen it, and he had certainly never seen it being made.

"Yeeeeees," Jeff said, teasing him.

"That's speed?" David asked.

"Haven't you ever heard, 'mixed in a bathtub'?" asked Jeff.

"It's the worst kind there is, right?" asked David.

"Or the BEST kind. It's nasty, but it keep ya up when ya need it. And a lot of guys here need it."

"I thought you had X?" David asked.

"Right here." Jeff opened a drawer filled with little

baggies of white powder. He carefully poured some into an empty pill half and sealed it with the other h alf. He handed David the drug. "Twenty bucks."

David reached into his pocket, paid for the pill and immediately popped it down his throat. "Good thing they don't drug test in the fire department anymore," he said with a grin.

Chapter Nine

breathe

It rained the entire night while David worked. Morgan watched news reports of fallen trees and mudslides, always looking for David's face in the middle of a disaster. The bed was covered with suitcases in preparation for their upcoming Europe trip. Candles and the television lit the room. Wind whipped at the bay window and sirens echoed in the background. Morgan wanted to go to bed early. She wanted to fall quietly asleep to the rain. It was already three a.m. Sleep wouldn't happen until she knew David was home and safe. She situated herself on the chase lounge in front of the television. It was the first time she seriously contemplated what it would be like to be a fireman's wife. She had never wanted or even thought about marriage before this. It was a bad sign, she thought, that she only thought about marriage during a natural disaster.

The dogs didn't like the thunder. Boo shook and hid under the blankets every time it hit, while Delilah nestled more tightly into Morgan's armpit. "Don't worry Dee," Morgan said to the Bulldog, "you won't have to go out in this tonight. You get a reprieve from a long walk."

Delilah buried her head deeper. Boo opened her eyes and looked up at Morgan. Her velvety white ears were pinned to the sides of her head in fear and her tongues turned a dark shade of purplish-red from holding her breath. Morgan rubbed her neck and pulled her closer. "It's okay Boo. It's okay." The Bulldogs drifted off to sleep, snoring like buzz saws. Morgan tried to simulate their rhythmical breathing. Soon the three of them wee in sync, sleeping soundly. Thunder continued to pound the windows and lightning struck within feet of the flat. They still slept. Their breaths became slower and sweeter until it was a chorus of peacefulness. Daisy, the Rottweiler, had taken the bed. She found a space between the partially packed suitcases. Plastic bags of new socks sat unpacked. Daisy watched over Morgan and the Bulldogs.

At the first sign of light, Morgan's eyes opened. She always wondered if David was really going to come home. Somehow it seemed possible that he might someday just disappear, or she would get a call from the hospital or fire department. He kept telling her to go to one of the support groups for significant-others of firefighters, people who lived in fear that their loved ones might die on the job. She always wanted to go. It was just that the other people there were mostly wives of firemen. She wasn't a wife and felt intrusive going to a support group. Maybe if they got married she would go. For now, she tried to befriend as many of his work friends as possible, to see if they were the responsible type. She wasn't convinced that he was safe at work.

Daylight crept into the room. There was no sunshine, just light. She loved mornings when she didn't have to face bright sunlight, mornings that foretold days of dreary, rain, not-feel-guilty-for-not-leaving the house solitude.

It was after seven a.m. David should be home. Morgan maneuvered out from underneath the two dogs, carefully resituating them on the pillows. Boo groaned in disagreement and Delilah opened a tentative eye. She quickly closed it at the prospect of being discovered awake and having to go out into the dreaded rain. Morgan smiled at her trick. "I saw you Dee," she said. Delilah squeezed her eyes more tightly shut. Morgan tuned on the television. Every local channel showed a different disaster. Every disaster was surrounded by local firefighters. Homes slipped down hillsides into streets. Bridges collapsed. Trees blocked intersections. Power lines dangled near cable cars. David didn't come through the door. A slight panic welled inside her. She crawled back onto the chaise resituating the Bulldogs next to her and pulled the blanket almost over her head. She closed her yes and tried to breathe with the dogs again. They were already too advanced in their sleeping stage for her to catch up. They were extremely relaxed. She just lay there trying not to let her mind go crazy, trying to be as numb as possible.

Daisy knew the sound of David's van and of his footsteps. She didn't bother to get up when he came home. Morgan watched her pretend to sleep. Daisy knew he was going to go straight to bed and if she stayed calm she might get to remain there with him. Her tail wagged slightly and her eyes shone when he opened the bedroom door. He had a bouquet of flowers in his arms. They were white hyacinths and salmon colored roses. He wrapped his arms around Morgan, letting the flowers crinkle onto her lap. Water dripped from his new moustache onto her lips.

"This thing is getting kinda hairy," she said, brushing her lips against the thick, black moustache.

"Don't you like it? I thought it would make me look older."

"I thought it might help at work."

"Are there problems at work?" she asked.

"I just don't want to look like a rookie."

"The flowers are beautiful. You always know what I like." She exhaled a sigh of relief. He was home. He was safe. She had flowers.

David peeled his wet clothes off and wrapped a towel around his waist. His skin was brownish olive colored and his mother's Nicaraguan heritage glistened off his dark chest. His eyes, usually dark and brooding, darted toward the bedroom door. "I'm jumping in a hot shower."

"Wake me when you come to bed," Morgan called. It was six a.m. She had waited for him to come home all night. This is what is what always like, being a fireman had no regular hours. It was a person's life. The sun started coming up.

"Why don't you get up so we can get a start on the day," he suggested.

"It's eight a.m. and pouring rain. The city is a disaster zone. You want to go back into that rain?" asked Morgan.

"I think we should get our errands done. We leave in two days," he said with an air of annoyance in his voice. The door shut behind him. Morgan heard the shower start. The whole flat resounded with running water. The pipes swallowed loudly within the walls. The slightest tooth-brushing or toilet flushing alerted all inhabitants that someone was up and functioning. That didn't mean hot water was available. Hot water was hit or miss. It sounded as if water was running directly behind Morgan's head. She laid still, listening to the water run. She knew David would be in there for a long time, with or without hot water, his shower seemed interminable to her. She had waited all those hours for him to come home, then he walked right away. She tried not to think about it and instead rattled off a check list in her head of what needed to be done before they left for Europe. A smile crept across her face. "He's scared," she said to herself. She realized that David was having pre-travel jitters.

She remembered how she was the first time she left for Europe. She was only eighteen and traveling by herself. It took months of planning and weeks of packing, right down to which books she should read in which countries. And now it was David's turn to go. He has no idea what he's doing, she thought. "Everybody dreams of their first trip to Europe and his trip is in forty-hours. He must bee losing his mind with anxiety." She jumped up, smiled to herself, and pounded on the bathroom door. "Hey, what's taking so long? We've got a list a mile long. Let's go!"

Morgan slipped into a pair of Levi's and a black turtleneck sweater. She finished lacing up her boots when David appeared in the bedroom. His eyes were red and the circles were getting darker. His olive complexion was more greenish than usual. Morgan watched as he too put on jeans and hiking boots, topped with a San Francisco firefighter t-shirt, again. He filled it out nicely, his arms slightly bulging beneath the sleeves.

"I need to go to the visa office first," he said.

"Why? Which one?" she asked.

"Whichever. The one for the Czech Republic."

"We don't need visas where we're going. Plus we are American," she said.

"My mom and dad said this it's better to be safe than sorry. What if we can't get in, or out?" David said.

"I'm sure we don't need them," she said. "I'm not gonna run around all day in the rain and stand in lines for something that is ridiculous. Call the embassies if you are really worried." Morgan threw her arms up in the air.

"Okay, traveler's check," he said, trying to dismiss the visa issue.

"Yeah," she said. "Let's go to that breakfast place by the bank, then the bank."

"I think we should go to the American Express office," David said.

"The bank carries reputable traveler's checks." She saw anxiety sweep over his face. She remembered her first time; a new back-pack, guide books for all the major cities, a Eurail pass, student i.d.s for discounts at all the museums and art galleries, a hostel guide, a money belt, and, of course, America Express travelers checks. "You're right. Never leave home without 'em," she recited the American Express jingle. She took a deep breath. It felt right to understand what he was feeling and be able to help him. It made sense to Morgan, somehow, that finally her experiences abroad could be put to good use. She could make it easier on David. She could read the train schedules and make sense of the military way of telling time. He wouldn't have to feel as desperate and lost as she did. And he wouldn't have to experience it all alone, as she did. She wrapped er arms around him. "Thank you for going to Europe with me," she said.

"No, thank *you*. I know my friends will love you," he said. Se had almost forgotten that they were visiting some of his college buddies in Prague, and that David still thought she would be "crashing on the floor" of the cement laden flat.

"Are they even going to have time for us? I mean, they both work right?"

"Yeah, they teach English," David said.

"Oh, so they have pretty flexible hours," Morgan said. "Well, I've taken the liberty of checking on a few hotels in Prague. They are a little pricey, but after a long flight we might wasn't to refresh before we impose on them. Besides, I can't sleep on the floor for ten nights."

"Jim said he has a blow up mattress."

"He could go with us to a nice hotel. We could have a vodka tonic in our hands within two hours of landing."

"He thinks we are staying with him."

"Where does he live in relation to the city?"

"He said it's pretty far out. We'll take a bus."

"David please," Morgan begged. "I've done this. We will be soooo tired after an eleven hour flight. We can't then travel to the middle of nowhere in below zero temperature. If we must stay at his apartment, at least promise me that we can take a taxi. I don't mean to sound spoiled. It's just that I know what I'm doing. A taxi ride will cost nothing in Czech money and I don't have the energy to pretend I'm a struggling student." David's brow furrowed. Confusion was apparent as he poured himself a cup of coffee and opened the newspaper.

Morgan sat down next to him and took his hand. She began rubbing it in a massaging fashion. He looked up from his a massaging fashion. He looked up from his paper.

"That feels good," he said. "My hands are tense from driving the right last night."

"I'll be right back," she said. Morgan walked into the bathroom and retrieved a jar of hand cream. She poured some coffee into an oversized mug and sat down next to David. She squirted some hand cream onto her hands and rubbed them rigorously together in order to warm the cream. David's hands trembled slightly as he held the newspaper. She gently reached over and took one of them in hers. "Let me make them feel better," she said, as she worked her thumb into his palm.

"Oh, that feels good," he said, then he quickly yanked his hand away.

"What's wrong?"

"What's that gooey stuff," he said.

"Hand cream."

David hastily went to the sink and washed his hands.

"I thought it felt good," she said.

It did. I just don't want any on that stuff on my skin."

"Why not? It makes it easier to massage them."

"They'll be all soft. I don't want sissy hands. Do you know how long I had to work for these calluses?"

"People spend a lot of money to keep their hands soft."

"Not firemen," he said.

"Why not?"

"It seems like you aren't working hard enough if your hands are in good shape."

"The majority of cuts on your hands are from chopping vegetables, David."

So I work hard at making good dinners." He smiled one of 'it's gong to be okay' smiles. Morgan beamed back at him.

The day flew by. They arrived home with arms

full of necessary travel accessories: passport holders, a travel alarm clock, two money belts, Pepto-Bismol, aspirin, sample sized shampoos, magazines, best-selling novels for each, a neck pillow, sleeping bags, and more socks than they could possibly wear in a month. The rain still beat on the windows. The dogs needed to be walked. Morgan watched Daisy, Boo and Delilah stand patiently at the door. Even if it was raining, they still knew it was time to go out. Morgan looked at David. They each snapped a leash onto one of the dog's collars. Delilah was obedient enough to walk without a leash, however she occasionally veered dangerously close to the curb when she knew the walk was coming to an end. Morgan stepped onto the porch, shook out the already wet umbrella, and with a deep breath, ventured into the elements. David jumped behind her, grabbing her waist and causing a splash. They huddled under the umbrella, dogs pulling them back and forth in a serpentine pattern. Delilah led the pack.

It was a wet, chilly night. Morgan could smell the moss growing. Spring would be here soon enough. Tulips and roses would pop up around the constantly blooming bougainvillea. Corn colored mustard fields would appear next to straggly twisted grapevines and orange blossoms would highlight the background with blotches of white, decorating the wine country just north of them and spreading south enough for this terrain to be part of their lives. The rain seemed so cold. It seemed like there was still so much to go through before Morgan could discard her heavy sweaters. It was early March. Winter in Prague was still in full gust. It would have been nice to take their vacation locally, Morgan thought, to not have to go so far, to not have to expend so much energy. Europe was what David wanted and Prague was where his friends were teaching English. He was like a European virgin, desperate to do it, clueless as to how to not screw it up, literally. "One piece of advice," Morgan thought to herself, remembering what her grandpa told her when she was seventeen, "stay away from the northern countries in winter."

"Why not Italy or Greece? Any place where I don't have to wear thermal underwear just to get a cup of coffee," she said to David. "That is, if they even have coffee shops." The San Francisco dampness crept into her clothes, sinking into her bones. Czechoslovakia was sounding worse and worse. "Oops," she thought, "now the new Czech Republic and Slovakia." As she had been continually reminded. Even their first stop in London seemed ominously bleak. Santa Barbara would have been nice. David could've taken her to all his old haunts, since he went to college at UCSB. She always heard they had great Mexican food in Santa Barbara. That sounded so much better than deciphering "goulash" off a Slovakian menu. Boo looked up at her, eyes squinted shut due to the rain.

She too shivered. Delilah ran ahead in search of the shelter of the door. Daisy dragged David, pulling as if she was walking up a hill. They passed the same flowering bush that they always did; only the usual magenta blooms lay on the sidewalk, having been beaten off the branches by the rain.

"It's nice to not have to worry when I walk on this side of the street," David said.

"Oh yeah, we usually cross over," Moran said.'
"Yeah we don't have to when it rains," David said.

"I don't get it," Morgan said.

"The bees," David said. "They usually hide in that bush. They don't come out in this weather."

"The bees?"

"Yeah, I can't get stung. I'll die," David said. "I told you this."

"Yeah, you also told me you were going to get one of those kits."

"Just call 911. I can't deal with keeping a syringe on me all the time," David said.

"What will happen if I'm not near a phone?"

"Last time it was three minutes before I went into anaphylactic shock. I was in intensive care for days. Just a few years ago, right before we started dating. My head swelled up like a melon. My fingers and toes looked like sausages. I had a bunch of allergy shots when I was a kid, every week for years. All types of shots. Allergies to cats, plants, dust, smoke, whatever.

They couldn't test me to see if the shots worked for bee stings without injecting me. So I found out the hard way."

"You're kidding. Then how could you smoke so much pot?"

"It's one of the reasons I quit. It made my allergies worse. I knew how bad it was for me," David lied.

They joined Delilah in the front awning's shelter. She sat on the welcome mat, staring up at the doorknob. Boo and Daisy shook the water off their silky wet backs as Morgan folded up the umbrella.

The house was warm and peaceful. Morgan took a deep breath. Irrespective of the newspapers littering the floor, shopping bags lining the hallway, and unpacked suitcases strewn over the bed, things were in order, she thought. At least for the present, her life seemed manageable. She noticed David fussing in the kitchen making hot tea. They settled onto the sofa together, still in their damp clothes. Their arms and legs slowly became entangled. The tea warmed their bodies and calmed them.

"David?"

"Umm?"

"What if something happened and we couldn't be together?"

"Nothing is going to happen."

"Just what if?" Morgan asked.

"I'm very safe at work," David said.

"I don't mean that," she said. He pulled her tighter into him. She felt him trying to soothe and quiet her. The television was blaring intrusively loud commercials. She fumbled between their stomachs for the remote control. "I hate it when they do that. Make the commercials louder so you have to hear them. That's so rude," Morgan said.

"They do that so if you leave the room you still hear the ad," David said. Two cars screeched to an ear-shattering crash as a "Classic Collision" commercial flashed a phone number. David's heart raced. The television screen quickly cut to an emergency room filled with crying people. David closed his eyes, pretending to not see the commercial. Morgan could see his chest heaving. He became helpless in that one instance. A mere commercial agitated him to such a degree that he practically hyperventilated. The part that made him sweat was the emergency room scene. David knew that that was the end of the injured victim, and David knew he couldn't stop the television actor from dramatically, painfully and falsely dying. As hard as he tried, some of the people he was paid to keep safe ended up in emergency rooms, just like the one flashing on the screen in the cheesy commercial. There was no room for error, yet there were errors. And there were many times when he knew he couldn't save his victims, just as he couldn't save himself from being sexually molested by Mr. Foster. His mother didn't do her job. Maybe she didn't know how without disgracing the family, Morgan thought.

"I'm not going anywhere Morgan," David said calmly. He had stilled his rapid pulse quickly. The commercial was over.

"But what if David? What if one of us just disappeared, like all those people on the news?"

"He gave her a big bear hug, completely engulfing her. "You know I am stuck with you forever. I would slowly crumble away," he said. "I wouldn't know it at first. I would just be frantic looking for you and I would miss you, but I wouldn't really think you were gone. Then one day I would wake up and my life would be over without you. It would be gone. I would be gone. You are a part of my life that allows me to survive."

"She looked at him in amazement. He was right. They were bound by some inextricable force which she desperately wanted to understand. She nestled her head deeper into his damp chest. She breathed in the blue silence. She breathed in the oneness. It was a oneness of salty ocean waves carrying them to where they belonged. Soon their breaths fell in sync with the dogs and the rain. The trees tapped on their window, telling them to go to Tomales bay, until they fell asleep. They dreamt of the rolling waves. They dreamt of burgundy majestic robes and billowy sales. They dreamt of deep, blue royalty and laughing children. Their dreams were one; one dream of a magnificent man who sailed the seas and breathed life into everything he touched. They dreamt of Antonio.

CHAPTER TEN

hard floors

David packed the last of the suitcases into the white van. He had opted for no backseat when he purchased it, thinking it unnecessary. Now the dogs were squashed against each other, heads pressed forward, competing for control of the small opening to the front seats, luckily not knowing they were headed for the kennel instead of a camping trip, as was usually the case when suitcases were involved. Morgan tossed in a worn, black leather backpack that she had specially bought for the trip. David settled into the driver's seat and took out a strange, white face mask, the kind painter or paranoid city-dwelling people wear. It covered his nose and moth. He kept his eyes forward, as if nothing was out of the ordinary. He could feel Morgan staring at him. He didn't look over.

The silence got to her. "What's that?" she finally asked.

"A mask," he mumbled.

"A mask?"

"Yes. A mask!"

"I can see it's a mask. What's it for?"

"My aaa-rrr-gies."

"What?" she asked.

"My aaaal-er-gies," he said through the paper. He lifted the mask from his mouth. "The dogs aggravate my allergies, especially when they are wet and confined to this small space. I can't breathe with them all in the car. I don't want to have an allergy attack before flying." He snapped the mask back, wincing a bit as it his face.

"We'll be to the kennel soon," she said.

"I should have taken them to my parent's yesterday," he said.

"You know I don't feel safe with the bulldogs there. They will drown. Your mom thinks that since your Yellow Lab can swim all dogs should be able. She doesn't keep a close enough eye on them"

"Yeah," David conceded in order to avoid the conversation. He wished he hadn't brought it up. He was becoming slight nauseas.

"She just doesn't pay attention," Morgan said.

David quickly ripped the mask from his face and

threw it in the backset. Morgan looked at him in amazement. He continued to drive as if nothing had happened. Morgan looked in the back of the van. The mask was tangled on Delilah's foot.

"Do you want me to take it away from the dogs? They will chew it up."

"No, we're almost there," David said calmly.

What happened? Did the elastic start bothering you?" Morgan asked.

"Nothing," he said.

"Do you want the mask back?"

"No."

"I'm going to crawl in the back and get it." Morgan unbuckled her seatbelt.

"Nooooooo neeeeeed," he said calmly. He turned the corner onto a side street and jumped out of the car. Morgan went after him.

"David? What's going on?"

He was bent over trying to breath. He slowly stood up, averting her yes. "I shouldn't have taken the mask off."

"Why did you?"

"The car in front of us had a firefighter sticker on the back."

"So?" she said.

"Soooo, it was probably a firefighter," David said.

"So, I don't want him to think I am a geek for wearing that thing."

"Yeah, I'm fine. Let's go." David brushed off the event. He quickly rolled the windows down. "We're almost there." His embarrassment faded with the prospect of sympathy. He drove with his head out the window. The dogs chewed on the remaining pieces of the mask. Bits of white paper were all over the back of the van. As he turned into the kennel he desperately wanted to take a hit ecstasy, or maybe just a valium. They dropped off the dogs, after happily carrying blankets, food, toys and pillows into the concrete enclosures. David's eyes were red and he wheezed heavily.

"Next stop: the airport," David said. He smiled at Morgan who was digging through her purse. Her hands emerged with the plane tickets and passports. She playfully waved them in the air.

"Can you believe we're going to Europe together? I always wanted to have someone to go with," Morgan said.

"We should try to enjoy ourselves as much as possible," David said.

"Of course we will."

I mean," David paused, "I'm a little nervous."

"To fly?"

"Yeah, to fly," said David, thinking that was as good an excuse as any to take ecstasy.

"Make sure you bring a good book. It'll your mind off things," Morgan said.

"I was thinking of taking something that would

make me relax a little. You know, take the edge off. A xanax or something."

"Like what?" Morgan asked, perplexed that David had drugs on him.

"Or maybe just a valium or something," David covered.

"That's a good idea, once you get on the plane," Morgan said. "Then you can go right to sleep."

"Do you want to join me?" David asked.

"If I can't get to sleep I will." Morgan examined the tickets.

"These things take a little while to kick in. Maybe we better take them now." David reached across Morgan, opening the glove compartment. He pulled out a bag of yellow and white chipping pills. Maybe we should have a little fun?" He slid his hand softly up her thigh, swerving on the road slightly. He regained his driving composure. "Let's do something crazy together," he said.

"Okay, what did you have in mind?"

David turned onto the 380 freeway, the San Francisco turnpike. "Let's take something with a little kick to it. This stuff won't let us keep our hands off each other for the whole flight. We can join the Mile-High Club."

"I already can't keep my hands off of you," she said.

"It'll be even more fun with these," he said, pouring two pills into his hand.

Morgan took the bag from his hand. She looked at the pills. He handed her one from his palm. Succumbing to the possibility of finally good sex she popped it into her mouth. "Cheers," she said.

"Cheers," he said, as he too popped one down his throat. He exhaled a sigh of relief and swallowed. He had already thrown several tablets of ecstasy into the fingers of his traveling gloves. Now if he was caught at least he wouldn't have to explain it to Morgan.

The plane smelled like a used rental car. The upholstery had seen days when smoking was allowed. There was a yellow tinge to the beige arm pieces and fold out trays. The lamination on the literature was worn around the edges and the safety card in David's compartment was missing the last section. The stewardess pointed to what seemed to David to resemble bird-like gestures at the doors and windows. He was tripping. He searched the aisles for a bar. He'd heard his friends tell stories about drinking on long flights, about the stewardesses having to wake them up and roll them out of their seats when the plane landed, but there was no bar in sight. He slightly panicked.

"Hey," he nudged Morgan, "how do we get a drink?" Moran burst out laughing. She reached up and pushed the stewardess light overhead. It turned red.

She laughed harder. The stewardess appeared looming over them.

"See," Morgan said, "that's all you have to do." Her laughter continued. David didn't know what to do. He looked at Morgan for help. The stewardess showed up. "Order," she said to David. At this, she slightly laughed and put her head between her knees to conceal her growing laughter and the fact that she couldn't form sentences. It became apparent to David that she would not be lifting her head soon and he was on his own. The X had kicked in. He looked up at the stewardess.

"Could we get a couple of drinks please?" His voice didn't sound like his own. It was garbled like an old movie soundtrack. He tried to maintain his composure. Morgan's laughter wasn't helping.

"The drink cart will be coming around shortly. But, what would you like?" the stewardess asked.

"Ooooooh, a drink cart. I forgot about that. Could I get two vodka tonics?" Morgan belted out. The stewardess left. Moran buckled back over in laughter. "She thinks we're out of our heads," Morgan laughed. David sank into his seat, unsure what he had done to Morgan and what to next. Eleven hours. His fingers danced on his knees. His eyes rolled slightly back into his head. The X was hitting hard. The stewardess looked more and more voluptuous, and more and more like a rabbit. As she bent over to deposit his drinks on the fold-out tray, David made an effort to look out the window. This proximity of cleavage wasn't what he needed to calm down. He handed her some cash. It could have bee a ten dollar bill or a hundred dollar bill. He trusted her to return the correct change. The vodka bottles looked like something out of Alice in Wonderland's tea party. They were miniature, yet grew large and annoying as he tried to open them. Morgan's laughter turned to snorting. He knew everyone was watching them. He edged Morgan again to quiet her.

"Shhhhhh," he said.

She moved closer to him and nuzzled his ear. "Let's go," she said. He was still concentrating on the drinks. The first bottle burst open and he quickly emptied it into the tonic. He handed her the drink.

"Go where?" he asked.

"The bathroom," she said, her drink spilling over a bit. He retried her glass from her hands and downed it.

"I'll pour you another one," he said.

"I don't want another one. Let's go to the bathroom."

"Together?"

Yeah, I'll go in first. You wait 'till no one is around then slip in behind me."

"I'll have to get the pills out of my bag. They're in my gloves," he said.

"I don't want more," said Morgan. "For goodness sakes. And I'm not even going to touch the glove issue.

Look at my perma-grin," she whispered. "I want to join The Mile-High Club."

"Ohhh." He looked again at the stewardesses sort skirt and then at Morgan's snug jeans. "I'm right behind you," he said. Morgan waited until there was no line for the bathroom. She then crawled over David into the aisle. At the lavatory she motioned to David that she was entering the first door. He followed not far behind and slid the "occupied" sign to the red position. Morgan was wiping water off the countertop. She had her back to him. He grabbed hold of her hips and reached around her waist until he found her blue jean buttons. With one tug, the buttons all pulled loose. Oh, how he loved 501s. The airplane bathroom was damp, but still clean because it was early in the flight. It smelled of cleaning supplies and cheap metal. He looked over Morgan's into the mirror as she kissed his neck and chest. The mirror made his skin appear green and pale. The bags under his eyes were black and because of the fluorescent lighting and the mirror's magnification he could see every blackhead and impending blemish. The top of Morgan's head looked like a new mop, white with a dreadlock quality, as it tousled back and forth in an effort to unbutton his pants with her teeth. He lifted her up to him and kissed her. He could taste the lavatory's sterility. He tried to lift her up onto the counter, but it was impossible in the small space and with her jeans wrapped around her knees. He bent down and pulled her jeans off.

David bumped the "occupied" latch. It slid to the 'vacant' position, causing the lights to go off as if the room was empty. The door popped slightly ajar. He quickly pushed it shut and corrected the latch. "Let there be light," he said. Morgan beamed up at him. Her eyes were slightly dilated and her lips encrusted in a perpetual smile. She unbuttoned her blouse. Her skin seemed a start white, rather than having its creamy hue, due to the fluorescent lighting. Her breasts seemed to no longer long in the lacey black bra. They spilled out. All of a sudden both of their senses seemed to overload. The sound of their breathing amplified and they both sounded like Darth Vader. The extreme satisfaction of touch was so amplified that it seemed as if their hands and partially naked bodies were glued to each other. The sterile lavatory smelled burned their noses. David could hardly contain himself with the extreme sensory overload taking control of him. He turned her around. She bent over and grabbed the back of the toilet. David watched his pale green, alien like face move back and forth in the mirror, As Morgan's breathing became so loud that David had to cover her mouth with his hand. In the mirror, their bodies looked to David like a sculpture he had once seen, fitting perfectly together, seemingly fluid and moving in plaster, until all at once their breathing slowed. Morgan turned around and wrapped her arms around his neck.

They were half naked and quickly becoming uncomfortable pressed against the cold metal counter with bright lighting illuminating them. Anything even remotely resembling a stretch mark or blemish was accentuated. David became self conscious. The drug was wearing off and the paranoia was beginning. He needed his clothes back on. He fumbled with his jeans and helped Morgan with hers.

"I'll sneak out first," she said. "Then you wait a couple of minutes, okay?" She didn't show any signs of paranoia. That's what it was like for first-timers, he thought. They don't know how bad the comedown from X us sit get don't fear it and don't slip into paranoia. He was already planning how to avoid it while she was ordering another drink. Either a lot of cocktails, or, the more appealing solution to David; another hit. It was hard for David to resist the idea. Usually the option of more drugs wasn't available to a user who was on a come-down. It seemed almost too good to be true. Not having to page a dealer and wait for a call back. No decision of having to drive or beg for a home delivery, at an extremely inflated cost, which he would suffer for the next week when bills were due. This time, all he had to do was rip open the lining to his gloves and in the right hand index finger there would be ecstasy, literally and figuratively.

"I'll be there in a minute," he said. He kissed her and for a brief second held her close to him. He could feel their hearts racing. He slid the door open and she squeezed out. A woman tried to enter hind her, but David slammed the latch back to the 'occupied' position. He reached into his fanny pack for his gloves.

The woman was still waiting when David exited. He could feel her hard star on the back of his neck as he walked to his seat. It made him more paranoid. The plane bounced a bit, throwing David off balance. He grabbed hold of the nearest stability; a headrest in front him. H awakened the front, slumbering passenger. He could hear Morgan laughing. The aisle seemed small upon his return to his seat. He needed orange juice, both to wash down the pill and to enhance it's effect. This one should be a good one, he thought. "I was already on an empty stomach and the last one almost completely wore off." He looked forward to the upcoming high, especially because he didn't have to hide it. His peculiar behavior was already explainable to Morgan.

"Alright folks," the pilot said, "we're over half way to London." David couldn't make out the rest of the announcement. The words garbled together as he searched for his seat. When he found it, he slouched down and rested his head on Morgan's shoulder. The shrunken movie screen displayed North America and Europe with a small red arrow chugging across the

Atlantic Ocean. He closed his eyes. He could hear the conversations in the rows behind and in front of hi. They merged into incoherent ramblings. Morgan moved closer to him.

"It's nice to do nothing together," she said. Her voice sounded calm and normal. He could hardly sit still. He snapped open a magazine. "What's the matter?" she asked.

"Nothing."

"I just mean that it's nice to feel comfortable doing noting with you," she said. His hands trembled. It seemed as if he was trapped in a bubble and someone was trying to pop it. He couldn't get up and walk the aisles again. That woman who followed him from the bathroom was eyeing him like a hungry lizard whose tongue could zap him at any moment, and the snoring oaf that he awakened had it in for him. Morgan continued poking at the fragile bubble exterior. She tugged at his arm. "Wanna play cards?" she asked.

"No…I can't."

"How 'bout backgammon?" she suggested. They had always enjoyed this together. Some nights they sat for hours, never knowing who was the final winner, competing fiercely just for the sake of fun together.

"No," he said.

"Let's get more drinks," she said.

"Good idea." He pushed the stewardess call button. His eyes darted around. The second hit wasn't helping as much as he thought it would. It was creating anxiety instead of easing the come-down. That can happen, he thought. That happens when you've done too much, your synapses get all scrambled, and not in a good way with colors and smiles. It was in a fucked up, scared-you-might-never-come-back-to-earth way.

"How do you feel?" he asked Morgan, with the slight hope that maybe they were in this living euphoric hell together.

"Fine," she said, loud and laughing.

"Do you want another hit?"

"Do you?"

"I already did one." There was no hiding it. She wasn't going to get mad at him this early in the trip and even if she did it couldn't be as bad as his own private misery. Besides, he didn't think he was capable of talking to the stewardess when she came to take their order.

"How do you feel?"

"Like *you* better order the cocktails."

"Morgan smiled. "How many should I order? I guess a better question is 'how many do you think she will bring us?'" David smiled back at her. She *was* on his wavelength. Why did he ever think she wouldn't be? She never really played mind games like other girls that couldn't understand him. She was really independent and didn't seem to expect that much from him. To David, it seemed that every problem could easily be solved by flowers and affection, no matter how badly he messed up. Morgan didn't deserve to be lied to. He was going to try to not lie to her anymore, to trust her.

"How 'bout that card game," he said. The stewardess never showed up. The movie ended. The food trays circulated. The lights came up. David and Morgan played cards and stared into each other's eyes. The plan landed. Almost everyone exited. The plane was littered with shrunken pillows and blankets. David imagined little people wrapped in them. As they exited the plane everything became blurry. There were lines and papers and questions. Even the voices around him were muffled through English accents. This couldn't be English, he thought. It might as well have been pig-Latin as far as he was concerned. Luckily, Morgan could take care of things. She filled our his paper work, which consisted of a very small piece of paper with declaration and immigration questions on it and retrieved his passport from his fanny pack when necessary. He became a little more anxious when they had to separate. They had to go individually to a man at a plexy glass protected podium. The line ended at a box with a man in it who asked questions about what David was doing there. Seeing as how he had no idea when he was doing, or for that matter where he had last stashed his drugs, this man and these questions made him sweat. As soon as he could he grabbed Morgan's hand. He chose not to let go no matter how sweaty they became. He even forewent finding a bathroom for fear of separating from her again.

This dilemma became reality when their plane landed. Morgan was doubled over in pain. "I need to find a bathroom," she said. He followed her. The signs looked like hieroglyphics to David. They dodged people who were dressed so heavily that their eyes could barely peek through their turtle-necks, scarves, hats and coats. As Morgan ran into the Czech Republic airport bathroom, hand covering her mouth, David followed.

"What's the matter?"

"I don't know. I think it's the drugs," she said. Morgan continued to wretch, kneeling on the dirty bathroom floor. She heaved and vomited three times. The floor was damp with muddy salt and snow. Her knees were dirty and she felt disgusting. The cold was already setting into their bodies. Morgan regained her composure. David helped her and wiped her hair off her face. He had two backpacks slung, one on each shoulder, and an armful of winter clothing. Thanks to David's parents, the couple came prepared for anything.

Jim, David's college roommate, waved eagerly as

David and Morgan departed the customs area. Jim was raised in Northern California also, a Marin local, also a Marin Catholic school alumni, and therefore not a foreigner to the warmth of California sunshine and a healthy color one one's cheeks. He now stood in front of them, pale and grey. He stared at David and Morgan, white as a ghost, wrapped n gray goose down jacket, dirty jeans and muddy boots. He blended into the crowd.

The bus ride to his apartment was long and cold. There was no seating room on the bus and Morgan could feel her toes going numb as dizziness swept over her. Upon arriving at the cardboard like dwelling Jim lived in, Morgan shivered. It was worse that she thought. They all peeled off their layers of clothing and slowly, very slowly began to thaw. Jim crawled into his sofa bed. Morgan and David blew up an air mattress and placed it next to the bathroom door, the only place with enough room for it. "Please David?" she pleaded, "We aren't broke. I lived like this when I was twenty. Tomorrow tell me we can go get a nice hotel? Please?"

"I don't want to disappoint my friend. He's tried so hard to accommodate us."

"I know honey, but I feel like I'm going to get sick. I need warmth, comfort, pillows," Morgan said. David didn't respond. They fell asleep clutching each other.

Her tears ran down his chest, until she had no more energy.

The next day and night came and went without any change in grayness. As they settled into their third night Morgan felt an ache inside her. The tears wouldn't stop. She couldn't believe David would expect her to live with this level of material discomfort. She quietly sobbed, shaking and shuddering. The sobs became audible. Her nerves become frazzled. Her mental state became unstable. She was lost.

"Please, don't do this," David begged as Morgan rocked to the sounds of her own sobbing. "Jim will hear you. He's tried so hard."

"I can't help it!!! David I have to go home. It's too cold here. I feel pneumonia setting in again. Something is wrong with me. I can't stay. You stay," she sobbed. "There's no reason for you to leave. Just get me on the plane. Then I can rest. I will recover on the plane." Morgan was frantic and confused.

"No, no. I'll go with you," David said. They heard sirens on the street and Jim snoring. Wind bit at the walls of the Prague building. The next day they checked into a palatial old Czech hotel. The fine china looked like it was from Disney land with pictures of Mickey Mouse on the tea cups. The bed and showers were warm. Morgan slept for three days. Jim checked on her regularly, seeming genuinely concerned. David didn't say or do much. He was embarrassed of her behavior, as if she had a choice.

In bed, Morgan clutched her aching stomach and shivered a lot. She couldn't think straight. Jim brought her soup. She was in full swing of a nervous breakdown. David took a few more pills. Nothing seemed to matter to him. They didn't speak. David watched movies in the hotel. Whenever he was gone, Morgan watched Czech television and tried to absorb the culture through a screen. David toured Prague with Jim when Morgan slept. They cut off the rest of their trip and flew back to California. It was a long, arduous flight. Morgan's felt as if she was PMSing the whole time, with cramps and stomach pain. She threw up constantly.

When they arrived at the luggage carousel David politely excused himself. "I need to make a phone call," he said. He went to call his parents. "Yeah, she was sick. I know Jim called you. I know. I know. I know. I'll go back. Yeah. Yeah. Yeah," he said, in response to the usual parental questions.

After the long flight and drive back to San Fran., Morgan ran a bath. She wrapped herself in a robe and meshed into the sofa. They didn't speak the entire way home. Two days passed before she got off the sofa. Since David was still on vacation, she didn't know where he was when she woke up. He was gone. There was blood on the sofa. Not a lot of blood, but enough: Enough for her to know why she was sick. There was blood between her legs. She got up to run another bath. As she slowly walked past the kitchen she noticed wilting flowers on the table, still in plastic from the grocery. The white lilies never made it into a vase. On top of them was a note from David. It said; "I'm not coming back."

CHAPTER ELEVEN

connections

Morgan knew that what was to come was bleak. She saw gas prices creeping up to over $2.50 per gallon and she felt David's emptiness. She called the fire station. His fellow firefighters told her lame alibis. On about the tenth call, David answered the station phone himself. She told him about the accidental loss of life inside her. His response was, "I didn't want this to happen." That was all she remembered from the conversation.

Waves of nausea came back frequently. He was now living at the firehouse. There was no discussion of where she would live. The San Francisco apartment was his. She barely liked living there when he *was* there. There was no point in staying, or in hoping. He wouldn't talk to her and had seemingly disappeared from their life together. Almost all food caused aches inside her body and shiver. Her skin crawled with confusion. The pregnancy had passed and she was constantly cold. She walked around the city; buying linens, comforters, flannel sheets, a portable electric fireplace; anything to keep her warm.

David was gone. All the little things ate away at her. Where were her insurance papers that she left in his van? She wanted her mail from the back of his van. Was she still supposed to care for his mother's dog while Gina went to Hawaii? What about her birthday looming ahead and their reservations up the coast? The worst part was that she couldn't get answers to these questions. He had just disappeared. The questions should have been easy. There was no rational reason for anything unkind. She didn't understand and he wouldn't explain.

Her upcoming birthday was one of the weirdest things haunting her. They were supposed to go to St. Ore. It was a resort comprised of private glass houses on a Northern California beach decorated with Russian architecture. Hundreds of years ago, a small number of Russian settlers had decided to start lives on the Northern California coast. Only a few remained.

Months ago she had seen her birthday and a confirmation number scribbled in David's handwriting across the front of one of the St. Ore's brochures. She had been so excited to go. Yesterday she found the brochure in a drawer, torn in half. He had to have purposely placed it there, she thought. She was the only one who ever opened that desk drawer. There were other odd things popping up, malicious things. Her favorite dress, which he numerously mentioned showed a little too much cleavage, was missing and some of her lingerie. Her friends had recently told her that they left messages personally with him numerous times and that he never relayed the messages to her. Another friend told Morgan that he had stopped by her flat to visit and David refused to let him in and threatened to call the police. A casino manager called offering complimentary rooms for their "high roller" players at The Venetian in Las Vegas.

The dogs had started begging for table scraps, which she never gave them, so she could only assume that David had given table food to the dogs so that they would love him, or so he could bribe them when he snuck in and out.

The worst and weirdest was still creeping up on her in subtle ways. There was this daunting feeling that she was being shunned. People started asking is she was 'okay' in a very odd tone. It wasn't just "Hi Morgan, how's it going?" It was more like, "Are you making it through this? Are you crazy yet? Are you a drug addict?" Then when Morgan responded with whatever the latest piece of news was regarding her recently uprooted life, mysteriously missing belongings or odd turning of events, the inquiring friends would excuse themselves. Finally Morgan figured out, by way of a possibly well-meaning and nosy friend, that David had indeed not disappeared but was telling everyone Morgan had checked herself into drug rehab. Then it all began making sense. There were nights when he used to wake up shaking and sweating. Morgan would embrace him and ask him what was wrong. He held her until her skin ached with numbness and he swore up and down that he never had dreams. He's never had one in his life, he said. Morgan heard him utter names and commands and odd things about Marin Catholic School in his sleep.

His clothes were still at their apartment. He never came back for them. Their lives, their future, it was all over and all gone without one bit of closure or reason. She decided it was time to leave. She grabbed a few things that mattered to her: her books, her shoes, the Bulldogs and her favorite blankets and pillows. When she opened the car trunk to load up her things she found a disorganized disarray of items. David had tossed everything of Morgan's from the van into her car trunk with no concern for their well-being. Morgan sighed. It was the final sign of how little he cared about her. He didn't even bother to carefully place her belongings in her car. He just threw them like trash into a heap. She cracked the window to her car to get some fresh air. It seemed to curb the nausea. She drove calmly, stoically over the highway 92 bridge into Half Moon Bay. The nurseries and pumpkin patches reminded her that summer was ending and orange, yellow hues would soon cover the hills. The end of summer was warm in Northern California. Even the water was swimmable and waves delicious. They could rock a person back to places in their soul before time existed. White crests jolted Main Street with thundering finales. Santa Ana winds settled into her body, removing her chills. She stopped at a local family farm. The hot wind touched her throat. It was a tonic to the past few weeks of retching and vomiting and choking down tears. Her eyes eased softly into the setting of the fresh fruits' and vegetables' vibrant colors. The beach was only a half block up the street. The local fruit and vegetable stand had bins filled with oddly shaped herbivorous foods. She decided on sweet corn. It would be easy to eat and would remind her of where she came from, who she was before David broke her. It reminded her of a place she could go back to that would be the same with or without him. "Knee high by the Fourth of July," all the farmers in Indiana used to say in order to gauge the strength of their corn crops. This corn was well over her shoulders and ready to be harvested. There were vats of corn, waiting to be bought or ground into grain. The vats were miniature versions of the grain sheds, used to make moonshine in the evening hours, she had seen on school field trips growing up back n the Midwestern United States. "In California you go to the beach or Disneyland for fieldtrips," she said to herself. "In Indiana they teach you how to make booze from day one." The vats were modern sterling silver and the floor of the market was bleak, grey cement. The contrast between the smell of fresh squeezed juiced and fermenting grain was practically indistinguishable. She asked if she could go into the field to pick her own corn. The woman at the counter was reluctant. Morgan insisted, "I know good, strong stalks and I have time on my hands. It'll save you the trouble." Morgan returned with ten ears. She husked them in front of the woman. She picked out an apple and some pumpkin seeds and paid for everything.

Back in the car she had the nagging feeling that she should call Gina to check on the dog babysitting thing. She didn't want to call, but she had promised to watch this dog and that promise was the only thing keeping her in Northern California right now. She needed to get away. She'd promised to care for Baily, the Petite Vendeen Bussels Giffon mix, when David's parents vacationed in Hawaii. David and Morgan were supposed to live in his parent's house. They were going to play house while watching the dog. It was supposed to be kind of like a testing ground for marriage, or something. There was a pay phone at the local market. Morgan took a deep breath and dialed.

"Hello," Gina answered.

"Hi Gina, it's Morgan."

"Oh Morgan. David isn't here."

"I'm calling about Baily. Do you still want me to sit for him when you're go on vacation. I know I promised. I just wondered if maybe David was going to do it. I'm still happy to. It's just…under the circumstances," Morgan was rambling.

"Uh no, uh Morgan we cancelled our trip. We'll be staying home that week. David won't be here…here at the house. You can't find him here. I don't know where he is," Gina said.

"What do you mean?" Morgan asked, finding it hard to believe that Gina, whom David talked to three times a day, didn't know where he was.

"I said: I don't know where he is!"

"Now I'm a little worried about him, Gina. He might need some help."

"No, he's fine."

"What?" Morgan said. "I thought you didn't know where he was. How do you know he is fine?"

"He's fine! He's just not here right now," Gina said.

"Okay Gina, call me if you need anything or if you change your mind and need a dog sitter."

"Oh. That won't happen," Gina said. "Someone will **always** be here at the house." Morgan realized

Gina was lying to her. It was getting weird. Morgan didn't deserve to be treated like a potential thief.

"Gina, do you want me to send David's things to your house? I'm sure he will be there at some point."

"Oh no. He doesn't need that stuff. You just keep it. He has plenty of clothes here."

"Okaaaaaaay," Morgan paused. "I'll talk to you later."

"Oh that won't be necessary," Gina said and abruptly hung up.

Morgan had no idea how to respond to this rudeness. She was being treated as if she was doing something wrong for having a miscarriage, as if she planned on ruining David's trip to Europe. As far as Morgan could tell there was no reason for anyone to shun her or lie to her. Tears welled in her eyes. The tenderness she felt for David was replaced with anger and confusion. Was it at all real? She thought. "This is stupid," she said out loud. "I never even liked his mom. She knows that her son messed up and will hide it from the world forever, just like she hid David being molested by the Catholic priest. She is going to make sure the secret stays in the family. Just like when she fabricated the date of her birthday. She made it the same as her mother-in-law's, David's paternal grandma, so that the woman would like her. Gina wanted so much to be accepted by the white Roman Catholic Irish family that she changed hr birthday and let her son be sexually abused the school priest. Gina knew all the time. And when David acted odd with girls and bent over in strange positions; positions which Mr. Foster praised him for, Gina pretended not to notice. Now he's run away from the only woman he loved. The only one who could handle his past, his pain, his shame and again his mother will take that away from him. She will take *me* away from him for fear of her own exposure. She failed to protect him. 'Not going to Hawaii my ass!'" Morgan put the phone down. She had been talking to an empty line for this whole time and was starting to feel a little crazy. She pulled into the beach parking lot. Her mouth was wide open and her eyes too wide to fill with tears anymore. Her life suddenly took on a surreal aspect, everything she new to be good and true about herself was in question. She wasn't a drug addict. She loved dogs and would gladly have cared for Baily no matter what the situation with David. Of course she would return his things, although he was telling people that he was afraid to come back to the apartment and get them. This character bashing was odd. She never realized David not only didn't love her, but actually wanted to hurt her. She had bizarrely become the focus of his paranoia. This couldn't be real. Every morning since he left she opened her eyes with a sense of hesitancy, not sure what she would have to face. Then the heaviness sank back in and she realized he was gone. Next came the fear. The fear of wondering what awful thing she would encounter that day regarding their past relationship. She had to get away from the lies and craziness. The dogs were always there to warm her feet, so she knew she could still feel goodness around her. The days flew by without answers as to why he left. She had ended up, weeks later, in Half Moon Bay Beach, with two dogs, some produce and a Mexican blanket in hand. David had abandoned the dogs also, except Daisy. They were now her responsibility.

She threw herself onto the sand. The dogs settled in next to her. She felt safe with them on each side of her, like gargoyles guarding a castle. No one would mistake her for a vulnerable, single person and approach her without Delilah wrinkling her nose and curling her lips into a low growl. Also, the dogs provided the added benefit of looking beautifully cared for. They had gorgeous coats and decorative brown leather collars embossed with brass flowers. The collars looked expensive and the dogs looked like they belonged exactly where they were. There was no mistaking them for strays, hence no one would mistake her for a vagrant or threat to society by sleeping on a Mexican blanket on the beach. She smiled to herself and thought out loud, "even my brother and closest friends sometimes treat me like an outcast." She thought of one of her favorite quotes;

The true measure of genius is found in the
confederacy of dunces against him.
—John Milton

She felt as if everyone was against her. Her battle was now a fight to remember who she was. She had to slay her demons, which she never even knew she had. No longer would she be able to waste her time saving David from his past and himself. He was on his own.

"He hates me," she said out loud. "His love turned to contempt." She wondered how long his mother actually let the awful sexual abuse continue. How long did she pretend it didn't exist in order to just fit in to the Marin social crowd? That wicked woman." Morgan so desperately wanted to help David, to let him know that she understood what happened. At this point she didn't know even if he was heterosexual or not. Their sex had been less than passionate, almost dutiful. She wanted to let him know that if he was gay they could be friends, and that he could 'come out' to her. Maybe his shame lied in enjoying what had happened with the priest? Maybe, just maybe he ran from his shame and not her. It didn't make sense why he would just up and disappear and spend so much time trying to justify his disappearance by making her look bad. "It had to be the drugs," she said, loudly. She wanted to help him with every fiber of her being, but she was smart enough to know that she needed to save herself. Their life together had been but a stumbling stone and it was time for her to find her own path. This life and these people were shunning her and mistreating her for their own amusement.

The crashing waves lulled her back to sleep. She slipped into a semi-conscious, meditative state. It was a time before this, when the cycles of nature and the waves decided who lived and died, a time when the ocean worked magic. She dreamt of two children, frolicking in the surf. They were young, five and six years old. No adult was around to watch them. There was a small brown, leather book. Beautiful blue bands surrounded the children's heads, turquoise halos.

Chapter Twelve

genetics of the soul

The body of water, near the Marin wetlands, where animals came for all means of survival split into two bodies decades ago, then it was gone. So much of it dried up that the median sand bar was the land winner. The sole survivor. As one large lake, this body of water could have sustained most any life form. Fish reproduced and thrived there. Trees tilted toward and grew underneath the water providing shade for the visiting thirsty animals and their offspring. Birds came to visit, bathing and basking in the oasis while chirping and calling to each other. These mating calls and social connections would not have existed without this body of water. As one half of the lake began to dry up the other formed narrow tributaries emptying out into the sands. Animosity and tension grew as nature became more and more thirsty. The trees had to reroute their roots causing wilting and browning leaves. The Aspen trees' trunks turned a deep, marshy red. There was enough water for the Aspens to survive. They displayed a gorgeous, glorious portrait of family life. All their colors meshed together, having the same roots and same vitamin supplies. Delilah and Boo sat in the middle of the huge Aspen grove. Morgan had decided to take the dogs there for a run.

The smaller animals; squirrel, mice, raccoon and a few domestically wild ferrets could no longer freely drink from the watering hole. Coyote mainly owned the rights via survival of the fittest. And so, without love and water, the smaller creatures, and the smaller dreams died off. No children or grandchildren arrived. Strong, enduring, glorious Aspen trees overtook the area. Aspen roots have the potential for infinite growth. Their roots will reach toward life-sustaining water, even though there is no water within their grasp. The roots always correctly sense which tangled direction to take to find it. Aspens possess instinctual perfection. All Aspen groves have the potential to outgrow their environment. Souls too, have infinite growth potential and quickly outgrow their earthly bodies. Each soul's light gets brighter and larger with each growth spurt. Every drop of learning adds light to a soul's composition. Every drop of water adds a twig to a growing Aspen. The trees remember where the drops of life-sustaining energy came from and they find their way back to their liquid life-source. Souls remember every ounce of love and pain that they have felt and they gravitate back to that emotion. The more a soul feels, the more it learns, enabling it to graduate to its next level. There is, of course, a point of diminishing returns. If the soul creates or gravitates toward too much darkness, its light flickers as a warning and it has to retrace a path back toward positive energy. The Aspens can, of course, drown if they are exposed to too much water.

At some point, everything gravitates toward what it is used to, unfortunately, frequently ending tragically. Due to 'survival of the fittest', every living thing must learn, at some point, to gravitate toward what is good for it, toward what is eternally sustainable, for it to survive. Socratic, instinctual souls are better at finding their sustainable paths. Old Aspen trees are deeply, intrinsically rooted in nourishing soil. Souls too need to find what nourishes them in order to flourish.

The wet-lands ground crusted over and the cellular memory of love sank into the crevices, waiting for some form of moist warmth to cause it to resurface. The body of water will always be there in memory. If it ever was there it will remain, with the fish skeletons and dried roots, the cellular memory of love and life lays dormant.

As DNA comprises a physical human being; cellular, molecular memories imprint the soul. The body of water will sink into the mud and ooze out the edges, like dreams which are never fully forgotten no matter how downtrodden they become. The good stuff doesn't go away. It lingers in a holding pattern, like the taste of cold, clean water. Always with the hope that with every glass of water we drink, we will find that perfect taste; crisp, fortifying and pure. It will pulsate like the smell of jasmine up our noses, through our veins, and run out our finger tips. We become one with the water and the cellular memories of its' effect on our bodies. We are all that there ever was and all that ever will be, in just one body of water, creating a family of *Populous Tremuloidus*, Aspen trees.

Bright, white balls of light dance in various physical forms at night, above the Aspens. The lights divide and reunite like flickering stars. Together they can light the path of knowing what's inside the building blocks which comprise our souls.

No matter how much betrayal, abandonment or loneliness Morgan had gone through, the love was still there. Her cells knew hot to feel it. She earned that eternal cellular knowledge. Even though David had left, he could not take that away. No one could take that away. Her soul was imprinted with the building blocks of true love centuries ago. Those building blocks were reactivated when she met David. She sat upright on her Mexican blanket under the Aspens. "It really is going to be okay," she said to herself. She felt the light of life inside her body and knew that she would never let it slip away again. She longed for her recently lost pregnancy to not be over. She longed for the light of life to engulf her, instead of the death and the shunning and the drugs and the lies which she had been forced to be surrounded with recently. No one could take away this beautiful light within her. Like a curse and a blessing she would always have it. She knew David was cursed too. She knew he felt it. She knew everywhere he went he took the curse of his malice was with him. Like the two dried up bodies of water in her dream they would both starve and crumble without staying connected to the eternal knowing inside of each of them. Without staying connected to it, they would become mere shells of their former selves. They would never be the same again. Their edges would become brittle and crack and break. Their skin would weather with more texturing than average for their ages. They were broken and out in a world that doesn't tolerate damaged goods. Neither of them had the time or place to recover. Their souls each needed a way-station for sanctuary until complete recovery was reached. Without recovery they were going to have to try to survive while being destined to make desperate decisions.

Their lives could have been full, rich, and

ceaselessly flowing toward harmony. Now she only had the former light of love within her. Her soul's cells ached for love's healing medicine.

The pain and release settled into her cells simultaneously. She was at once free with the ceaselessly loving, crashing ocean lulling her into timelessness while her human body fought her spiritual ease and forced pain down her chest, into her stomach and back up through her esophagus. She exhaled the darkness. The bile burned her throat as she heaved and vomited the blackness out of her being. Everything was heavy. She couldn't clear her head, although just minutes before she had felt that everything would be okay. Now she didn't feel safe. Her words were no longer safe. The people she used to trust were no longer safe. She would be mocked, yet she had to talk to someone. She needed David's hand on her throat to calm it, to warm its' aching. Yet he wasn't there. He was gone. The body of water was split. The animals were dehydrating and the trees dying. There were no children in her future. She couldn't swallow. She knelt with her face in her hand, aching for help. There was no longer the possibility of life as she had envisioned it. Everything had changed. Everything was gone. The cells of her soul which remembered being filled with and cared for by love, also remembered severe pain and loneliness. Unfortunately, all the emotions were stored inside her. By bringing the dark emotions to the surface she allowed her soul to feel them again, as it had done days before, months before and hundreds of years before. She needed to feel love. Morgan wrapped her arms tightly around her dogs, easing the pain in her throat. "There comes a time for letting go," she said.

Morgan remembered a story she had read in *Physician's Digest*. It was about cellular memory. A man's heart had stopped and an organ donor gave him a replacement heart. The man suddenly started having intense cravings for fried chicken. It turns out the donor was from the south and loved his mother's fried chicken. Finally the man went through the proper channels and contacted the donor's family. The man sent his regards and thanks and asked if he could bring the family a gift. The man arrived at the family's house with an armful of flowers and a bag of groceries. He talked to the mother of the deceased son who had graciously donated his heart, and told her that he had new, over-whelming cravings for fried chicken. She laughed and said, "You just gave me the best gift ever. My son is alive and well in you."

The man with the donated heart handed the mother a bag of groceries. It was filled with bread crumbs, flour, vegetable oil, Captain Crunch cereal, chicken breasts. "Please, please show me your recipe."

The mother laughed until tears ran down her face. "How did you know my baby liked cereal on his chicken," she asked?

"Because now I eat it everyday," the heart recipient said.

Morgan packed up her dogs and belongings from the beach. "Everything lives forever," she thought, afraid that she would always feel pain. She carefully loaded up her car for fear that with any quick movement could bring her to her knees. She got in the driver's seat and put the key in the ignition. She reached for the radio then quickly withdrew her hand. Any love song could debilitate her right now. She started driving north, not knowing where she was heading. She drove on Pacific Coast Highway 1, instead of heading inland and taking a quicker freeway north. There was no reason to go faster. She didn't even know where she was going. Besides, she needed to be able to see the ocean. The sound of the waves was the only thing keeping her grounded. She drove up the Pacific Coast highway until her vision blurred and she was forced to pull over. She stopped at a Bed & Breakfast/motel. *Sunrise Inn*, the sign said. The second '*n*' was tilted and hanging below the bottom of the faded blue and white sign. Sand and wind had both taken their tolls on the building. It made it more authentic. A seagull sat on top of the sign. She turned off her engine and walked trepidatus into the weathered lobby. To her amazement, there was a warmly rock fireplace and huge, comfy, inviting, brown leather chair. Morgan thought that she could collapse into the chair forever.

There were fresh flowers. White roses and white lilies on a table filled with coffee and cookies. The place was built for weary travelers.

"May I help you?" a lovely, well-manicured man said from behind a marble counter. He wasn't clad in a uniform. He wore a casual white button down shirt with the sleeves rolled up one cuff, khaki shorts, and loafers. This was the motel's idea of looking professional.

"Do you take pets?" Morgan asked.

"Fifty dollar deposit," he said.

"Okay. I need a room, preferably on the bottom floor."

"With or without a fireplace?" he asked.

"With," she answered quickly. She didn't care how much it cost. She needed the warmth. The thought of having a fire to fall asleep to melted Morgan's soul. For the first time in awhile she felt the possibility of peaceful slumber surround her.

He handed her a plastic key. "Breakfast is from seven to nine a.m.," he said. "Room 131."

"Thank you. Is there firewood?"

"A Duraflame log," he said. "You can purchase a bundle of wood for five dollars at the market up the street."

Morgan took the plastic key. She was grateful that David had taken Daisy, the Rottweiler, and left her with only the two Bulldogs. Delilah and Boo looked up at her as she drove to the nearby 7-11 convenience market. She bought two cans of dog food, a bundle of wood and some dried almonds. She didn't know what else to eat. She had already lost ten pounds since David left. "The benefit of being single," she thought. "No more four course dinners followed by bottles of wine and ice-cream." She contemplated picking up a *New York Times* until she saw the front page and realized the news was just going to depress her. The Middle East was entering a deadly crisis that she knew would inevitably escalate, as all wars do. She knew that soon half of the world would be inhospitable to tourists. The Czech Republic was nowhere she should have been. That's why she had fallen apart so quickly. Its' grey bleakness and deathly cold temperatures were too much for her to handle. She had sensed her own closeness to a war. She knew it before she went, yet he wouldn't listen. Just some warmth and beauty was all she had needed to survive. When she had told him that, he acted like she was trying to take something away from him, like she was trying to take away the college hitchhiking/hostile sleeping experience which had already passed him by. He seriously thought she would be okay sleeping on the floor of a dank, six story cardboard building. For the first time she started to resent him. The resentment got deeper as she remembered all of his disappearances and long days at work. Then, without even a proper break-up, he took off. No explanation. Just blame. His selfishness made her cheeks turn red and for the first time anger rose up in her throat. After all that, he had lied about her and caused other people to shun her. It was at this point she knew that she was never going back to San Francisco. All her belonging were in storage anyway. They didn't fit into the San Francisco apartment so she stored them a long time ago. The apartment was his. The Rottweiler was his. She knelt and cried for Daisy.

When she walked into her motel room she was overcome with gratefulness. It was a perfect beach cottage stuffed into a small room. A brightly colored, floral loveseat was the first thing she saw. Above the sofa was a watercolor painting of a white-washed covered bridge over a flowing brook. The brook was surrounded on both sides with yellow and lavender wildflowers. In the background of the painting was a tall, white lighthouse. The painting dared her to jump into it and start life fresh in a bubbling, alive place. Her eyes turned to the river-rock fireplace, covered with a wrought iron screen. It too dared her to fill it with wood and bask in its warmth and glow. She placed the complementary Duraflame log horizontally on the bottom then meticulously stacked the newly bought wood in a teepee style. The room even came with a six-inch long lighter. She clicked the red button and put the flame to the corner of the fake log. Soon amber and burnt orange hues filled the room, unwrapping the grey from her soul. She opened the pop top cans of dog food and filled the complementary plastic coffee cups with water. The dogs ate heartily by the fire. For the first time in a long time, she basked in the beauty of watching them eat, of seeing them nurture themselves. She laid out the blankets she had brought from the car and built a nest for them in front of the fire.

She took a steaming hot shower, rubbed complementary lavender lotion all over her body and climbed naked into the all white cotton, billowy bed. The huge white over-stuffed, down comforter blanketed her and like a bear crawling into a cave for winter hibernation, Morgan exhaled in deep, unmoving sleep. As she started to doze off her body convulsed. Her legs jumped wildly, uncontrollably around the bed and her body shook in seizure-like pain. She was so tired that she rose above her exhausted body and watched it lay there, convulsing. She was conscious of the fact that she was not able to move a muscle even if she tried, yet her body seized in desperate exhaustion. She lay in a lucid, meditative state wondering how long it would take to recover and rejuvenate. She felt the coolness of the white cotton combined with the heaviness of the comforter protecting her without smothering her. The dreams came slowly. At first all should could see were colors. Deep red circles encompassed her head.

As her beta waves deepened, the red circles drifted off her head, resembling beacons of deep rose lights. The red circles left her body in large circles and drifted into seemingly red polka dots which disappeared into nothingness. During this red doppelganger dream, a man's face became more and more visible. She saw a brown, leather book, then it quickly faded. The man's face resembled someone who lived in the mountains; a lumberjack or hunter, although he didn't have the spiritual energy of a hunter. His smile led Morgan's soul upward to room filled with fleeting memories; a sailboat, children, a beautiful white dog and love. Pure beautiful love surrounded her. It guided her back into her body as the pirate man led her soul back and allowed the red circles to fill his emptiness. The deep passionate love, felt in her dream, pinned her to her bed. She no longer convulsed. The love wrapped around her and held in under the cool, white cotton sheets. She felt perfect, light, and slightly whole again. The red lights broadcast off her head exactly like those off a satellite, every second sending a new circular signal. They softly ignited the way to a light pattern emanating from a lighthouse. The lighthouse emitted red doppelganger flashes. The flashes reflected onto the ocean water in one straight line of light leading to Morgan's heart. The lighthouse guided her into wakefulness.

She would have remained in bed for days if Delilah

had not nudged her. Warm morning light painted the bed yellow. She could hear the waves and smell the ocean. She patted the bed, inviting the dogs to jump up and snuggle with her, something David would have only allowed with irritation. She reprimanded herself for thinking of him.

Delilah was the first one on the bed. She curled next to Morgan. Boo jumped onto Morgan's feet, positioning herself perfectly on Morgan's calves to create pressure for a slight leg massaging effect. Boo's head wriggled into the back of Morgan's bent knee. Boo's heartbeat calmingly rubbed into Morgan's calf. The energy was perfectly peaceful. A symbiotic green auric wave rolled across their bodies. They all three fell back to sleep together. This time her sleep was restful. Instead of bouncing body parts, a heavy lull pulled her into the pillows. The dogs senses her immediate peaceful and sank into their usual bear-like slumber.

It was pitch black when Morgan opened her eyes. She could still hear the waves and smell the ocean. The darkness showed her no urgency to leave bed and start another day. She was not hungry. The dogs still snored. Morgan was amazed that they hadn't moved from the same positions they were in hours and hours before. They hadn't whined to go out or nudged her to get up. Finally, she felt no urgency or fear eating away at her. She knew her restorative sleep and calming dreams had given her the ability to move on. She closed her eyes and meditated until the sun came up.

She slowly stepped into the shower and let the healing water wash over her thirty-six hours of crusty eyes and matted hair. She put on her blue jeans. They hung loosely around her hips from two days without food. She walked and fed the Bulldogs.

She sat back down on the bed. As much as she wanted to get in to the car and go somewhere, anywhere, her body wouldn't let her. Exhaustion swept over her. She sat down on the same, unmade hotel bed. She flopped backward, her feet still touching the floor. Again, she fell into the type of sleep that bordered on a coma. Morgan and the Bulldogs slept so deeply that their dreams fused. The lighthouse reappeared and the beautiful white dog. Morgan eyes flashed quickly open with the realization that she had just had the same dream. Boo was staring at her when she woke up. Morgan was still so tired that she could barely lift any of her limbs. She was emotionally pinned to the bed. She felt as if she hadn't slept for years. Life wafted in through the windows. A beautiful Northern California sunset glowed life into her room. The book she was reading blew off the table as the ocean wind picked up. One by Richard Bach landed on the floor.

"One more night, okay?" she said to the dogs.

"I'd like to extend my reservation," she said into the hotel phone. "Yes, I'll be checking out tomorrow.

Yes, please bill my card now she said." Morgan hung up. She picked up the dog's leashes and headed for the sunset.

It was only six p.m. The sun still set early in late springtime. It was June already, three months since Prague. Time had warped the extreme inner pain at the expense of outer . Morgan spread out the blanket. She sat, legs crossed four times. Her ankles wrapped over her knees; meditation style. The horizon changed from orange, to pink, to bright rose; as the sun dropped into the sea. There was no fleeting burst of green light.

Chapter Thirteen

digging through drawers

David sat in his van, staring at their apartment. He had watched the apartment for days, for any sign of life. It looked dead to him. No lights turned on or off. Nobody entered or exited. As the days went by, the apartment's appearance didn't change. The front door housed multi-colored restaurant flyers, mostly Chinese, some Thai. He knew the foods' ethnicities because the same fliers littered the kitchen counter. The foreign kids who disseminated the colorful advertisements were mainly of Latin or Spanish descent. Each time someone walked up the apartment steps, David sunk lower into his seat, as if the steering wheel could conceal his identity. The restaurant workers never looked at the vehicles on the street. They used to spend hours carefully placing menus so that when the drivers got situated the first thing they saw was enticing Mu Shu Pork or savory Pad Thai. The good fliers had color pictures and were carefully placed on cars that regularly drove away during lunch or dinner times. The restaurant owners paid good money for information about the vehicles, the vehicles owners, and the times the vehicles were moved. Some vehicles were moved only once a day in order to erase the tire chalk marks and consequently foil the city's twenty-four hour parking limit. Good delivery boys knew to take extra time placing menus in just the right place, near expensive cars that regularly went out for meals. This meticulous process of littering luxury SUVs led to many complaints. The complaints started with the potential customers calling the establishments that besmirched their vehicles with advertisements. This attempt to stop the littering was misinterpreted by the ethnic restaurants as the restaurant being noticed, thereby having the opposite effect intended by the annoyed callers. The problem became so offensive to the vehicle owners that they contacted local environmental groups, asking for "green" backing in the support of citing restaurants whose fliers were found littering the San Francisco streets. At first, all the uproar over the randomly distributed menus gave the restaurant owners some hope that they were being noticed. Then the city imposed fines on them for littering. The restaurants were legally banned from putting menus on windshields or under windshield wiper blades, since that involved touching someone else's vehicle and the Marin city council had deemed this a form of vandalism. The delivery boys didn't bother to look at "modes of transportation" anymore. David was only hiding from himself.

David waited until it was dark outside then left the sanctuary of his car. After days of paranoid, relentlessly staring at the apartment his eyes were blurry and unfocussed. He couldn't get the key in the door. His vision blurred. It looked to him as if there were two locks and two doorknobs. He managed to stumble his way into the apartment. The Rottweiler stepped away from his side, cowering. His instability scared her. He looked down at Daisy. She shot him a glance filled with fear. Her ears were pinned down tightly and her brow furrowed. "Come on girl. It's okay," he said to coax the dog in the house. She darted in as fast as possible and ran directly under the bed. David stood in the entry way. He had come back to the apartment in search of his stash. His high was fading after all the time in the car and he began resenting Morgan for "bumming his high."

David ran to the bedroom. He yanked every drawer out of his dresser in order to glance at the contents. Some drawers he pulled so hard that they fell to the floor. He kicked them over to empty out the contents. None of the dresser drawers had what he was looking for. He moved onto the plastic hanging closet organizer. The cubbies were weak compared to David's forceful grabbing and throwing. He succeeded in breaking the hanging organizer and leaving the contents of his belongings all over the closet floor. His stuff was in a heap. What was left of Morgan's belongings; a few pairs of pantyhose, some black stilettos, old blue jeans, a bathing suit, and books which she never intended to read, were left on neatly organized on her side of the closet. Her organization and cleanliness enraged him, so he threw her belongings onto the floor, in the heap with his.

He pulled his sock drawer out. It fell to the floor. He ransacked the contents, as if they belonged to someone he hated or someone he was stealing from. He tossed each rolled up pair of socks over his should. Nothing. He began picking up the sock balls and unrolling them. "Maybe I put it inside one," he mumbled to himself. After tearing apart each roll, he randomly threw the socks in different directions. The room was empty except for a bed, dresser, light, television and his boxes of firehouse memorabilia. "It must be in there," he said, diving for the box of firefighter things. In his mind, he associated his job with the creation of the drugs, since that was where they entered his life, so, logically, he thought the drugs had to be buried within his box of work related accolades, newspaper clippings, old SFFD shirts, black rubber boots. Bingo. Inside the boots, he thought. He picked up one boot and turned it upside down. He shook it. Nothing. The next boot was more promising. Out fell a small baggie with a white powder and a small white rock located in it. Before emptying it any more or shaking it harder; he ran to the kitchen, took out a spoon, turned on the gas stove and began melting the powder in the spoon in order to "rock it up" and subsequently smoke it.

The bathroom floor was clean and comforting. He lied on the sparkling white, bleached clean ceramic tile, as he lit the glass pipe. Daisy lied in the hallway, on the floor, outside the bathroom. She whimpered to get in. "No," David said nicely. He had the decency to not let her inhale the toxic fumes.

Hours turned into morning. He opened the bathroom door. Daisy looked up at him, whining to go out. He found a leash and walked her up and down the sloped San Francisco street. He wore large sunglasses and dirty clothes. He carried a newspaper and pretended to be engrossed in it, so as not to have any communication with passersby. Daisy went to the bathroom. David stuffed it into a black plastic bag and walked back to the apartment, newspaper and feces in hand.

Once back into the apartment, the madness started again. David's venture into the outside world triggered paranoia. It used up all of his residual self-induced drug energy. The outside world triggered his brain's normal synapses to fire to already drug-filled receptors. His thoughts and emotions had nowhere to go. As he threw sofa cushions onto the floor and kicked over potted plants, the neurotransmitters in his brain fired double and triple the amount of synaptic bullets as usual. The bullets had no place to go. They drilled holes into parts of his brain not meant for damage. The holes sat empty, except for the drugs carried by the drug bullets which filled the healthy parts of his brain with unexplainable behavior. As the drugs wore off, the bullet holes craved being filled. Like a smoker craving nicotine to make the shakes go away, David craved crack cocaine to calm his brain. David was coming down and needed to find his other stash.

He convinced himself that Morgan had found it and flushed it down the toilet, so he got his tool box, turned off the main water and disassembled the bathroom pipes. He thought that somehow she missed the drugs in the baggies left the drugs in the baggies and that it was possible that the baggies got stuck in the pipes. David worked on the bathroom floor all day. Finally, the initial fix started wearing off. He fell asleep on the bathroom floor surrounded by dirty pipes and toilet water.

Chapter Fourteen

rest stop next exit

It had been days, probably more than a week, that Morgan had been traveling. All she knew was to keep heading away from San Francisco. North seemed best. The air got cooler as dusk fell and as she got farther north. She had driven slowly, not wanting to miss any sign that she should stop. Finally she pulled into a Mom & Pop type gas station. These type of road stops made her feel wholesome and real compared to the empty feeling she got when she entered a big, well-known oil company gas station. There were usually homemade cookies at the counter and kids selling lemonade. This evening it was too chilly for lemonade stands. The chill entered her bones. Her skin stung from the slight sunburn she got at Half Moon Bay. She popped the trunk in search of a sweatshirt.

She pushed aside sandy towels, unused sunscreen, dog water bowls, and worn blue jeans looking for something that could keep her warm. Her heart jumped, as she moved the blankets and saw the books from the general store. She gathered the books up into her arms. She was no longer cold. She placed the books in the passenger seat next to her and embarked on the two hour drive back to *Capricio's General Store.*

She fantasized about Elizabeth opening the door and breaking into a huge smile. Tears came to her eyes as she imagined Tibbs gluing himself to her leg and nuzzling into her in loving ecstasy. She didn't dare think of Sebastian.

Morgan rounded the curve on the Pacific Coast Highway and noticed that the hotel/restaurant where David stayed on her fateful, life-threatening night was named *Nick's Cove.* She wondered why she had never noticed the name before. She carefully rounded the bend where her car had careened off the highway. She didn't look down at the rocks, or the cliff, or the cold water. Instead she looked at the Bulldogs. They were fine. She had recovered. And, oddly, she was right back where she had started. "A full circle," she said to Delilah and Boo. "Only this time we are happy and we are heading the other direction."

Morgan excitedly pulled into the general store

parking lot. She had planned to not come back. It was the books, she told herself. She believed in her heart that it was disgraceful to not return barrowed books.

A few of the books' spines were separating. Morgan took a roll of tape, which she always carried with her, out of her glove compartment. She meticulously taped the books' backbones. She preserved the worn covers and smoothed out the dog-eared pages. She loaded more books than she could carry into her arms, making sure to not leave any behind. An Almost Wasted Life, fell from the top of her over stacked arms and landed in the parking lot. She could not bend down to pick it up. She tip toed over it.

The store was ominously dark. The sign read, "**Open 7-7 Everyday.**" It was only 6 p.m. The front stoop was sandy. It hadn't been swept. The small bookshelf, which before stood on the porch for anyone to use at anytime, was locked inside. There was no firewood propping the door open. She smelled old fish and upon closer observation saw that the freezers were unplugged. Tears welled in her eyes. She carefully stacked the books on the porch and sat down on the steps. She cried. She didn't know if she was crying because she hadn't read the books, or because she felt so alone, or because she hadn't returned when she promised. She did know that she desperately missed Elizabeth and Tibbs. The idea of never having Tibbs velveteen ears and pushy nose nudging into her leg made her cry harder. Morgan had promised them that she would return the day after their magical dinner together. They didn't know she had been in the hospital. They probably thought she just didn't want to come back. Large, lurching sobs wretched her body. Again she was freezing cold. She went to the car and got the Mexican blanket. She picked up <u>An Almost Wasted Life</u> and placed it in the book pile. She covered the books with the tattered blue, red and brown Tijuana, blanket. She pristinely tucked the blanket corners under the books to make sure no sand or fog or any natural elements could damage them. As she did so, she saw the bookshelf inside the door. One book caught her eye. It was a very old, antique looking, leather bound book with an extremely tattered gold tassel.

Morgan sat on the store steps for hours with Delilah and Boo. She didn't want to go anywhere else. It was her birthday and she wanted to be with the people and places she loved. To Morgan, there was nowhere else to go, except the beach with her dogs. If she couldn't be happy, she decided she would find happiness in watching her dogs be happy. It was at this decisive point, between altruistically finding happiness by caring for others and wallowing in utter aloneness, that she realized she needed to spend her birthday with the Capricios.

Because it was her birthday, Morgan had the

rarely acknowledged, slightly selfish, mysterious 'birthday strength' that people get on their birthdays. The strength that allows the birthday person to do feel entitled to do things that otherwise would seem selfish, or decadent...when, in reality, if the selfish act of acknowledging one's own birthday is not done, that horoscope privileged person will actually lose a sense of his or her self. This wallowing, passionate 'just do it' behavior is forgiven on one's birthday, but the true sense of what matters remains. That is the true reason birthdays must be celebrated. If not, it is as if the person's life no longer matters. As children, relatives shower gifts upon the birthday kids. As teenagers, many are treated to quinceneras, or sweet-sixteen parties, or 'coming out' celebrations, or extravagant debutant balls. Hence, the ritual of having other people organize celebrations to make the birthday boy or girl remember that the day he or she incarnated into this world matters, is established. As people grow past the age of twenty-one in the United States, it becomes necessary to have friends or significant others acknowledge and organize birthday celebrations for the recipient. If friends or relatives fail to do so, the indispensable light of hope slowly diminishes within the person's soul. As adults, it is viewed as egocentric to indulge in one's own birthday, yet without the acknowledgment of the importance of one's life: it may become a painful day. The forgetting won't happen at first. It starts by not having a candle to blow out and consequently not making a wish. With no wish there is no hope. This loss of hope leads to a slight empty feeling. The empty feeling grows into not making birthday plans the next year for oneself and simply going to bed early, or worse, being dragged by drunken friends to a bar and forced to do shots as a means to entertain the friends. Then the birthday person simply begins, year by year to pretend that it is just another day and that it really doesn't matter. With this action, the brain starts to believe the actions. The soul then starts to feel that maybe it 'really doesn't matter.' Soon enough, life doesn't really matter and a magical day becomes a pretend day of nothingness. The problem buries itself, unknowingly and seemingly unselfishly, into the soul; who slowly turns cynical and bitter. A gentle soul can become a bitter, scary entity without the birthday remembrance by some soul, any soul, that birthdays are historical events, never to be forgotten. Although the common trend has been to gracefully pretend that a birthday doesn't matter and that forcing others to celebrate is embarrassing, the truth is, anything that is harmful to the soul is harmful to all of humankind. It is necessary to be where a soul is content on the birthday of its present incarnation in order to set the tone of acceptance for the following year. Morgan pontificated whether or not she should light a match, make a wish, and blow out the match. She opened a tattered, paper match pack which read **Red's Bar and Grill**. She tried to light one. The fog and wind didn't allow it.

Then it crossed her mind to look for Elizabeth and Tibbs at the beach. Maybe, just maybe, they were at the beach. She ran down the cliff in search of Tibbs, in search of a warm fire, in search of Sebastian, in search of the hope her soul entered this world with on a warm June afternoon decades ago.

It was eleven p.m. by this point. Fog covered the beach. There was a large bonfire surrounded by drunken teenagers who looked at her warily. She picked up a stick and walked toward the fire. The teenagers looked at her as if she was going to strike them. She placed the tip of the stick in the fire. "It's my birthday," she said.

The teenagers yelled a drunken, "Make a wish. Make a wish. Make a wish." Morgan blew out the end of the stick and they cheered. "Do a shot. Do a shot. Do a shot." One beautiful, young girl blond girl didn't cheer. She looked sadly at Morgan. They recognized that they physically resembled each other. Morgan walked toward her. The girl stood frozen. Morgan gently kissed each of the college girl's cheeks.

"Don't worry," Morgan said. "I have someone to love." The girl's lips parted and a huge set of perfectly aligned white teeth flashed a brilliant, high priced orthodontic smile.

The Bulldogs bounded for the water, unusually happy under the circumstances. Morgan followed. The tide rolled in and she began to worry about the dogs with the current. She ran farther into the water than she had planned. Her jeans were soaked. She called to the dogs. They came dutifully back. The three of them sat at the water's edge. Staring at the rumbling, tumultuous sea filled with oysters, abalone, frolicking sea otters and life. "Tomales," she said to the dogs. "Body of Water. That's what it means." The three wet souls sat on the beach. Clumps of wet sand stuck to them. Morgan and the dogs simultaneously shivered in the sand. She hugged her knees in close to her chest. Waves broke with deafening, ominous thunder.

The lighthouse in the distance blinked its safety beacon for weary travelers. It shone the same perfect white landing strip light down the same miles of water that weary travelers sailed hopefully toward land for over a hundred years. It was built in 1896, when the ocean became wilder on the adjacent rocks and civilization became equipped enough to know that it had the resources available to guide enthusiastic and lost travelers to safety.

"Let's go," she said to the dogs. "There has to be a hotel somewhere nearby." It was after four a.m. as they continued to drive north up the pacific coast. The road curved slightly inland and the ocean was no longer visible. Without the ocean she had no bearings. A gravel road appeared on her left. The weather beaten driftwood sign was originally painted white. It had no words. It was three pieces of chipping wood tied together in the shape an arrow. The arrow pointed slightly west, toward the ocean, down the gravel road. She followed it. The road was overrun with unmanicured, long grass. The grass moved back and forth with the blowing wind. Her eyes started playing tricks on her. The long, blowing grass looked like waves. She considered stopping and sleeping in her car. Her eyes burned, from fatigue and tears.

Finding the general store closed was so emotionally devastating that for the first time in her life, she felt completely lost. She was alone, on a dark gravel path, with wind whipping her car from side to side. She stopped and burst into tears. She cried, with her head in her hands until her nose dripped so profusely that she was forced to look for a napkin, or something to blow her nose with. She reached for the old Mexican blanket. It was gone. She used an old paper towel to blow her nose. Her head cleared and her eyes hurt less as she blew the congestion from her head. She looked up and noticed the sun starting to rise.

With the sunrise, she saw wildflowers growing long and unruly in the unkempt grass. As she looked further she noticed that the grasses dissipated and all the remaining shrubbery was comprised of wildflowers.

She drove further down the gravel road. The wildflowers became more prolific. Long pussy willows, yellow mustard seeds, and incredibly purple daisies swayed in the same wind. Ahead the flowers turned brighter. White rose bushes that seemingly had grown for decades spilled fully bloomed roses onto the gravel road. The gravel was coved in white rose petals. The sun rose higher and, her jaw dropped open in amazement. The grey, ocean colored, lighthouse was directly in front of her.

She sat in awe. The dogs didn't move. The lighthouse beacon didn't blink, because it was almost daylight. Her pain washed out of her body into the ocean worn cement walls. As she sat, upright and tingling with the excitement of discovering another lighthouse, the front door opened.

Elizabeth stood in the lighthouse entrance. A catharsis of compete painlessness swept over Morgan. Morgan stepped from the car. Elizabeth screamed. It was almost ecstasy, almost pain, "She's here. **Tibbs**! Tibbs! She's here."

A white streak flew from the lighthouse door into Morgan's arms. Tears ran down Morgan's face as she cradled Tibbs. He licked the tears from her face.

Elizabeth ran to the car to greet her. She threw her arms around Morgan, "No more crying. No more. Let's get you cleaned up," Elizabeth said.

"It's okay," Morgan said, holding Elizabeth tightly,

"we can cry. I thought I would never see you again. These are good tears."

"I know. I know. But let's clean you up. I don't want him to see you like this," Elizabeth said. She took a step back. "Have you been sleeping in your car? You look like hell...and beautiful, of course." They both laughed.

"It's been a long trip. I don't need to get cleaned up. It's okay," Morgan said.

"No," Elizabeth said, "When you didn't come back he gave up. It was only a day or two, then he just stopped. He has to see you."

Morgan's eyes filled with tears. "Please tell me he is okay. Please Elizabeth. Where is he?"

"He is sitting by the fire. That's all he ever does anymore."

"Take me to him," Morgan said. Tibbs was already tugging at her sleeve.

"Let's clean you up first," Elizabeth said. The two woman walked quietly into the cement lighthouse. "Shhhhhh, this way," Elizabeth whispered. She led Morgan up what seemed to be an ancient winding staircase to a small, bedroom. It was originally the Lighthouse Keeper's quarters. It was now filled with teenage rock-star posters. The bed was small. It was covered with shiny pink and purple striped sheets and a handmade quilt. Each square had a different crustacean shell on it.

Elizabeth dampened a wash cloth and wiped Morgan's face, then applied a little lipstick and sparkly white eye-shadow to Morgan. It wasn't Morgan's style, but she was so happy having Elizabeth touch her and care for her that she would have let Elizabeth paint her face black. Elizabeth brushed Morgan's long blond hair and went to her closet to find some clean clothes. Morgan picked up the hairbrush and finished her own hair.

"Hey, Elizabeth, come sit," Morgan said, motioning for her to sit at the make-up table. Elizabeth sat down. Morgan carefully separated Elizabeth's hair into long, think chunks and slowly brushed them into straight perfection. When they looked in the mirror together they noticed that their hair was exactly the same. They laughed.

"Elizabeth, please, take me to him."

They walked down the stone steps and just before entering the living room Morgan darted outside. "Just one sec," she said. Morgan picked an armful of flowers.

They walked into the living room. The huge fire was blazing. All they could see was the high, back of a distressed leather chair. Tibbs ran to Sebastian's chair. Barely moving, Sebastian reached over and placed his hand on Tibbs head. Morgan looked at a thirty something man who ran a lighthouse, huge fishing company and general store. He was immobile. A roaring fire was blazing in the fire place exactly like the one Antonio and Isabel had slept and conceived their son in front of. It is Antonio. The time since Morgan left significantly aged him. He had chosen the hellish life on enlightenment in an earthly body, so as not to miss this life with Isabel and, after searching for years across oceans for her he had learned to wait for Isabel, to find him. When she did find him, his life was perfect completion for a few hours. When she didn't return he sank into confusion and despair.

Sebastian turned and looked at Morgan. Tiberius knew, as did Sebastian, that their destiny walked back into their life and their hell was over. Blue waves encircled the room. Morgan watched, speechless, as green beads danced around her head and purple stripes wrapped around her body. Elizabeth was filled with white, glowing light.

Morgan walked up to the side of the chair and placed the flowers in Sebastian's lap. He looked like he had aged ten years in the past few months. Their eyes met. He stood up and embraced her in front of the fireplace. "Please listen to me, please trust your instincts," he said. He put his hands on her shoulders and placed her delicately into the leather chair. "We have traveled many lifetimes together."

"I have loved you for a thousand years and that I will love you for a thousand more." He placed his hand over her heart and felt it pulsating. She instinctively reached back and did the same to his heart. It is at this point that she remembered what love felt like. Red and grey waves lifted from the floors to the ceiling. She watched the red and grey overlay disintegrate above their heads. She broke down in tears.

"I'm sorry," Morgan said. "I was in a car accident when I left that night. I'm sorry."

"I knew I should have driven you home," he said. He stood up and placed his hands on her shoulders. "Sit. Please sit. Are you okay. What hurt? Are you okay?" he knelt down in front of her, as she sat in his spot, in his huge, distressed, leather chair. He placed the flowers on her lap. "Are you hungry? Let me feed you."

"I'm fine now," she said. "When I saw the store…I went to the general store. What happened?"

Elizabeth stepped closer. "He won't go back there without you," she said.

"I couldn't bear it when you didn't come back. Now I know it was my fault. I always knew I should never have let you leave."

"You didn't have a choice. I had to go. I had someone waiting for me." Sebastian grimaced and winced. "But that is no more," she said.

He threw her arms around her. "Wait. Oh Iz, it's after midnight. We missed your birthday." He ran to the kitchen and brought back a doughnut with a lit candle in it. He sang *'Happy Birthday'* and Elizabeth joined it. "Now make a wish," he said, kissing her forehead. She sheepishly smiled up at him.

"I don't even want to know how you know this," she said, as she took blew out the candle. She softly intertwined her fingers with his. She picked the doughnut up to take a bite, and laughingly shoved a bite into his mouth. Sugar and dough smashed onto his lips and cheeks. They both laughed so hard that they doubled over.

Elizabeth stared, awe struck that Sebastian could still laugh. "Oh, you think I'm too old to laugh," he jokingly said to her. Before she could answer he smashed the rest of the doughnut into her mouth. She laughed so hard she spit it across the room. Tibbs licked up the gooey, split laden pieces.

"Let's go walk on the beach," he said excitedly.

"The dogs," she said. "They are in the car."

"Tibbs, go get Delilah and Boo. Take your friends to the beach," Sebastian said to Tiberious. Morgan looked at him in astonishment that Tibbs would understand this. Tibbs was already on his way to the car.

"I'm so tired," she said. "I don't think I can walk another step. May I just sleep here, in front of the fire for awhile?"

"Yes, yes, sleep, sleep, I will make you food," Sebastian said. He so desperately wanted to take her to the bedroom specifically built and decorated for her. He restrained himself. He wrapped her in a tan, herringbone blanket and placed a pillow on the armrest. "Elizabeth, please put the flowers in water," he said. "When you wake up it will be like your birthday morning, all over again, filled with flowers, and love and doughnuts," he chided. Morgan smiled and squeezed his hand tightly. She was asleep by the time Sebastian placed the flowers on the table next to the huge leather chair. He wrapped her shoulders and feet in the herringbone blanket. Sebastian lied down on the white alpaca rug in front of the fire, near Morgan's feet. The exhausted, happy dogs wiggled in from the beach and fell asleep at his feet.

CHAPTER FIFTEEN

searching for Pat

As they all slept, the dreams came. The fire flickered into their subconscious, reminding them, as fires do, of times long ago. The usual prehistoric memories of dancing figures with spheres and large animals danced in the flames. Elizabeth sat and watched the five souls melt into one. When Tibbs twitched, the other four souls slightly moved. When Sebastian rearranged himself on the alpaca rug, the others physically moved in rhythm with him. Elizabeth watched them, mesmerized at their closeness. She wondered where she fit into this family sleeping in front of her. She too was tired. She wanted to clean the kitchen and have a mouth-watering breakfast ready for them when they woke up. Even more, she wanted to sleep with them.

She didn't want to go up to her bedroom. She wanted to be part of their pile. She wrapped herself in a tan herringbone blanket, which exactly matched the one covering Morgan. Elizabeth crawled onto the alpaca rug. She softly moved Delilah to one side and nestled into Tibbs back. Within seconds Elizabeth's mind slipped into the same dream state.

It was Elizabeth's sleep that allowed them to dream together. The knowing essence of the dreams could not be achieved if one of the members was missing. The six of them all dreamt of their last incarnation. They heard waves and felt laughter. As they slept together, they dreamt together. They became one functioning, cellular unit. They saw each other, as they had been, five hundred years ago. Elizabeth felt Morgan lift her from the basinet. She felt her mother clutch her small, infant body to her breast. Elizabeth felt her mother's tears fall onto her head. She felt her mother's pain and love wrap around her. "Know that you are loved," her mother whispered into her ear. It was Morgan whispering. in her dream and saw the pages of a book blow open and close.

Morgan's breaths deepened. Her chest rose and fell. She slipped into the deepest slumber of her present life, dreaming of Sebastian's arms around her. He held her as if she was in a cocoon of all-knowing love. She was completely wrapped in love. In the dream, she could not only feel him around her, she could see his face. Morgan's dream then collided with Elizabeth's dream. Morgan dreamt of holding her baby daughter. She wrapped her daughter in a white, cashmere blanket. Morgan saw herself pacing the room with her daughter in her arms. Morgan saw herself cry as she paced the room, tears falling onto her infant daughter's head. Morgan saw herself sobbing. And Morgan saw the leather journal on the bed stand. That is when she abruptly awoke. She sat straight up in the comfy leather chair. The fire still burned and Sebastian was asleep at her feet. When she looked over at Elizabeth, Elizabeth awoke abruptly. They stared at each other for what seemed like an eternity. They did not want to confess their dreams.

Sebastian awoke and saw the two girls staring at each other. "Do you remember?" he said to Morgan. She stared blankly at him and began to cry.

"Who are you?" she asked softly through her tears.

"You won't believe me," he said.

"I might," she said. "I have seen things in my dreams for years."

"What kind of things?"

"A book."

"And Pat? Have you seen Pat?" Sebastian asked.

"Who is Pat?" Morgan asked.

"He is an old friend of ours. He can explain everything. Elizabeth, what about you?" The women simultaneously felt the same energized tingle go up their spines.

"Breakfast Time. Breakfast Time," came a bright, sunshiny voice from the kitchen. Sebastian leapt up and ran to the kitchen, the girls and dogs followed him. An eight foot long, picnic style table made of driftwood was formally set for brunch. A bright sunflower yellow table cloth covered the table. Three carafes of fresh squeezed tangerine juice were filled to the brim. Eggs and steaks sizzled on the kitchen grill. Fresh fruit plates filled with bright red strawberries, deep blue blueberries, lollaberries from the northern Californian coastal bushes, white jicama, sweet orange mangoes and over-sized green grapes spilled out of a white, porcelain washtub. The pitcher, which was hand-crafted and kiln fired to fit inside the white washtub was stuffed full of wild, unpruned, white hydrangeas and matching white hyacinths for olfactory stimulation.

"Well it's about time," Sebastian said to the curmudgeonly man cooking in the kitchen. "How long were you going to let me go at this alone?!" Sebastian reached out to hug Pat.

"Careful," Pat said as Sebastian threw his arms around him. "You almost spilled my mimosa." Sebastian laughed. "Mimosa's for everyone, I assume?" Pat said. "Even you, my darling princess," he said, looking at Elizabeth. Pat filled up the champagne glasses. The girls still stood looked at Pat blankly. "They don't know?" Pat said to Sebastian.

"She just got here last night," he said nodding at Morgan. "And I wanted to wait until they were together, so 'No', Elizabeth doesn't know either. Pat, why is Tibbs acting so normal? He doesn't even seem excited to see you." Tibbs wasn't wiggling or shaking or dancing. He was sitting by the grill, patiently waiting for his steak.

"Oh Tibbs and I have been meeting at the beach all his life," Pat said. "He has needed some help taking care of you. You haven't made it easy on us, with all your grumpiness and long nights. You gave us quite a bit to worry about," Pat said to Sebastian. Tibbs looked at Sebastian and nodded.

"So, let's eat," Pat said. He put three steaks in the dogs' dishes. "Okay, Antonio you sit at the head of the table," he said. Everyone glanced at each other as if Pat was crazy. "Don't you all look at me like that. His name is Antonio. He is a great Italian sailor and he will sit at the head of the table. Unless…unless," he mused to Sebastian, "Unless you want your queen to sit there. She does have more royalty than you." Pat led Morgan to the head of the table. His touch on her shoulder was warm and comforting to both of them. "Don't worry, my dear Isabel, you are where you are supposed to be."

"Now, Isabel II, you sit next to your mother,"

Pat said. The girls looked inquisitively at each other. Sebastian knew he better slow this down.

"Pat, Elizabeth lost her mother in an accident. This is new to her. I adopted her," Sebastian said slowly and cautioningly.

"So, she doesn't know anything?" Pat said.

"Nope." Sebastian said.

Pat seated Elizabeth at the table next to Morgan. He wrapped his arms around her and whispered in her ear, "My dear, you are no longer without a mother. Morgan, or rather 'Isabel' is your mother. She gave birth to you five hundred years ago and died of heartbreak when you were an infant. She has spent the last half a millennium watching over you and reincarnating on this earth to care for you. You lost a lifetime together, now you have an entirely knew and beautiful one in front of you."

Morgan still had not spoken. Deep down she knew everything this short, old man was saying was true. She desperately wanted to believe it. She wanted Elizabeth to be hers and only hers. She wanted a daughter. She wanted a *real* daughter.

Sebastian said to Lizzy, "That's why I was nearby when you needed a parent and that's why it made sense for you to live with me. I am supposed to watch over you, for all of eternity. Your mother died five hundred years ago because of me. It was my karmic debt and my pleasure to care for you."

"So,....you are really my dad somehow?" Elizabeth asked.

"Unfortunately not. Your father was the King of Portugal. And your mother the Queen. She is sitting right next to you." Sebastian said.

Morgan understood her role in this unfolding of events. She reached over and placed her hand on top of Elizabeth's. "I don't remember yet, but I know they are right. I feel it when I look at you and I know it when I touch you. We even dream the same dreams. I know we are meant to be together. I am your mother from a past life. I did not give birth to you in this life. You biological mother loved you with all her life, but you and I also share the same genetics. Our souls are genetically similar. We have the same cellular memories. The woman who gave birth to you in this life knew I would find you and care for you. We equally share our love for you. You must show me pictures of her and someday I will remember when she and I decided to care for you. At this point, I cannot remember. I will though. And she knew that I would find you and love you and raise you properly. I didn't get to raise you in our past life. I don't know much more right now. My head is a little foggy," Morgan said.

"We made a choice five hundred years ago to let you be raised as Princess of Portugal. We had to leave you with the king for your own safety. Our love for each other put you and your brother in danger," Sebastian said.

"My *brother*? I have a brother?" Elizabeth said.

Morgan and Sebastian looked at each other. Sebastian saw that Morgan was searching her memories for a little boy. "You had a brother in your past life. You were raised together as Prince and Princess. You were very close. Almost like twins," Sebastian said. Elizabeth's mouth was wide open. She was silent.

There was a long, collective, freeing silence. It wasn't awkward. It was cathartic. They were all able to sit quietly and understand who they really were, who they really are. Knowing who they truly are immediately opened doors for them to become who they wanted to be. They all saw paths of understanding paved in front of them. Except Morgan. Morgan felt a pit in her stomach that brought tears to her eyes.

She looked at Pat. "He was mine, wasn't he? Elizabeth's brother had to be my little boy."

"Yes," Pat said. "You only held him for a few breaths before you died. You made sure he was taken care of before you died. You were a good mother." Sebastian watched her closely, wondering if she knew the baby boy was not just *hers*, but also *their's*.

"And he is not here. Have any of you ever met him?"

"No," said Pat.

"So he is lost?" Morgan said, crying, "Lost with no family and no home." She sobbed.

Sebastian got up from the table and went to Morgan. He wrapped his arms around her. "We will find him. He was *our* son. We will find him and make him happy." She grabbed hold of Sebastian's arms and wept with sobs.

"No, he is gone," Morgan said.

"We don't know that," Sebastian said, consolingly. "See, I chose to be born with a gift and a curse. I can see peoples' entire histories when they are around me. I know when I meet someone if I am bound to them eternally and karmicly. I know if that person is necessary for our group of souls to grow. I knew the minute I saw you that you that we had each followed our instincts and trusted our souls enough to find each other. That's why I couldn't stop talking when we had dinner together. I was so nervous. I wanted to tell you. I wanted to tell you so badly that I almost exploded." She cried harder. "It's okay. I will open the general store and someday he will walk through that door and we will never be without him again."

Morgan clung tightly to Sebastian. She looked in his eyes and could see her past and present. She felt guilty for feeling so complete. "Sebastian, now there is something I have to tell you; I was pregnant, just recently, since I met you, and I lost the baby. I lost our son."

No one moved or breathed. "Oh no," said Pat. "Did you conceive this baby since you met Sebastian in this earthly lifetime."

"Yes," Morgan said. Sebastian flinched at the idea that she had been with someone else. "I was with a man for less than a year. I thought I loved him. Something was always off. Something was always not right in my stomach. The break-up was strange. He just took off. He decided he couldn't be with me and didn't give me any explanation. I know he was using drugs. I know he was a very lost soul." Delilah, the Bulldog, yelped. Pat looked at her. Pat held Delilah's gaze for a very long time. Brilliant colored, thick waves encircled Delilah's head. Everyone in the room could see the bright scarves wrap around the Bulldog. Pat continued looking into her soul until he understood.

"Morgan, this man, did he run into danger a lot?" Pat asked.

"Well, he is a fireman," Morgan said.

"I mean," Pat continued. "Did he run into chaos instead of away from it? Like reaching out to people who seemed dangerous? Or running into catastrophes to save people?

"He did tend to want to save people. But really Pat, he was the one who needed saving," Morgan said.

"He has a death wish," Pat said. "That's what happens to a soul betrayed by a parent. He is not free. He will either kill his betrayer, or save his own soul."

Solemnly, carefully, Sebastian said, "And I am his betrayer."

"Yes, Seb, without knowing it you are his abandoner. You left him in a past life." Delilah pinned herself against Sebastian's leg.

"Really Pat," Morgan said, "the fireman only wants to hurt me…and himself. He believes our love is the source of his pain."

"That's what I wanted to tell you!! Any love makes him feel too much pain. So he hurts himself. You are too advanced for my teaching," Pat said to Morgan.

"Teaching?" she inquired.

"Yes, do you understand that I am your spirit guide? You and I have consulted on many lifetimes," Pat said to Morgan.

"If you are supposed to 'guide' me, why have I felt so much pain?" Morgan said. "I have no one. I've been so lost."

"Not really," Pat said. "You have never been lost my dear. You just hadn't yet found your path."

"Now, back to this firefighter. And did he like drama?" Pat asked.

"Well, his life as a firefighter was pretty dramatic," Morgan said.

"And did he have 'abandonment issues'?" Pat asked.

"I don't know. He used drugs to mask some kind of pain," Morgan said.

"Did he eat poorly and drink a bit too much," Pat asked.

"Yeeees," Morgan said slowly.

"Is his name 'David'?" asked Pat.

Morgan flinched. "Yes, why?" Morgan asked.

"Because this man is Sebastian's son," Pat said.

"What!!!!!!!????" Sebastian yelled.

Morgan stared calmly at Pat until Sebastian stopped looking shocked. "Then he was my son too?" Morgan asked, afraid of the answer, afraid that she had crossed into some sickening oedipal karmic mishap which could not be undone.

"A long time ago, you taught your soul to be instinctually aware of crossing familial boundaries. It is actually one of your best qualities," Pat said. "So 'no', David was Sebastian's son, but not yours."

"So you must have lived a life without me," Morgan said, staring into Sebastian's eyes.

"Unfortunately my love, it was during our last lifetime together that we were separated for a very long time. And you were married to the King. You were a queen. I was a sailor. I had sailed to the Seychelles, off the coast of what is now Kenya. We were apart for a long time," Sebastian pleaded for forgiveness. Morgan cringed. A wave of emotions over-powered her. She felt jealousy, without having a relationship with this man. She felt the rage and betrayal without knowing why. Anger welled up inside her body, forcing blood to rush to her face. She was amazed that she could be so mad at a man she hardly knew. "What?!" she yelled at Sebastian. "You cheated on me. I knew this was too good to be true." Morgan yelled at Sebastian, like an old married couple. "You left me for someone else and now you think you can just walk back into my life and expect me to love you." The room went silent.

Sebastian knelt in front of Morgan and took her hand. He kissed it. "I do not expect you to love me. I only pray for it every second of every day of every life. Please, forgive me. Please give me a chance. I will show you how much I love you."

Suddenly, calmly and gracefully, Morgan composed herself. She looked down at Sebastian kneeling before her. "We will see. You have a lot of making up to do," she said, knowing that she had just left a relationship with another man and that Sebastian could just as easily accuse her of cheating. She knew they were even and ready to move on.

"Come with me," Sebastian asked. "I have something to show you."

"I am not going anywhere with you right know," Morgan said, indignantly.

"Please Isabel, please. I will show you that I have been waiting for you forever. I have built something for you," Sebastian said. He held more tightly to her hand and tugged at her. Tibbs nudged at her leg.

"You are right. I was and always will be royalty and

must act as such. I remember this grace. I remember this power. I remember missing you. You were gone so, so long. That pain is inside me. That pain of wanting something that I couldn't have brought me here. It instinctively has pushed me my entire life, to look for more, to want more, to find more, and to know that I can feel more than pain when I close my eyes. This intuitive strength led me here, to this lighthouse."

"YES, yes, yes, my Isabel. Our intuitions and strength led us here, as we agreed five hundred years ago. Yes, Izzy, Yes," Sebastian proclaimed. He threw his arms around her. "You are home. We are home." She returned his tight embrace with slight trepidation. It was all so much to find a daughter, a home and a lover within hours. Sebastian slowly pulled away, giving her the space she needed. He held her hand. He cautiously intertwined his fingers with hers. He would never let completely go again. "Just give it a chance here. I promise you will be happy," he said. "Now please, come with me? The rest of you, clean the kitchen for our queen." Sebastian clapped his hands. "Chop Chop." Morgan laughed. Pat rolled his eyes.

Sebastian practically picked Morgan up out of her chair. "I will carry you if you like," he said. She stood up. Tibbs bounded ahead of them.

They walked toward the winding, cement staircase. "Wait," Morgan said, "I want my daughter with me."

"No," Elizabeth said. "You go with Dad. He has

something to show you. He has been working on it for a long time and I never understood what he was doing up there with all those tool until now. You go with Dad." Morgan looked longingly at her daughter. "I will be here when you come back," Elizabeth assured everyone. Morgan still didn't want to move. "Go.... Mom," Elizabeth ordered. With that, Morgan smiled and squeezed Sebastian's hand.

The two lovers ascended the staircase. Morgan's heart pulsated blood into her tired body. They walked upward for what seemed interminable. They passed cement door after grey, cement door, until they reached the top of the lighthouse. Sebastian opened the last door, displaying a three-hundred and sixty degree view of the ocean and Tomales bay. Morgan was awestruck with it's beauty.

"I have sat here, day after day, year after year, with this ancient telescope, watching for you," Sebastian said, holding the telescope from his initial voyage from Lisbon, around the horn or Africa to the French islands, five hundred years ago. I chose to incarnate into the same family, providing me with the same cellular memories as those experienced by my physical ancestor, Antonio. That made it easier for us to find each other so easily. With this you can't doubt our reality. Our history of the Capricio family and the Queen of Portugal is documented in history books. We come from the same place. Our souls came into being at the same time, meaning our energy and strength evolved from the same molecular surroundings. Millennia before our ancestors migrated from Africa together onto the colder European continent. Souls with cellular and karmic connections are rarely parted. You wrote your heavenly chart so as to never get lost and to guide the Caripicio family toward reconciliation with the Italian government. After our political exile from Italy in the late 1400's, we chose to relocate to Portugal. Lisbon, specifically. The family continued on, in spite of the religious persecution, many spiritual masters guided us toward the greatness of knowing who we are, and who we come from and where we belong in this earthly world. You waited hundreds of years to incarnate back onto earth in order to join us and never be separated. I stayed within the Carpricio bloodline to make sure that physically and spiritually our building blocks remained consistent. I did this so we could find each other."

"And here we are," she said, softly, trying to comprehend this connection to the universe and all of its connections.

"No, my love. *Here* we are." Sebastian swung open a door to a master suite. Morgan walked slowly in. She gazed at the mahogany bed, adorned with sea shell carvings and a white, eye-lit, puffy down comforter. The chairs were covered in white satin. Morgan tip toed into the room, as if a baby was sleeping in it, and she began to remember. She looked at Sebastian and began to sob. "No. No. Don't be sad. I built this all for you. I carved this window out of the cement so you could hear the ocean when you sleep," he said, pulling back the white, flowing curtains. "And I brought the silk from Europe. And I found the silver brush and mirror in a Sotheby's Portuguese antique auction. They claim to be from Portuguese royalty, so they were probably yours or Elizabeth's." Morgan cried harder. "Stop," he said, wrapping her in his arms.

She abruptly pushed him away and screamed, "How can I stop? How? The last time I saw you, you were cold and dead in this bed. I was alone in this room. I cried and cried next to your body that I knew would never hold me again."

He reached out and pulled her into him. She sobbed. "I'm holding you Isabel. I'm holding you. And I will never let go."

She looked up at him. He had a huge smile on his face, as he embraced her. "What do you think is so funny? You left me here."

"Iz," he said slowly and firmly, "You remember." Her tears stopped.

Her face softened. She buried her face in his chest. "Yes, Antonio, I remember."

Chapter Sixteen

the universe hates a void

"We have to find David," Sebastian said.

"Well, he certainly won't return my calls and his family hates me. I have even called the firehouse," Morgan said.

"I know where he is," Pat said. "The key is to get him to come here. You can't go to him. It will frighten him away and he will never recover. I will go to him." Pat swooshed out of the room and into thin air before anyone could protest. The family and dogs all sat around the large driftwood table, quietly eating. Elizabeth finished and sat silently until Morgan and Sebastian were done.

"Anyone for a game of chess?" Elizabeth asked.

"Oh, I don't really know how to play," Morgan said. "But you could teach me."

Sebastian looked at Morgan in amazement. Not everything had come back to her. Her memories were coming in pieces. "Let's set up the board together," he said. He wanted to move slowly with her, to let her remember everything, but not at the cost of losing her. It was better to rush, he thought, better to push a little and wear my heart on my sleeve that it would be to lose her. The idea of losing her swept through his body. He ached with coldness. He knew he could not go back to living without her. He knew this was his last chance. If she left, if she drove away from the lighthouse his life would end.

The three of them walked outside onto the circular, wrap around deck. Two white Adirondack chairs were placed on the sides of a wooden chess board. The board had drawers underneath it to hold the pieces. Games didn't last for days or weeks, as real chess games did. The games lasted only as long as the players sat at the table due to the ocean breezes blowing over the chess pieces.

Elizabeth opened a slightly hidden drawer under the chess table and pulled out some sea shells. Sebastian looked at Morgan for any sign of recollection of their childhood chess pieces. Sebastian watched green beads dance over Morgan's head. Morgan simply followed Elizabeth's lead and opened the drawer on her side of the table.

"Just set the pieces up exactly identical to mine on

your squares," Elizabeth said. Morgan set up her pieces. They pieces were sea shells as pawns, abalone shells as queens, mussels as rooks, huge white sand dollars as kings, and dead sea horses as knights. Morgan mulled the dead sea animals over in her hands. She rolled the shells through her fingers. Purple auric waves wrapped around her. When Morgan picked up the sand dollar she began to cry. She looked at Sebastian, who was staring intently at her, waiting for some glimmer of recollection. Morgan threw her arms around him and sobbed into his shoulder. "I remember," she said.

"Hey, no need to cry. This is great. I think you forgot your queen. Look in the drawer."

"Antonio, did you hear me? I remember. We played beach chess as kids. Just kids. That's all we were. Just kids." Morgan fumbled through the sandy objects.

"The queen is on the board," she said through her tears.

"No, there is a better queen saved in the back of the drawer so this one won't break."

"What's going on?" Elizabeth said.

She reached all the way to the back of the drawer. Morgan found a small black box with a gold clasp on it in the back of the drawer. It looked a hundred years old. "An abalone shell won't fit in here," she said, putting the box back into the drawer.

Sebastian kneeled down and looked into Morgan's eyes. "Just open the box, please?"

Morgan opened the box. She immediately showed it to Elizabeth. They gasped.

"Oh yeah, it's too small for an abalone shell," Sebastian said nonchalantly, "so, will you please marry me?"

"Oh say 'yes', say 'yes'," Elizabeth said.

Morgan sat staring at the diamond ring. She couldn't speak.

"I know it is soon. I know you don't remember everything. But we were in love. We are in love. Please, Iz. Please marry me?" A rainbow of energy wrapped around the two lovers. They were engulfed in vibrancy, in full knowing, and beautiful blue love.

She watched blue and green ocean breezes swirl around his body. "Yes," she said.

Elizabeth grabbed the ring and put it on Morgan's finger. Morgan threw her arms around Sebastian. "I'm never letting go," she said. Elizabeth quietly backed off the deck and closed the sliding door.

Sebastian cradled Morgan head into his neck. Her head fit perfectly in his hand. He wrapped his other hand around her waste. They looked like a picturesque statue with the sun setting behind the waves and their bodies. With each thunderous crash of a wave their bodies clutched each other more tightly. Morgan craned her neck upward. Sebastian took her face in his hands and kissed her. Their lips touched and their bodies moved. To them, they seemed motionless in time.

A car horn honked in the distance. Morgan looked up. She knew that horn. "What is it?" Sebastian asked.

"That's David's van," Morgan said.

"Are you kidding? I've waited five hundred years for this moment, Iz. And now your ex boyfriend and my son are in our driveway?"

"*Our* driveway?" she mused.

"Yes," Sebastian said, "this is *our* lighthouse. And this is *our* beach and that cottage over there," he said pointing to a far off white beach house, "is *our* home."

Morgan laughed. "You can't be serious?"

"Yep. My family and I bought the oyster business out here a decade ago. I built the cottage right away and, of course, it is all next to the lighthouse because that's what we agreed upon."

"What?"

"Oh Isabel, we will work on your memory. Right now we have other things to deal with." They ran down the gravel driveway to meet the van. Pat was parking the white van. Or rather, Pat beached the white van with an abrupt halt in the lighthouse meadow. Pat got out, surveying the damage. He had mutilated a large number of wildflowers. He got down on his hand and knees and started picking what was salvageable of the flowers.

"What the hell?" Sebastian said.

"I found him on the bathroom floor of the apartment. He was near dead," Pat said. He handed the mangled bunch of flowers to Morgan.

"What?! David," she said to Sebastian. "He's talking about David. This is David's van."

"My son was on a bathroom floor dying," Sebastian said. "Get him inside." They opened the sliding van door. Daisy jumped out and ran into Morgan's arms. The stench of vomit overpowered the air. Red circles encompassed David's head. Delilah whimpered as Sebastian and Pat carried David to the living room. They placed him on the hard wood floor with a bucket next to his face. Morgan put a pillow under his head. Delilah curled into a ball at his feet. Sebastian pulled up a chair and solemnly stared at his own son, wondering what could cause this emptiness. Then Sebastian remembered how he had felt without Morgan and realized that simple loneliness could cause this self-destruction. Sebastian knew David's was much deeper. He knew that David had been wresting with abandonment demons all his life. Now David was here, in front of the man who had left him, lying face down on a hardwood floor, close to an overdose, in the home of his demons. Sebastian felt this was his fault.

Morgan looked at David with little emotion. She remembered how David's mother had treated her. Morgan remembered how David had tried to make her feel the pain of abandonment that he was suffering. She walked into the kitchen. Elizabeth was roasting garlic and slicing vegetables.

"Did you really date that guy?" Elizabeth said to Morgan.

"Everybody makes mistakes. I was drawn to him because he is part of our karmic group. We are drawn to people for a mess of reasons. I guess I agreed to watch over him for Sebastian in a past life. I didn't do a very good job. Hey, at least he is alive. I'm trying really hard right now to forgive him for the pain he put me through."

"That pain led you to me," Elizabeth said.

"Oh my god, you're right. I fled him and found the books and the lighthouse."

"And the ring," Elizabeth added with a huge smile.

"The ring means nothing without you, Elizabeth. I remember having to leave you when you where an infant. I can never live without you again. You are my daughter. You are mine. And I am yours."

"I'm really glad you and Dad are together," Elizabeth said.

"If you weren't happy about it, I wouldn't stay with him. This is for us. For all of us. We are a family. We have always been a family. I remember everything now."

"Will you teach me how to remember my past lives?" Elizabeth asked.

"Mediate. And follow your true instincts. You have all the answers inside you. Listen to your inner Knowledge. Know that you are loved. We can work on it together. Now… you tell me about your present life.

What about 'boys'? Are you interested in that boy I saw you laughing with at the general store?" Morgan chided.

Elizabeth blushed. She sliced the green ends off some strawberries. "Life has been lonely since my biological parents died. I feel like I have had to take care of Sebastian. Tibbs has been my best friend."

"Elizabeth, have your dreams given you any solace?"

"A little. I dream of the beach a lot. When I can't sleep, I pretend to dive into a perfect blue wave and pop up surrounded by white beach foam. Usually that puts me to sleep. Then I dream of living under in the ocean. White waves and beautiful sailboats take me anywhere I want to go in my dreams."

"Those white waves might be the flowing white curtains than blew over your basinet as a baby. Do you remember?"

"No, I remember being alone," Elizabeth said, looking down at the counter, afraid to meet her mother's eyes and cause pain for both of them. "And I remember a brother a little bit. He made me laugh. I remember loving him."

"That won't happen anymore. Sebastian will be fine from now on. I will take care of him and you. And all the dogs will live long lives on the beach and in the waves. You just worry about your grades. No more loneliness. I will fill this house with love and laughter." Morgan hugged Elizabeth and stroked her hair.

Elizabeth hadn't felt a motherly touch for so long that she broke down in tears. Morgan hugged her harder. "I will always be there for you, and for your children, and grandchildren. You will never be lost or lonely again."

Elizabeth cried harder, "but what if something happens to you? What if I lose another family?"

"I should have seen this coming. We lost each other before. You absorbed all the loneliness and pain into your soul memory as my tears fell onto your miniature head as an infant, then you lost your family in this life when you were only ten. But Elizabeth, look around. This is all yours. This land. This house. And Pat. Pat will be with all of us forever. I promise, you will never be alone again."

"Can you just, just please not leave for awhile? No matter what happens. Please?"

"Elizabeth, if we ever leave here we are leaving together." Morgan buried her nose in Elizabeth's hair. "Has anybody every told you that your hair smells funny?" Morgan mused.

"What?"

"As a baby, I used to kiss your head so much that it smelled like my spit and people thought your hair was dirty."

"Oh Mom, that's gross. Why didn't you wash my hair?

"Of course I washed your hair. Everyday. You didn't have much."

"What? I was a bald baby?"

"You had a few, beautiful gold ringlets and really big ears. I was just so afraid to put you down that I held you every minute of every day and kissed your head all the time. Everyday, by afternoon, you smelled like dried spit. It was worse than dirty diapers. And back then we didn't have a disposable diaper, that's for sure." Morgan ran her fingers through Elizabeth's gorgeous flowing locks. "It must have worked. Even in this incarnation the love and kisses made your hair grow thick and beautiful. You know, 'good hair is the best revenge'." They both laughed.

The world seemed hopeful again. Their souls were full and their smiles were real. "Wanna try on the ring?" Morgan asked, slipping it off her finger.

"Yeeaah, of course." Elizabeth put it on. It fit perfectly.

"See, we are both size five and a half. Small hands and big souls. That's all a girl needs in life," Morgan said.

"No matter what F.Scott Fitzgerald or Daisy Buchanan says," Elizabeth chided.

"You read my mind," Morgan said. "Let's amend that 'small hands, big souls and gigantic libraries.'"

"It was really the books that brought us together, wasn't it?" Lizzy said.

I know where it is," Elizabeth said

"So do I," Morgan said, winking at Elizabeth. "It's

where we met. When I pulled the Richard Bach books off your bookshelf it touched my hand."

"Liz," Morgan said seriously, "when I went back to the general store I saw the leather book with the gold tassel. Have you read it? It can't really be the same book from five hundred years ago, can it?" Morgan asked.

"I read bits of it. I didn't know it was about us."

They looked at each other, grabbed their purses, rushed out of the house, past the white van parked crookedly in the meadow and quickly past unconscious David. "We gotta go to the general store. Need anything?" Morgan called to Sebastian, as the two girls jumped into Morgan's car. Sebastian asked a few questions to the girls. They nodded a pretend acknowledgement and drove speedily down the driveway.

"What are they doing?" Sebastian asked Pat.

"It's time for the journal reading. Isabel remembers," Pat said.

"Oh no, now is not a good time. The journal has all the stuff about Victoria in it. Morgan doesn't need that after we just got engaged. It's too much too soon."

"Engaged! Congratulations."

"Thank you," Sebastian said somberly. "Pat, I can't lose her. Maybe you should do your swooping magic thing and go get the journal before they find it. It really is just too much, too soon."

"She is stronger than you think. Don't ever forget that she is a queen. And as for 'too much, too soon', her unconscious ex-boyfriend is passed out in the meadow, close to a drug overdose, a flying spirit guide is in her driveway, and the love of her eternal life is trying to revive this ex-boyfriend who happens to be *his* son. She and her daughter finding a five hundred year old journal is the best thing to take her mind off her presently crazy life. Just life her go. She will be back in a couple hours," Pat said. "Maybe by then we can have this mess cleaned up," he said looking at David.

"Hey, by the way, it's time for you to read your own journal again, Sebastian. You can read it with them. It will be good for your soul," Pat said.

"You mean the one Isabel read when I died?" Sebastian asked. Then he stopped himself. "That's right. I wrote things in it not just about my travels but about my love. I kept a diary back in Portugal. I learned how to turn the pages with my spirit breath. I saved it and gave it to Elizabeth to read, hoping that she would figure out who she really *was*. I mean *is*. But how did it get here?"

Pat, I seriously don't have time for this now." Sebastian crawled into the back of the van and covered up David. Sebastian placed a pillow under his shivering child's head. Delilah jumped into the van. Her old dog bed sat smashed into a corner with a suitcase on top of it. Delilah head butted the suitcase off the bed and, using her teeth, pulled it next to David. Delilah curled into a ball, nestled as close to David as physically possible. Delilah watched in vain as her son shuddered and shivered the drugs out of his system. Delilah knew what she had to do. They fell into the same breath rhythm. Sebastian watched them, comforted by the sound of his own son's breath.

Like all related sleeping souls do if they share the same bed, David's and Delilah's dreams meshed. The French islands, colorful beads, a lifetime of exquisite sunsets and extreme poverty flowed into their psyches. They dreamt of picking wild fresh fruit and playing all day in the waves of the Indian Ocean. In their simultaneous and shared dream they dived down deep into the green, clear water. They communicated with hand signals, like S.C.U.B.A. divers. In the dream, Delilah, in the body of Victoria, motioned for David to go back to the surface. She pointed her thumb upward, seemingly giving him the "thumbs up/okay" signal. David started to ascend. She waved good-bye to him. He did not panic. He quickly dove back down and embraced her. She wrapped a blue scarf around his neck and pointed upward. He smiled and made a heart with an index finger and thumbs. She reciprocated with the same symbol. The sleeping souls knew who they were, at least in their dreams, and Delilah knew that Sebastian would now care for her son.

Delilah breathed an audible sigh of relief. She got up from her dog bed and nestled into Sebastian's lap. Her breathing became labored. Her eyes watered. She rested her head very heavily in Sebastian's hand. Her duty was close to done. They knew who her son, David, was and they knew he was in trouble.

Morgan and Elizabeth pulled into the driveway. They ran over to the van waving the journal at Sebastian. Morgan took one look at Delilah and broke into tears.

"We have to get her to the vet," Elizabeth screamed.

Morgan sat down next to Sebastian. She ignored David snoring in front of her. Sebastian slowly lifted Delilah's listless, but still alive, body onto Morgan's lap. Morgan and Sebastian wrapped their arms around Delilah. Morgan placed her index finger on Delilah's heart. Sebastian placed his large hand on Delilah's neck and pulse. "No," Sebastian said. "She is right where she is supposed to be." The two of them began to recite the historical ablution to help ease Delilah's pain.

"Angels of Love
Our guardians dear
To whom your love
Lifts us from here,

Please be by Delilah's side,
To Light, To Love, To Guard and Guide"

"You will be fine Dee. I am always with you," Morgan started crying. "Delilah please watch over my baby Isabel, my Elizabeth, please Dee? And please hang around and run on the beach a little. Please lay on my bed. Please, if your soul has to move on, just visit a little." Morgan broke into tears.

Morgan shook David with her foot. "Wake up."

"What's going on? Where am I?" he said. They all sat in the van; Morgan, Elizabeth, Sebastian, Tibbs, and Pat, staring over David.

"David, touch her before it's too late. Delilah had a heart attack. She is about to move on," Morgan said. David reached out and cupped the beautiful Bulldog's face in his hands. He cried as he rubbed noses with her and stroked her forehead. Delilah was still in Morgan's lap. She now had Morgan's hand on her heart, Sebastian's hand on her pulse, David's hands wrapped around her face, and Tibbs staring at her. "Kiss her again, David," Morgan asked.

David kissed her and Morgan felt Delilah's last heart beat. Sebastian looked at Morgan. He too had felt her last ounce of life when he felt her pulse stop at the exact moment David kissed the dog.

They all sat in the back of the white van, clutching Delilah's dead body, crying. Sebastian reached out and hugged David. David cried on Sebastian's shoulder. Delilah's purpose was fulfilled. Her soul hovered over her body, not wanting to miss one second of watching her son be loved by his father.

Pat quietly said, "She is gone."

Sebastian, Morgan and David could not compose themselves enough to speak. Tibbs sat majestically, head tilted upward, as he heard Delilah above him. "Sebastian will take care of my son. Tibbs, please take care of my Boo. She loves you. Run on the beach with her." At that, Tibbs head-butted Boo and they ran from the lighthouse meadow to the open ocean. Daisy followed them. Delilah floated over them.

CHAPTER SEVENTEEN

fluttering leaves

I am still here.
I did not leave.
My existence echoes in the Aspen leaves.
I am still here.
I did not die.
I am now a million molecules,
floating above us in the divided sky.
Do not stand at my grave and cry.
I am not there.
I did not die.
Stand beneath the Aspen trees.
You will hear me in the fluttering leaves.
As the wind blows, my spirit will shake
and quiver on the branches, but never break.

Resembling the quaking, tremulous sound of rain
I will no longer feel human pain.
As the fragile floor boards grow old and creak,
My love will enter your soul while you sleep.
I am always there.
I did not die.
I am waiting for you in our divided sky.

-anonymous

Sebastian carried the epitaph, carved into driftwood, and a shovel to the burial place. "We can't dig right under the Aspens. We might hit one of their roots. It's better to dig a little farther away. The roots of this tree will fuse with the others," he said. They had hiked a few miles east of the lighthouse meadow, over a small rolling sand dune. They were all heavily panting.

David insisted on carrying Delilah's body himself. It was wrapped in the Mexican blanket, which Elizabeth had retrieved from the book shelf at the general store.

Morgan pulled a wheel barrel filled with a teenage Aspen sapling, gardening gloves, yellow citronella candles, coffee, ceramic mugs, fold out cots, sleeping bags, nutrient filled soil, a jug of vitamin B solution to add to the soil, Delilah's fleece bed and favorite bunny, and vinegar to pour on Delilah's body. Morgan had mixed up a bug preventing potion of dish soap and water to spray on the old, mature Aspens. Next to the unplanted Aspen was Delilah's fleece bed and four sleeping bags. Tibbs, Boo and Daisy walked in step with David as he methodically put one foot in front of the other with Delilah's body in his arms.

Pat followed behind with hemp bound, white sage smudges. He chanted as he walked. This one was harder than most for him because of the extremity of personal grief. He already missed her more than he knew. He thought about her gentle brown eyes and knowing, dainty walk. It was hard for him to lose an enlightened soul, especially one whose express purpose was to save her child. These special souls made of unconditional love were hard to come by. He couldn't bear it when one moved on. Pat looked at Tibbs, knowing that Tibbs would miss Delilah more than anyone.

"She was never even here. She liked the other Aspen grove," Pat protested.

"This one is on our property and we can visit her all the time. She can hear the leaves flutter and feel the ocean breeze at the same time. She will be happy here," said Sebastian.

"Let's start digging," David said. He placed Delilah's body carefully in a shady spot, so as not to increase the death smell, naturally increased by heat. "I don't want the smell of cooked dog around us. It will attract coyotes."

Everyone looked at David, stunned at his blatancy. "It comes from the firehouse," Morgan said. Morgan carefully unwrapped Delilah from the Mexican blanket. She used an eye dropper to cover her in citronella oil. Morgan recovered her tightly, taking special care to prop her head up.

"He's right," Sebastian said. "She should decompose in the ground so her body disintegrates directly onto the roots."

Elizabeth started building camp. The five of them, plus Tibbs and Boo were staying at the burial spot to prevent the coyotes from digging up Delilah's body. Elizabeth built a small bonfire to keep away the bugs away and lit sage brush on all four corners of the grave site to purify the air for an easier soul's ascent. It seemed a little ridiculous to her to light the sage bundles. She knew Delilah wasn't going to have any trouble traveling down whatever path she chose.

"Dig until we hit the underground source of water. If we go that deep the roots will always be nourished," Sebastian said.

"That will take forever," Morgan said.

"He's right," David said. "It's actually a really good idea." David looked at Sebastian for approval. It was obvious that David was the strongest and most trained in survival skills due to his paramedic training. It was also obvious that Sebastian was the leader of this group. Morgan took a shovel out of the wheel barrel and started to dig.

"No way," Sebastian said. "You help Elizabeth and Pat keep get the Aspen tree ready for planting."

"Oh come on. I can dig. I want to help. I'm not a sissy," Morgan said.

Sebastian knew he was treading on this ice. He also knew that Morgan was pregnant. He put down his shovel. With a tip of his head he motioned for Morgan to follow him. They walked away from the others. "Hey, Elizabeth and Pat need you with them. And, well, David and I really need this bonding experience. Just please, please let us do the digging. I'm not being chauvinist. I just want to be with David."

"Fine. I will make myself invisible. Poof," she said with a dramatic arm gesture. Sebastian laughed. It was all he could do to not kiss her, but neither of them wanted to disturb David.

"I see moisture," David yelled to the others.

Sebastian lay on the ground, stomach flat, and reached into the hole. He ground some gravelly, black soil around between his fingers. "Yep," he said.

Pat poured a vitamin B mixture into the hole to nourish the soil. The girls put Delilah's fleece bed down. Sebastian and David slowly lifted Delilah into the earth. Morgan and Elizabeth reached deep into the hole and unwrapped the Mexican blanket. They placed Delilah's favorite bunny under her head. They poured vinegar and vitamin B directly onto her body in order to increase the decomposition time naturally.

David and Sebastian placed the six-foot-tall, baby Aspen tree on top of Delilah's body. David stood, holding the Aspen upright, as the other threw handfuls and shovelfuls of dirt into the remaining empty circle. Even Tibbs kicked dirt at the hole. "Tibbs!!!" Everyone screamed simultaneously.

Tibbs saw that he had covered all his friends with dirt. He laughed. Tibbs and Boo sat next to the grave until the humans had finished filling it. "I'm exhausted. Tibbs you take first watch," Sebastian said. "We will have a proper ceremony in the morning. Tonight we take turns keeping coyotes away from the grave... and you and Boo. I don't want either of you chasing coyotes. Come wake me if any show up. Don't let Boo be lured by their fake injury noises." Tibbs nodded, knowing that coyotes faked loud yelps, as if they were in need of help, to draw their prey out into the open.

Daisy stood, gargoyle like, guarding the grave. "I think Daisy has it," Sebastian said. "Just stay with her." Tibbs nodded again.

As it got dark, coyotes howled. They sounded like sirens. One noise set off the other. The dogs twitched. Tibbs reminded the others not to move. David went and sat on the grave with the dogs. Tears streamed down his face. He didn't know what exactly had happened. Delilah was gone. That was all he felt.

Nothing else mattered. He didn't understand why or how he could feel so sad and so comforted at the same time.

Sebastian woke up and went to the grave. The moon was full and exactly above them in the sky. Coyotes and wolves howled. Sebastian munched on an apple. He picked the seeds out then ate the entire core. He used his thumb to push holes in the grave. He placed the seeds in the holes and covered them with dirt.

"It would be nice if apple trees grew with her. She always loved finishing my apples," David said.

"I know," Sebastian said. They sat for hours in silence as the sun came up.

Elizabeth built a fire from sticks she and Morgan had gathered. They made coffee. When they handed the mugs to the boys no one said anything.

Eventually, Sebastian asked everyone to come and sit by the grave. He read the epitaph. They lit the white candles and planted them into the soil. The scented wax would be a good camouflage for the smell of death.

"I would like to say something," Morgan said. "I put Delilah's favorite bunny by her head because whenever she got tired she used to suck on it. She held it in her front paws and kneaded at it like a cat making dough balls. She could always fall asleep with her bunny. Hopefully, she can rest peacefully now, knowing that we will always care for David." A strange, cool breeze fluttered through the trees. A catharsis went from the trembling leaves into David's body. For the first time, in this lifetime, he was becoming one with the earth. With his mother dead, part of him was now buried, happily forever.

But his cells felt the loss. After all, they had the same cellular and soulful memories, so part of him left. Part of him was empty. His body occasionally twitched and he spontaneously cried without understanding what exactly triggered it. Literally, part of his earthly body was taken away from him. Like an amputation, or a life-altering disease, he had to learn to live with this new life, with drastically altered fewer cells.

At the same time the gift of love was given to him. He did not know that Sebastian was his dad. He just knew that he felt okay for once in his life. He didn't have any desire to do drugs or return to the firehouse. He sat, calmly, under the baby Aspen and enjoyed the world around him.

Elizabeth said, "I think we should walk back to water the roses and keep an eye on the firehouse. We will hike back here tomorrow morning to bring you food and coffee."

"That's a good idea. We have this under control. You take Tibbs and Boo for protection. We will keep Daisy. You don't have to come back. We will sit shiva for the requisite time and come back," Sebastian said.

"That's ridiculous. You aren't staying here a week," Morgan said.

Sebastian saw that her eyes were pleading with him to not be away for that long. "Okay, three more nights. Then we will be home," he said.

"Okay," Morgan agreed.

"Besides, she needs to do some school shopping. You guys can go, right?" Sebastian asked.

Morgan smiled, holding back tears of glee. She threw her arms around Sebastian. "I will take her!"

Sebastian walked the girls and dogs to the edge of the grove. He had to push aside wild, unruly branches for the girls to get though. He walked for a half hour with them. They he couldn't take it anymore. He grabbed Morgan and pulled her to him. They embraced and kissed with the passion of teenagers. "When I get back, we will start our life. I promise."

"It's already started," she said, looking at her fingers. They stood in silence, holding hands and smelling the ocean.

Sebastian looked down at Tibbs, "Take good care of our girls." Tibbs nodded.

The girls hiked over the sand dune and back to the lighthouse. They watered the roses, cleaned the kitchen, fed the dogs, and opened the journal.

CHAPTER EIGHTEEN

life happens

The women opened the half a millennium old, leather bound journal. Morgan read about her own knowledge of her impending death. Elizabeth read unbearable passages about her mother's pain of knowing that she was going to die. They read about Isabel and Antonio's love. And Elizabeth realized, for the first time, that they both had to die in order for the King to not be suspicious. Life began to make sense to both of them.

Tibbs and Boo bounded in from the ocean. They were wiggling. Morgan began humming a tune from long ago. Tibbs perked up. "What is that," Elizabeth said. The girls turned to each other and started clapping their hands against each other's. First a normal clap, with all four hand touching. Then they simultaneously flipped their hands and clapped the backs of all four hands together. They reflipped their hands and clapped them twice together. They turned their hands over and touched the backs together twice. They repeated this movement, adding a clap on each turn. At seven claps, Morgan messed up and flipped her hands the wrong way too soon. They laughed. "You made it to seven. Let's go again," she said. The next time they made it to ten and fell onto the floor uproariously laughing.

"We used to do this when you were a baby," Morgan said to Elizabeth.

"How high did we make it?" she asked.

"Twenty-two," Morgan said.

"Oh, we can easily do that again. Let's go," Elizabeth said. They sat on the kitchen floor playing paddy-cake and school girl games the rest of the afternoon. The sunset filled the lighthouse kitchen with soft pink and lavender iridescence. They played until it was dark, then went to their respective bedrooms. Boo followed Morgan. Tibbs followed Elizabeth. The dogs stopped and looked at each other. They walked away from their masters and nestled together onto a dog bed in the living room.

Morgan walked into her perfect room. She began to cry. It was too much to sleep without Sebastian in that room. She walked into Elizabeth's room. "Can I sleep in here?" she asked.

"I thought you would never ask." Elizabeth pulled out a purple, fuzzy pillow and matching blanket. They fell asleep, contentedly in her bed. Their minds were on the same thing as they drifted off, so, instead of the past, they dreamt of Sebastian. They could see him, sitting on the Delilah's grave eating an apple. They saw him make up David's cot with a sleeping bag and a pillow and tell David to get some rest. The girls slept with an image of Sebastian hovering over them. They felt that all he wanted to do was come home to them. They felt that he couldn't stand to be away from them. They awoke. "I am used to feeling him hover over me like a protective father," she said.

"I've never known what this felt like," Morgan said. "I miss him more than anything and know how much he misses me. It's strange to know someone loves you."

"Tell me about it," she said to Morgan. They laughed and fell back to sleep. In their dreams they could see David's hands moving while David stroked Daisy's head. It was deafening, maddening silence between the men. Their identities, their lives didn't come up. The girls felt the boys' unfinished business.

As Sebastian fell asleep in the dirt, Morgan could access his dreams. And he could enter hers. Their love put them on the same telepathic wave and they could see everything. Sebastian showed her their past together. Morgan drank in the beauty of Portugal and lavished in their love.

When Morgan awoke she was afraid Elizabeth had seen the dream in which she was with Sebastian in a past life. Elizabeth showed no signs of knowing anything. "I slept like the dead," she said to Morgan. Morgan was relieved and comforted that she and Sebastian could have an entire life of dreams together. She wanted to go back to sleep and not wake until he returned. It was the only way she could be with him.

Sebastian felt this too, as he awoke. He realized that he and Morgan had been communicating telepathically and that he had shown her their past life. He then realized that he could show her their life on the other side in their next set of dreams. He had to find a way to stay lucid in his dream state. He had to learn to guide his dreams in the direction he wanted them to go in order to comfort Morgan and be with her. He decided to practice meditation and lucid thought all day.

CHAPTER NINETEEN

with one more look at you

Sebastian sat in the lotus position on the moist earth of the newly planted Aspen tree. Delilah lay beneath him. "Are you with me?" he said. The baby tree's leaves jingled above him, like bells that sounded like a light rain shower. "I knew you were there," he said. "Is it time for us to go?" There was no answer. Sebastian stayed seated on the soil, waiting.

The men had spent the entire day walking to and from the nearby creek, filling their coffee mugs with water to empty onto the new Aspen. When Delilah's burial place was moist, the men continued to walk through the Aspen grove, emptying their mugs onto all the baby fledging Aspens.

"I can smell death," David said. "It smells dank,

dark, and moldy. Kinda like skunk weed. The moon is full and the coyotes will be out. We should urinate around the area to keep them away."

"Good idea," Sebastian said. "I smell it too. This smell is too familiar for me. It is hurting my soul. I smelled it on the ships when men couldn't make the passage."

"What passage?" David said.

"It was a long, long time ago. It's when I met your mother in a different life. A more dangerous life. A life without antibiotics," Sebastian said.

"When did you meet my mother?" David asked. Sebastian couldn't bring himself to tell David everything.

"Pat will tell you everything," he said. "And maybe pour some more B complex vitamin potion around the grove, to mask the smell," David said. "You know, when she looked at me, I felt like I was someone worth loving. She gave me the confidence to survive. Another good idea. I will mix it up in the blue bucket," Sebastian said.

"Ya know, I just needed to hold her one more time. To let her know that I didn't leave her. I left Morgan, not her. I would give anything to let her know that," David said.

"She knows," Sebastian said.

"No, she doesn't. She died because I left," David said.

"Oh boy, we have a lot to talk about," Pat said.

"She left because she knew you were safe. Can't you get that? She was your spirit animal, your protector. David she was your mother in a past life. She stayed here until she knew you were safe," Pat said.

"I do feel safe," David said. "But I don't know why. And I damn sure don't know how you got me here."

"You are safe," Sebastian said. "You take the last shift. Sleep on your mother's grave and let her know that you love her. It's your turn to protect her. By tomorrow the scent will be gone and the moon will drop. I want to go home tomorrow. I can't be away anymore. If you want to stay, I understand. I must leave in the morning."

Sebastian rolled out his sleeping bag and tried desperately to lucidly dream with Morgan. He thought of every aspect of Morgan to connect them. He thought of her small hands, huge eyes, chocolate that they loved to share, Tibbs, and all the flowers. He forced himself to dream of handing her bunches and bunches of brightly colored flowers. He hoped that she was asleep and receiving the flowers in her dreams.

Morgan still slept in Elizabeth's room. It was less lonely for her. As she drifted off the flowers came into her head. Tibbs nestled at her feet. She knew Sebastian would be home in the morning.

He woke up in a cold sweat. He couldn't wait for daylight. "Pat, watch over this situation. I can't leave

Isabel and Tibbs anymore. Something is wrong. I have to go."

"No problem," I will bring David back to you. "We will be fine. You have done well," Pat said. "Follow your instincts and go."

Sebastian walked into the lighthouse before the sun came up. He had picked wildflowers from the meadow. He looked into Morgan's bedroom. When he found it empty he panicked. Life passed before his eyes. Luckily, Tibbs heard him come in and went to get him. "She's with Elizabeth," Tibbs said telepathically.

Sebastian ran up the stairs. He saw Morgan quietly sleeping next to Elizabeth. He carefully picked Morgan up. She woke up. "Your flowers are already by the bed," he said, as he carried her to their bedroom.

For the first time since they reincarnated they lay in the same bed together. They watched the sun rise and the flowing white curtains blow in the breeze.

"We did it," he said.

Morgan turned her head up to his. "I was so scared to come back here, to this earth. Without you I would have been miserable. Very few people every do this. How did we do it?

"Love," he answered. "And a little help from Tibbs and Pat." At that he heard a yelp from the beach. They both flew out of bed and went to the window. Tibbs was lying on the sand. Boo licked him and howled for help.

Sebastian got to Tibbs first. The tide rolled in around Tibbs and Sebastian could see that the dog was entangled in a jellyfish. Tibbs had been stung in the heart, while frolicking in the waves with Boo. Sebastian lifted him out of the water. "It's not time yet, big guy. Please. Not yet. Morgan and I aren't married. We need you. I thought you were a goner when you darted under her car and brought her to me. This isn't the time. This just isn't the time, Tibbs." Sebastian performed hard CPR on Tibbs heart. "Tibbs, please. I know we made a deal. It just isn't time. Please don't leave me yet. Please. The best is yet to come and I need to share it with you." Sebastian collapsed in exhaustion onto Tibb's body. He was stoically, quietly, heaving sobs by the time Morgan got there.

"No," she said. "No!!!" Boo frantically licked Tibb's face. "He's too young. It's not time. Wait. You knew about this," she said to Sebastian.

"No, well 'yes', but not like this. Not this soon. Tibbs was here mainly to bring us together. He was our bond."

"Not yet, Tibbs, please not yet," Morgan cried as she kissed his head. "I can't take it Tibbs. It's too much pain. First Delilah, then you. Tibbs we might not survive all this pain without you." Morgan tried everything.

Sebastian picked up the majestic, white Bullmastiff's, one-hundred pound body and slowly walked across the beach. Boo and Morgan sat traumatized together in the surf. Sebastian kept walking. He walked across the meadow with the dog in his arms, then over the sand dunes, then back into the Aspen grove. He collapsed. Tibb's body rolled out of his arms and onto the grave. Tibbs head bounced as they hit the ground. Sebastian picked him up and hugged him, until Pat pulled them apart.

"Carefully dig up the Aspen and put him with Delilah," Pat said to David. David was speechless. He had not seen Sebastian come up behind him. He picked up the shovel and started digging.

"You knew!" Sebastian yelled at Pat.

"You made the deal. You knew you would have to watch him die in this lifetime. I can't change your chart. You know that," Pat said. "Our darkest moments hold the deepest truths. He gave you Isabel."

"But it wasn't supposed to happen yet. I still needed him."

David lifted the Aspen tree out of the grave. "Sebastian, *you* should be the one to do this." Sebastian placed Tibbs on top of Delilah and replaced the Aspen tree. He recited the 'prayer for the grieving,' then broke down. "Not yet, Tibbs. Please, I can't live with this pain and grief inside me. I need *you* to overcome my anger and my selfishness. I need one more day with you, one more run on the beach, just one more look at you, looking back at me, trusting in me to be there for you."

CHAPTER TWENTY

life finds a way

Elizabeth could not leave her bed. Morgan waited on her hand and foot. Boo stayed pinned to her under the blankets. When she slept, she could feel Tibbs. She could touch him, run with him, play with him and feed him. In their dreams she made him huge bowls of lamb stew and sat at the ocean's edge with him. When she awoke, Tibb's hair was in the bed. Morgan changed her blankets everyday and everyday his hair was in the same spot. A small circle, where he used to nest as Lizzy's feet, on the right corner of the bed, was covered in white Bullmastiff hair. He had come to her because he knew it would be hardest on her. He knew she wouldn't understand why he left. It wasn't part of her destiny that he had taken into consideration when he wrote his chart. She was the innocent victim of other people's destinies.

It was days before the boys returned. Ships filled with lost, disoriented boat people landed at the lighthouse in search of refuge. Morgan fed and cared for them and sent them on their way, while she waited for Sebastian to come home. At least she had Elizabeth and Boo to console her.

Every morning, while Morgan made a cup of tea, Boo stared up at her, waiting for breakfast. Morgan relished spoiling Boo. She made lavish salmon and steak breakfasts for Boo, complete with steamed carrots and broccoli. Boo devoured everything.

One morning while Morgan was placing a breakfast tray across Elizabeth's lap she said, "Liz, do you notice Boo looking larger?"

"Well, she hasn't had much exercise. She will run more when Daisy returns."

"Plus, I've been feeding her a lot. She seems to eat everything. She used to eat what she wanted and leave the rest in her bowl for the others. Now she finishes every crumb. Maybe you should take her for a walk today?"

"I will try," she said. As they were finishing breakfast, Sebastian walked into the room. He was dirty, with a graying beard and crow's feet of pain surrounding his red, tired eyes. He collapsed onto the floor in front of Elizabeth's bed. Morgan put a pillow under his head, covered him with the soft, cotton herringbone blanket and lay down next to him. As he slept, Morgan crept downstairs to make him food.

When she entered the kitchen David was sitting at the long picnic style table eating a sandwich. "Hey Guaymas," he said to her, as if all pain was forgotten and forgiven, "how did you get here?"

"I live here," she said softly. "And you are welcome to stay."

"Stay? I can't stay. I have to get back to work."

Pat walked into the kitchen. "David, I think it would be a good idea if you stay awhile."

"Or what, you are going to swoop down and bring me back."

"I thought you learned something in the forest," Pat said. "You are loved. Very loved here."

"Did Sebastian explain things to you," Morgan asked.

David's demeanor became more loving and accepting. "What kind of things?"

"David, did he explain who you are?"

"I know who I am."

Morgan began, "David, you are Sebastian's true son in a past live. He did not know about you. Please believe me that had he known of your existence during your previous life he would have loved and cared for you. Thank you for waiting to give him this opportunity. Your mother was a wonderful Seychellois woman who gave you all the love you ever needed. That is why you were able to grow from her love and give your father another chance. She chose to stay with her family in the Seychelles. Many souls who go there never leave. You two had no karmic balances to work out, so she was free. She earned her freedom by truly loving everything and everyone. That is true freedom. You should visit the Seychelles again. Victoria has been with you this lifetime. She was Delilah and she recognized you immediately. Your cells and auras match hers. You have hues of brilliant purple around you now."

"That is why her death hurt so much," David said, starting to understand.

"Yes, brilliant," Pat said. "When one of your own dies, some of your cells literally die too. It's usually the cells that have the most love in them. This is why you feel so empty and lost when someone you love dies. Cells that carry love die too. Part of you literally dies with them."

David's eyes teared up. "I did love her…so much."

"Well, all is not lost. Her daughter, Boo, is still here. Boo has Delilah's cell's also. She shares your pain and your love."

"Morgan, let me take Boo with me when I leave?" David asked. Morgan shot a sharp glance at Pat.

Pat said, "We have a better idea. See, the firehouse seems to be a source that gives rise to your demons.

We have a job for you here. Just for awhile. You can leave if you don't like it."

"What is it?"

"Why don't you run the general store for awhile? See if you like it?" Pat said.

"I can do that, for Sebastian," David said, without batting an eye.

"Great," Morgan said, as she carried a plate of food out of the kitchen.

Sebastian lay passed out on Elizabeth's floor. Elizabeth and Boo moved to the floor to be with him. As Morgan opened the door, Sebastian opened his eyes. Boo licked his face. He took the Bulldog's beautiful velveteen ears in his hands and petted her head. Then a loving smile came over his face. Morgan bent to kiss him.

"Tibbs didn't die," he said. Morgan was scared that Sebastian couldn't handle all the heartbreak and was having a nervous breakdown.

"I'm right here with you. I'm not going anywhere," she said.

"No really," he said, "Look at Boo." Boo was looking a little large. "She has some little Tibbs in there."

"What? Are you sure," Morgan and Elizabeth simultaneously said.

"Sure as I am that I can't live without you," he said, pulling the girls next to him.

"How far along is she?" Morgan asked.

Sebastian put his hand on Boo's stomach. He sat quietly for awhile. "Six weeks or so," he said.

"That means Tibbs and Boo found each other and hooked up while we had dinner at the general store," Morgan said. "What do you mean 'or so'?"

"No one, not even an enlightened soul can tell how long it takes to create life. Life works at its own pace. If the conditions are right it works on pace, if not life might not form at all. It's all about the right energy."

"We've had too much heartbreak. The puppies won't make it. They couldn't have survived in this grieving environment," Morgan said.

"I think it will be okay," Elizabeth said. "Boo has stayed in bed nesting with me. She seems happy."

"Six weeks. That's forty-two days. The gestation is sixty-three days. We could have Tibbs babies in less than three weeks." Morgan rushed out of the room.

"Where are you going," Sebastian yelled.

"To cook for her and make her a bed. She needs folic acid. I have to go to the store."

Morgan ran downstairs and told David and Pat. They stared at her in amazement. "I'm going to the store with you," David said.

The two of them jumped in Morgan's car and drove to Petaluma, the closest grocery store. "Now, she loves ground sirloin and lamb. Nothing with bones. Plenty of cottage cheese. And puppy food. Don't forget puppy food." As Morgan rattled off Boo's needs, David filled the cart. "Folic acid. 800 mg a day." David ran to the pharmacy.

They rushed back to the lighthouse. David ran upstairs to Elizabeth's bedroom. He stepped over Sebastian asleep on the floor. "Excuse me," he said. David picked up Boo and carried her down to the kitchen. Everyone started cooking for her. Morgan poured pure salmon oil on her food. David sautéed lamb and diced it in little pieces. He hid the folic acid in the cottage cheese. They placed in the bowl in front of her. Boo looked up at them, like they were crazy. She didn't touch the food. "She can smell the prenatal folic acid. Canned dog food. She needs canned puppy food to hide the vitamins in," Morgan said. David knelt on the floor, mixed canned dog food into her bowl, and spoon fed the little white Bulldog.

"She does look a little chunky," David said. They both laughed.

Sebastian and Pat came into the kitchen with boards, hammers and nails. "We are going to build a whelping box."

"I'll help," David said.

"Let's just get a plastic kiddy pool. That way the puppies can't get stuck under the wood if it lifts up," Morgan said.

"Nope," Pat said. "We are doing this right. There will be a wooden bottom and triangular corner seats." The three men went outside. A zen mood took over. The corners were measured and cut perfectly. The bottom didn't have an inch of open space for a miniature puppy paw to get stuck.

Morgan and Elizabth prepared blankets and fleece pads for the puppies to get their footing. "It will be perfect," Elizabeth said. "No more sadness in this house."

The five hopeful souls doted on Boo; taking her temperature every two hours, feeding her vitamins, taking her on slow walks, putting steps next to the bed so she wouldn't jump, sleeping next to her. Finally, the time seemed to be getting near, so Morgan started sleeping in the whelping pen with Boo. They huddled together in the whelping box all night and snored loudly. Sebastian turned his big leather chair toward the birthing area in the living room and slept sitting next to them.

Morgan awoke at three a.m. one night. "Light a small fire, my love, and wake Elizabeth. Her temperature is dropping. She was at 98 degrees at midnight. Now she is at 97."

"Maybe she just has to go to the bathroom. Morgan, it is too early for the puppies. We should go to a vet hospital," Sebastian said.

"Not enough time at 97 degrees. I knew the distress of losing Delilah would do this. Please, get me scissors to cut the umbilical cords and dental floss to tie them off. Oh, I also need a small kitchen baster to aspirate the tiny noses." Sebastian ran.

By time he and Elizabeth returned Morgan was holding a small purple puppy. He was born with a greenish tint and no placental sack. She cut the umbilical cord. It wasn't crying. Morgan held tightly to the puppy and flung it into her should to push all the liquid from its' lungs. "Give me something to do," she said.

"Pet Boo, talk to her." Morgan flung the puppy again. Still no crying. Morgan desperately put the puppy's head into her own mouth and exhaled as long and as hard as she could. Sebastian saw the puppy's lungs lift with Morgan's breath.

"Do it again," he said. Morgan flung the puppy and again breathed into its mouth.

"Another one is coming," Elizabeth said.

"Catch it," Morgan said. She handed the first puppy to Sebastian. It was purple and limp. "Do exactly what I was doing and rub it vigorously. Get it's oxygen and blood flow going."

The second puppy emerged. It was in a grey placental bag. Morgan cut the bag away and began to aspirate the baby. It too was not crying. Morgan aspirated it and cut the umbilical cord. "Hold it in front of Boo's face. Let her lick it to life while I tie off the umbilical cord." Morgan could see that this puppy had pink gums, unlike the purple one in Sebastian's hands. Morgan used dental floss to stop the umbilical cord from breaking too short. She took the puppy from Elizabeth's hands and Boo's mouth and placed it to suckle. The puppy latched on immediately. Boo contorted her body to lick the puppy while it nursed. Milk bubbled out of the puppy's mouth. Morgan carefully lifted its' back leg. "It's a girl," she said.

"How is that one," she said to Sebastian.

"Still purple," he said. Morgan took the first puppy and rubbed it so hard that it looked as if she was hurting it. He started crying. She attached the puppy to Boo's breast and carefully lifted his back leg. "It's a boy. You kept him alive," she said to Sebastian.

"The nursing will induce further labor to help the other's be born," Morgan said. They sat for an hour watching the puppies nurse and Boo clean them. Morgan asked her to go get David and Pat.

"I'm right here," Pat said from behind her. "You don't think I would miss this."

The clock ticked and no more puppies came out. Boo still panted as if she was in labor. "There could be a puppy stuck inside which she can't pass. It could be stuck. She could go septic," Morgan said. "I can handle anything, but not losing her. I'm driving her to the vet in Petaluma for a c-section."

Just then Boo's pants turned to deep prahna breaths. She sounded like she was gargling and coughing at the same time. It was the sound of her making milk for the babies.

"5:05 a.m.," Morgan said looking at Elizabeth. "That is the exact time you were born five hundred years ago." No longer did anything seem odd about this piece of information. Elizabeth hugged Boo and stroked a puppy. The babies were both pure white, with huge white wrinkles on top of their pink noses and miniature velveteen ears.

"Careful, Boo will bite you. She will tear anyone's arm off if they get near those babies," Morgan said.

"Oh, not us," Elizabeth said. "Boo knows I won't hurt her."

"I would have killed anyone who came near you when you were born," Morgan said. "Don't ever underestimate what a mother will do for her off-spring."

David over-heard this. "Can we name the little girl, Delilah?" he said.

Sebastian and Pat mixed up Boo's favorite food and carefully slipped the bowl of fresh lamb, ground beef, cottage cheese and salmon, under Boo's face. She bowed and took one bite. Milk bubbled from the puppies mouths and noses. As the milk slowed, Boo ate more.

Boo was served her favorite foods and fresh blankets were put in her bed every four hours. Morgan slept next to the whelping box. Sebastian slept in the chair. They took turns, every four hours staring at Boo.

Bulldog mothers can easily fall asleep and crush their young. Sebastian and Morgan were taking no chances. When David saw Sebastian's head dropping, he removed Sebastian from the chair and sent him to bed. David and Morgan kept watch.

Ten days later, the puppies were getting their feet underneath them and Boo stopped growling at anyone who came near the pen. She started letting the family love Little Delilah and Little Tibbs. The puppies never had a chance of being put down until Boo barked for their return. Boo could sense when the puppies needed cleaning and feeding and no one was going to argue with her. Once, the doorbell rang. Boo lunged at the door and practically cracked her teeth trying to tear through it. She would kill anyone who entered.

Soon enough, the puppies had their shots and could run around the house freely.

Morgan's pregnancy was also starting to show. Her jeans didn't button as easily and her breasts were getting bigger. At dinner Pat said, "It is time we had a talk. We all know many of the things I am going to tell you. Elizabeth, you were the heir princess to Portugal in the year 1493. You are Princess Isabel. You and Stephano took over control of Portugal when your father, the king died. Your mother died when you were one year old giving birth to Stephano.

You are the true miracle of this life. Sebastian has raised you and loved you like his own daughter in a past life and his biological daughter in this life. You both chose to embrace love and fulfill your earthly lessons.

When we were on the other side and we all decided to incarnate together in this life we made many compromises which have proved to teach us many lessons. We chose to pay off our karmic debt; this news was understood by you. Now, that we have embraced love, as we did on the other side, we can move on and make sure we learned the lessons we chose to learn in this life-time together. We took this leap of faith together to return to this painful learning planet in the hopes that we could save each other. We all did good." Pat raised his glass. "A toast to love and life."

"To love and life," everyone said.

"Now it is time for me to go," Pat said. And with a *swoosh* he was gone.

"Now, if you will excuse us; Isabel and I have waited five hundred years to be together," Antonio said. Boo groaned and walked over and licked his face. It was the unconditional love of the dogs and children that allowed this disjointed family to understand what true unconditional acceptance and love can do for lost souls.

"I did good, didn't I Iz? I promised you I would take care of Isabel II and I did it. She is wonderful. Just like you."

"I didn't do such a great job of taking care of your son, but I brought him to you. We kept our promises to each other."

"Now, what about that promise to marry me," Antonio said. "It's about time we start planning that."

"I'm thinking of a little something, ummm…more life altering," Isabel said.

Antonio gazed at her. He already knew. "There are benefits to reincarnating with partial enlightenment."

"You know! Why didn't you tell me. You knew before me! You made me pee on that stick and wait and be nervous without you"

"You were never without me," Antonio said. "I waited to tell you until you were ready."

"Well,…I'm ready. And I'm happy. And I kinda hope it is a boy. But it doesn't matter, of course," Isabel said.

Antonio stared deep into her eyes. The centuries flashed back and forth between them. They saw each other's aura and souls. "We will love and live forever," Antonio said. The couple strolled out of the lighthouse, onto the beach. The waves crashed and the sun burst its beautiful green dot as it sank into the ocean.

"Until we are ball of white lights, then we will fuse into one larger form of energy," Isabel said. In their conscious memories they remembered their beach cottage on the other side of the sky, as they looked at their beautiful beach cottage in front of them, just down the meadow from the lighthouse. They remembered their childhoods on the Lisbon beach.

"There is something I have to tell you," Antonio said. "You will be happier than ever in your life."

Isabel lay on the sand, afraid to breath.

"The baby inside you is the son we had to leave five hundred years ago for his own safety. First we made him prince. Now we are making him our son. He has forgiven us for leaving him and has come home. He is inside you, and he is ours Isabel. He is ours." Tears rolled down both their cheeks.

Isabel finally spoke, "Elizabeth will have her true brother back."

"Yes," Antonio said, "and we will have our family."

The two lovers, Antonia and Isabel, walked inside and lay down in front of the fire. They entangled their bodies together into one blue mass. Pink waves reverberated off them. Their singular, mutual aura matched the sunset; burnt orange, magnificent red and just a touch of vibrant green. As the sun departed into the sea, the lovers wrapped themselves in a white, down quilt. Boo spun in circles next to their feet until she had made a proper nest for her and babies.

"Meet you at the hearth," Sebastian said.

"Tonight we are going to the center of the universe," Morgan said.

"We've already been there," Sebastian said. "I like it here."

"Then let's never close our eyes," Morgan said.

"I don't want to miss one more minute," Sebastian said.

Boo and Little Tibbs watched the waves beating ceaselessly onto Tomales Bay. Daisy made nesting circles on her fleece bed. The bed was filled with Tibb's soft hair. The five of them were lulled to sleep, knowing that they had planned this moment for over five hundred years. "This is our last chance," Sebastian said.

"Then don't blink. Don't ever blink," Morgan whispered into Sebastian's ear as they faded off.